JENNA KERNAN

"Kernan does a great job of mixing action,
suspense, romance and the exciting details
of the Alaskan gold rush."
—*RT Book Reviews* on *Gold Rush Groom*

"Opposites attract in this adventurous western
set against a blistering Texas landscape,
with authentic dialogue, energetic protagonists
and gun-toting outlaws."
—*RT Book Reviews* on *The Texas Ranger's Daughter*

KATHRYN ALBRIGHT

"Fans of western and marriage-of-convenience
romances have it all in this…quick-paced love story."
—*RT Book Reviews* on
Texas Wedding for Their Baby's Sake

"Set against the Battle of the Alamo…
The Rebel and the Lady manages to tell a tender
love story against an intense, grim background."
—*All About Romance*

LYNNA BANNING

"Banning pens another delightful,
quick and heartwarming read."
—*RT Book Reviews* on *Smoke River Bride*

"Flowing, beautiful, intelligent,
and always historically accurate."
—*Goodreads.com* on *Lady Lavender*

JENNA KERNAN spent much of her childhood wandering in the woods of the Catskill Mountains, navigating the forest at her father's instruction, and so books of adventure and romance hold a special place in Jenna's heart. Outdoorsmen have always been irresistible, and her husband, James, is no exception. Jenna now lives north of New York City in the Hudson Valley, U.S.A., across the river from her beloved Catskill Mountains. She visits the grassy meadows and quiet groves often in her imagination. You can contact Jenna on www.jennakernan.com.

An obstetrical nurse, sonographer and medical writer, **KATHRYN ALBRIGHT** was delighted to add "published novelist" to her bio when her first completed manuscript made the finals in the Romance Writers of America Golden Heart Contest and was picked up by Harlequin. She writes American-set historical romance, and her award-winning books are inspired by the real people and events of the past. She lives in the Midwest and loves to hear from her readers at www.kathrynalbright.com.

LYNNA BANNING has combined a lifelong love of history and literature into a satisfying career as a writer. Born in Oregon, she has lived in Northern California most of her life. After graduating from Scripps College she embarked on a career as an editor and technical writer, and later as a high school English teacher. An amateur pianist and harpsichordist, Lynna performs on psaltery and harp in a medieval music ensemble and coaches in her spare time. She enjoys hearing from her readers. You may write to her directly at P.O. Box 324, Felton, CA 95018, USA, email her at carowoolston@att.net or visit Lynna's website at www.lynnabanning.com.

JENNA KERNAN
KATHRYN ALBRIGHT
LYNNA BANNING

WILD WEST CHRISTMAS

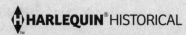

HARLEQUIN® HISTORICAL

ISBN-13: 978-0-373-29803-7

WILD WEST CHRISTMAS

Copyright © 2014 by Harlequin Books S.A.

The publisher acknowledges the copyright holders of the individual works as follows:

A FAMILY FOR THE RANCHER
Copyright © 2014 by Jeannette H. Monaco

DANCE WITH A COWBOY
Copyright © 2014 by Kathryn Albright

CHRISTMAS IN SMOKE RIVER
Copyright © 2014 by The Woolston Family Trust

PLEASE RECYCLE

THIS PRODUCT IS RECYCLABLE

Recycling programs for this product may not exist in your area.

Printed in U.S.A.

HARLEQUIN®
www.Harlequin.com

CONTENTS

A FAMILY
FOR THE RANCHER

JENNA KERNAN

Dear Reader,

This Christmas, I'm pleased to introduce you to an odd couple. Alice Truett is an entitled young miss, determined to prove her metal by bringing the orphaned nephews of her best friend to their uncle, the only man she's ever loved. She thinks he left her because she failed to tell him that she was a wealthy heiress, but the truth is very different.

Dillen Roach once had prospects, but that was before his father abandoned him, leaving Dillen to support his sister and mother. Dillen once held hope that he could make his fortune and return for Alice. But he failed, and now, instead of returning for her, she's returned for him with two little boys in tow. He thinks she's come out of Christian goodness, and she plans to be home for the holidays.

I'll promise that Alice will be with her family for Christmas, but it won't be the family she expected.

Come along as Dillen and Alice heal old wounds and give two boys a Christmas to remember.

If you enjoy my story, please let me know on Goodreads or Amazon. You can write to me at www.jennakernan.com. And for the very latest news, follow me on Twitter, @jennakernan, or find me on Facebook.

Merry Christmas!

Jenna Kernan

DEDICATION

For Jim, always

Chapter One

Blue River Junction, Colorado, 1880

Dillen Roach held a letter from Alice Truett in one hand and a half-empty bottle of whiskey in the other. The woman had a gift. Every time he had contact with her, she threw his world off-kilter. This time her correspondence marked a death. The whiskey buoyed him as the grief pressed down hard on his shoulders, chest and heart. According to Alice, his little sister, Sylvia, was gone. Dead and buried shortly after her husband, Ben Asher, who had come down with spinal fever. Sylvia had tried to nurse him and had caught the same damned thing. His end had been quick and Sylvia's had been slow or "exceedingly difficult," to use Alice's exact words.

But she'd had time to make out a will and leave her boys to him. Sylvia's brain fever was the only explanation for such a bad choice. But perhaps she had made it because he was her *only* choice. Dillen barely managed to keep himself alive and was in no position to take on two youngsters.

The December wind whipped down the street, threatening to tear his battered tan Stetson from his head. Dillen pressed down on the crown, keeping hold of his hat but releasing the front of his unfastened sheepskin coat. The wind sent the sides flapping like the wings of an agitated rooster. The bite of icy cold sobered him enough so that he thought he might reach his destination without falling again, but then he missed the first step to the telegraph office and folded over the sturdy banister. A gentleman, with a trim white beard and a charcoal-gray overcoat that was distinctly devoid of grime or snow, gave Dillen a wide berth and a sour look as he trotted down the stairs as agile as a mink. Dillen leaned against the wall before the door to catch his breath. He had business to attend.

Then he could finish the bottle. He was a big man, but the liquor was strong and his endurance for such indulgences was limited.

Dillen pressed the bottle under one armpit, clamping down tight to keep from losing the contents as he opened the door and staggered into the telegraph office. Good thing he had written out his responses before he'd hit that bottle, because he could no longer see straight.

The clerk spun around when Dillen got tangled up in the chair beside the writing desk provided for customers. He ended up kicking the chair harder than he'd intended, sending it sliding on its casters like a block of fresh-cut ice on a frozen lake.

"Now, see here," said the clerk, lifting the latched portion of the counter to step from the safety of his recessed sanctuary. Then, taking a good look at Dillen, he dropped the section back in place. Dillen had that effect on folks even when he wasn't drinking. His size accounted for some of it, he supposed, his pistol for the rest. Though he wasn't an outlaw or a lawman. Just a cowboy turned showman, trick rider and marksman. That and three years of his life had gotten him absolutely nowhere. In fact, he was further behind now than when he started. Glaring at the clerk, Dillen patted down his various pockets in search of the scraps of brown paper he'd salvaged from a package from the dry-goods store.

"I gotta send two telegrams," said Dillen, rocking forward against the counter and nearly sprawling across the polished walnut surface.

The clerk looked so young he barely had whiskers. But his blue eyes were clear and his movements steady as he pointed to the desk, now lacking a chair. "Just copy them down on the form you see there."

Dillen glanced over his shoulder at the twin desks, one now floating slightly higher and to the left of the first. He returned his gaze to the clerk. "How's about you copy them into your little form? Just take them down as I wrote them."

"That is very irregular," said the representative of the United Telegraph office.

Dillen slapped a silver dollar on the counter. "Make it worth your while."

The coin vanished and the clerk lifted his pen expectantly.

Dillen found the two ragged pieces of paper in his front left pants pocket and ironed them flat on the counter with the side of his broad hand. Then he examined them and set them side by side.

The clerk took down his name and filled in the necessary boxes. He needed Dillen to read the one he wrote to Alice because at the time Dillen had composed that particular missive he'd already been blind drunk.

"Says, 'Situation unstable. Unable to take them now.'" Dillen wiped his nose, feeling the guilt chewing on his guts again. He was their only living blood kin. "I'll take them, by God, but not now."

The clerk scribbled.

"Don't write that last part. Just what I said. 'Situation unstable. Will wire after the first of the year. Regards. Dillen Roach.' That's it. Read it back."

The clerk complied.

Dillen dictated the other message to the horse trainer in Cripple Creek. His boss wanted those three-year-olds as a Christmas gift for his ten-year-old twin boys. Dillen had seen the twin foals himself and given his report, promising to have them ready for riding by the thaw. He couldn't see to the ranch, break two horses and take custody of his nephews, Cody and Colin. He'd take them, but first he needed a different situation. How old were his sister's children now?

His brain was too fuzzy to do the math.

"You done scribbling?" asked Dillen. He was thinking about his sister, Sylvie, again. He retrieved the whiskey and set it on the counter, squeezing the neck of the bottle as his eyes burned. "Read it back."

"'Interested in taking the pair. Stop. Immediate delivery. Stop. Will pay for transport for both plus handler. Stop. Wire arrival date and time.'"

"Fine," said Dillen.

The bell above the door jangled merrily. Dillen turned to glare at the bell and then the young dandy who took one look at Dillen and decided he had pressing business elsewhere.

"I need the delivery information," said the clerk.

Dillen wondered what Alice would think of his reply. Disappointed, he decided and she had every right to be. He had been nothing to his former sweetheart but one giant disappointment. Still, he'd been straight with Alice. He couldn't say the same for her.

"The recipient?" asked the clerk, tapping his fountain pen now.

He recited the address from memory. "Miss Alice Pinter Truett, 1606 South 32nd Avenue, Hanscom Park, Omaha, Nebraska."

"And this one?"

"Mr. Todd Jackson, Horse Creek Crossing Ranch, Cripple Creek, Colorado."

"Send them right out."

Dillen paid the man and waited, dozing as the metallic tap of the telegraph set in motion the first in a string of dominoes that would lead directly back to his door.

His mission accomplished, Dillen staggered out into the blowing snow toward the lights of the Nugget Saloon.

Miss Alice Lorraine Pinter Truett stood on the icy platform of the Blue River Junction train station with her two charges, Cody and Colin Asher, braced against her dark skirts like flying buttresses. She had a horror that the departing train might suck the boys under those steel wheels and so gripped tight with her gloved hand to the narrow shoulders of each child.

Alice had never been outside Omaha, Nebraska—much less away from the safety of her family, who were less than supportive of her decision to escort her friend's offspring to their uncle.

The whistle shrieked and Alice startled as Colin began to wail. Cody jumped and clutched at her skirts, fumbling to find any purchase that was not taffeta or velvet, and failed. Alice squatted and scooped Colin into her arms and pulled Cody close. The little lambs had lost their mother and father, and she felt a poor substitute.

There the boys huddled like two blackbirds flanking one black crow. She'd bought the traveling clothing for the children, thinking it appropriate for them to wear black to mark the passing of their parents.

Steam blasted across the platform with a loud hiss as the train crept forward. Cody lifted his head to watch the monstrous metal marvel as it picked up speed. The grinding of the wheels on the track was positively deafening, and Alice clamped one hand to Colin's ear and pulled his other against her breast.

Alice hoped that Dillen had received her reply. He did instruct that she bring the children as soon as possible, so she had wired him their arrival details. She was not certain what bothered her more, being called the children's "handler" or his admission that he was interested in taking the pair, as if she would even entertain separating these two orphans. In her heart she feared that perhaps he did not want Colin. Men were funny about young children, feeling they required a woman's hand and so forth, all of which might be true, but…

She allowed herself a moment's fantasy in which Dillen would now need her help. The instant she realized what she was doing she cast off the ridiculous notion. Dillen Roach had once told her that he would not accept her help and that he did not expect her to wait for him. He could not have been blunter if he had told her that he saw no future for them. She still wondered how she could have misread him so completely. He had offered small hope, that he still held her in highest regard. But then he'd never come back. His actions spoke much louder than words.

Yet here she was, still turning down perfectly suitable gentlemen of her own class to chase the one man for whom the money did not eclipse her shortcomings. But she wasn't here for him, at least not directly. She was here for the children. Wasn't she?

Blast, where was the man?

Chapter Two

The engine puffed, belching black smoke skyward as steam blasted across the platform. Dillen stomped up the planking of the station stop that was so new he could still see the sawdust frozen to the seams. What the Sam Hill was Alice Lorraine Pinter Truett doing ferrying his sister's boys out here anyway? Couldn't she hire a servant to run her errands?

And then he saw her, and his feet stopped of their own volition as his heart took up pounding like a cobbler's hammer. He would recognize her anywhere, the way she moved, the inclination of her head.

She stood all in black in a perfectly tailored coat that clung to her in all the right places and showed that her figure had only improved in his two-year absence. He let his gaze wander appreciatively up from the expensive skirts hemmed in real velvet to the fur-trimmed coat. Was that sable at her cuffs and collar? Her head was capped with a felt-and-fur hat secured to her elegant upswept hair with a hatpin topped with a pearl the size of a pinto bean. It was a shock to see her as she really was, a wealthy woman who had come to do her duty by his sister.

He'd known from the instant he'd met Alice that she was uncommon, but how could he have failed to recognize *how* uncommon?

He wondered if her features had changed as he recalled her big, wide-set, green, earnest, intelligent eyes. He was so focused on trying to see her face that it wasn't until he caught movement at her side that he noticed that one child was pressed close to her skirts and she held the other one in her arms. His nephews, he realized. If he didn't know better, he would have sworn they were hers. He'd never thought of her that way, but now wondered what kind of a mother Alice might be.

With a stab of guilt he realized she would likely already be one now if he hadn't run like a colt in a summer meadow.

Alice lowered the little one to the ground and took each boy by the hand. Dillen looked at his sister's sons. The smaller one would be Colin, the youngest, he realized. Why, Dillen recalled when he was just a baby. And now Colin would be six. The child had thinned out and his hair was even a lighter brown than Sylvia's had been. Dillen looked at the other boy who was a few inches taller and clung to Alice's opposite hand as he strained for a better look at the departing engine. Cody, he recalled, was eight and was also in black right down to the high socks and shiny shoes. He looked to Dillen like a tiny undertaker in short pants. This one might be old enough to recall him. Cody's mink-brown hair curled from beneath his cap and was the same color exactly as his mother's had been. Dillen's smile faded as an unfamiliar stab of grief pierced him.

He wanted to go to his nephews and hug them and tell them that he'd take care of them, but the truth was he could barely take care of himself.

His attention turned back to Alice. He drank in the sight of her. Damn, he thought, what he wouldn't give to have a woman like Alice Truett. Everything, anything, but wanting didn't make that possible. He sure had learned that lesson well.

Dillen found the strength to step forward. This next part would sure be hard. But it had to be done, for the boys' sake.

As he neared her, he became aware of the mountain of luggage on the cart behind her. It looked like they'd emptied an entire freight car. He had a sudden horror that all that gear might belong to Alice. But that was impossible, wasn't it? Dillen counted four hatboxes and knew with cold certainty that they all belonged to the wealthy, entitled miss who might already be spoken for. That thought put a hitch in his stride. He fumbled in his pocket, feeling the two silver dollars knock together. How much would it cost to take all that gear to the hotel? Worse still, how much would it cost to rent her a room?

More than he had, he knew. Dillen gritted his teeth. He couldn't afford Alice for even one afternoon—let alone a lifetime. The truth bit into him with sharp teeth, but he couldn't shake it off.

He came to a stop before them. Colin leaned back to stare, his mouth dropping open as he gaped, looking very much like he might cry. Cody had also spotted his uncle and gave a sharp tug on Alice's sleeve before turning around, almost like a soldier awaiting inspection.

Colin likely knew his uncle only through stories, if his uncle ever came up at all. Dillen wondered which stories he might have heard and scowled as a series of possibilities danced through his mind. He met Cody's gaze. Two years was a long time to a child. Did the boy recall him?

Alice did not need Cody's warning for she now regarded him with a steady stare and a tight expression that took the lush, full curve from her enticing lips. Didn't matter. Even frowning, seeing Alice was like seeing a butterfly in December. He still felt dizzy with the effort of not reaching out to touch her. He noticed the hollows beneath her cheeks now. She'd lost weight and sleep, he realized, judging from the smudge marks under her eyes. Had she been at Sylvie's grave when they'd lowered his sister into the ground?

Sylvie had written him on occasion, when he had a place to receive mail. She had said that she and Alice had remained friends after his parting. Her presence here told him without words that this was true.

"Mr. Roach," said Alice, her voice formal, but still sweet music to his ears.

Had she really let him kiss her that Christmas Eve, before he'd met her family and everything had gone to hell?

He found himself reaching, clasping her by the shoulders and turning her so he could look at the face he thought of each night and every day on waking. Alice stared up at him, her mouth now slightly open as she drew in a surprised breath. He acted on instinct, pulling her in and holding her close, feeling her stiffen and then, an instant later, go as pliant as a willow branch. He inhaled the sweet fragrance of her skin and felt the soft brush of her hair on his face. Then she was stiffening again, turning to stone in his arms as she leaned away. She gave him a small shake of her head and then glanced to the boys, collecting their hands once more.

"I am exceedingly sorry for your loss, Mr. Roach," Alice said, her tone stiff with formality. "Your sister was a good friend, a loving wife and an exemplary mother."

Now Dillen felt awkward. He shouldn't have hugged her. He

had no right. She might even be spoken for, though Sylvie had not mentioned it. He glanced to her left hand and saw it sheathed in a finely made black leather glove, revealing nothing. He met her gaze, finding the small line between her brows that indicated concern. He waited, his stomach knotting as she pulled the boys forward so they stood shoulder to shoulder just before her now.

"These are your nephews." Then she spoke to the pair. "Colin and Cody Asher, this is your mother's only sibling, your uncle Dillen Roach."

The woman could make a formal introduction like nobody's business.

Dillen knelt down to meet the two at eye level. "Hello, boys. I'm your ma's brother." Colin stuck his thumb in his mouth as he fell back against Alice, huddling against her as if trying to disappear into the fine wool and velvet of her skirts. Dillen turned to Cody and extended his hand, open and up as he would to an unfamiliar dog. The boy looked at Dillen's empty hand. Confusion wrinkled his brow as he glanced from his uncle's empty hand back to his uncle. Why the devil hadn't he thought to buy a peppermint stick? Instead he had brought them nothing. How appropriate. "You remember me, son?"

Cody nodded. "Yes, sir. You use to come by Sundays for supper and play the fiddle. You used to pour medicine from a bottle into your coffee when Ma wasn't looking. Are you feeling better now?"

Dillen glanced to Alice, whose look showed reproach at this revelation. It was true. He had brought liquor into his sister's home. Young and dumb, he'd been. Now that memory shamed him, but it did serve to illustrate what he already believed. He'd make a terrible parent, maybe even worse than his own father, if that were possible.

Dillen gave the boy a gentle punch in the arm. "I still occasionally feel the need to take a dose."

Alice might as well know that he was not the man she hoped he'd become. Show her right off the disappointment he was and confirm in her mind that she was well rid of him. No use putting it off. Dillen rose to face her.

"The front of your coat is all wet." She lifted a gloved hand to touch him, and then hesitated. He looked at the finely made, fit-ted black leather sheathing her hand like a second skin. Had she bought her mourning attire especially for this journey? Of course she would have. Nothing but the best for the Truett family. Their eyes met and held.

"Why'd you bring them, Alice, when I asked you not to?"

She bristled as if he had struck her clean across the face. "You said nothing of the sort." She released Cody and rummaged in a small velvet reticule that hung from her slim wrist by a satin cord. A moment later her gloved hand reemerged holding a folded scrap of paper. She straightened the page and cleared her throat before reading aloud. "'Interested in taking the pair. Stop. Immediate delivery. Stop. Will pay for transport for both plus handler. Stop. Wire arrival date and time.'"

Dillen's stomach dropped six inches as he realized two things simultaneously. He'd sent Alice the wrong telegram, and that meant that the horses that his boss was expecting him to have purchased were not going to be delivered.

Dillen snatched the telegram and read. Then he threw down his hat and swore.

"Holy hell!"

Alice gasped and covered Colin's ears too late as Dillen pressed a hand to his forehead and swayed. He had two duties. Help Bill Roberts with the jobs he could no longer manage at the ranch and purchase and train those two green horses. How was he going to tell his boss that he'd failed to buy the twin Welsh ponies? Worse yet, how was he supposed to train two horses he didn't have?

What had he wired Alice exactly? Something about writing after the first of the year. He muttered a curse, because he knew the breeder had at least one other offer.

He retrieved his hat, turned to Alice and said, "I gotta go."

"What?" she yelped.

But Dillen didn't answer because he was already running over the icy platform toward the telegraph office.

Chapter Three

Dillen Roach ran to the telegraph station. If Alan Harvey found out that he'd sent that telegram, then he was out of his situation in the dead of winter.

Dillen waited in a panic for Morecastle's reply.

What had Sylvie done, leaving her boys to him? Surely there had to be a better situation than this. But maybe she didn't realize that. His sister couldn't know how hard his life was, for he'd kept it from her. He should have been honest. If he had told her the truth, she would never have left her children in his custody.

He thought of Alice and the boys waiting at the station and decided he'd best go fetch them. And bring them where? As he contemplated this, the telegraph sprang to life and his message came through. Mr. Morecastle now wanted him to come to Cripple Creek in person with cash immediately, or he would not hold the pair. Dillen sent his reply.

Now he needed to find a place for Alice and the boys while he headed up the line to Cripple Creek. His first thought was Mrs. Louise Pellet. She was his foreman's niece and ran a clean boardinghouse in town. Maybe she'd be willing to take the boys for a spell if he could persuade her to let him pay her on time. He and her Bill ate Sunday supper at Mrs. Pellet's table, which was a meal he anticipated all week. He couldn't think why she'd do him this favor, but she was a Christian woman. Maybe that was reason enough.

The only other person he thought might help him was a woman whose name he wasn't quite sure of. Alma, or Erma? He knew the last name was McCrery and he thought she was the wife of Sylvia's husband's uncle. He recalled she was a widow who lived alone in a big house in Chicago. He knew the street as well, since he'd met her at Sylvia's wedding and attended the reception there. She'd been ancient then and the connection was tenuous, but it was all he had.

The telegram that he sent to Mrs. Edna McCrery was brief. Just that since the death of Sylvia and Mrs. McCrery's nephew, Ben Asher, there were two orphan boys who he could not care for. Would she take them?

He didn't wait for a reply. Leaving Alice alone on the train station platform had been a combination of raw panic and bad judgment. If she was wise she would have boarded the next train heading down the mountain.

Dillen removed his hat before entering the railroad station and raked his fingers through his shaggy hair. He wished he'd had time for a cut and to shave off his three-days' growth of beard before seeing her again, because he knew he looked like what he was: a no-account bronc breaker. When he entered the depot and found it empty, Dillen broke out in a sweat.

He was still sweating when he heard someone call his name.

"You Dillen Roach?"

He turned to see a man in uniform shuffling forward. The stationmaster, he realized. The man was so stooped he appeared to be addressing Dillen's boots.

He nodded, then spoke up. "Yes, sir."

"She headed over to the hotel."

There were several hotels in Blue River Junction, and more than a few were wholly unsuitable for a lady to enter and all of which he could not afford.

"Which one?"

The man scowled. "Blue River Junction Hotel, course!"

Dillen replaced his hat.

"She left you a message." He slid a small white envelope across the counter.

Dillen had to remove his work gloves to open the tiny thing. Inside was her calling card with her name embossed in raised black font—Alice Lorraine Pinter Truett. He flipped the card and saw her neat looping script in pencil.

We are lunching at the hotel.
Please feel free to join us at your earliest convenience.

Alice secured a porter and, after speaking to the ticket operator, determined that the only acceptable hotel in this small oasis in the mountains was the Blue River. She was told the establishment was within easy walking distance, but the ice made travel a challenge. She was greatly relieved to see that the ladies seemed respectable and the male residents did not strut about with pistols on their hips like gunslingers, except Dillen. She had noted that he was armed.

The hotel itself was a pleasant surprise, opulent in a way that was not garish, but still it gleamed with polished wood, fine fabrics and chandeliers with sparkling crystals. The dining room appeared an inviting place to begin.

She gave her luggage to the bellman and saw it secured before tipping him for his trouble. Her father always handled the money and Alice had limited experience with such matters. Then she left word with the clerk at the front desk about her expectations that a Mr. Roach would be joining them in the dining room. She felt quite pleased at having conducted the business by herself. As long as no one could see how her knees were knocking beneath her skirts, she might almost be mistaken for a competent caregiver. It was a small step toward proving her mettle but she still counted it, along with making her trip from Omaha unescorted. Sylvia's death proved to Alice that her friend had managed more life in her short years than Alice had in her entire lifetime, and she was three years older than Dillen's sister had been. The realization disconcerted and had brought her to this place despite her mother's objections. She would see Dillen and reconcile what had passed between them one way or the other. From the look of him, he had not been pining for her. Even more annoying, he had run out on her a second time. It was enough to make her feel as if she carried some form of plague.

Once settled in the dining room, close to the woodstove, she had not even time to lift the menu before Colin tugged at her skirt. A few minutes later they had returned from the privy and prevailed on a waiter to allow them to wash their hands. This time she read the first menu item before Colin again tugged at her skirts.

"Where's Uncle Dillen?"

She knew that children should be seen and not heard. She knew because her mother had constantly said so. Still, she did not have the heart to shush him. At six, Colin was an inexhaustible sponge, soaking up everything around him and curious as a cat.

"I'm not sure, dear."

She redirected their attention toward lunch, and soon her selection was served. The fare was excellent, far better than the bustle and rush of the rail station meals. Alice savored her pot of gunpowder tea as the boys devoured their apple pie as if they had not already eaten everything on their plates. They seemed to be always hungry. Alice watched them with a mixture of pride and sorrow. Very soon she would have to give them up and return to her home. She had only had them for three weeks. Two after Sylvia took ill. And one since her friend's burial beside her husband, Ben Asher.

The hotel manager finally arrived, as she had requested, and she asked if he knew Dillen Roach.

"Roach, yes, ma'am. He took over the Harvey place, about three miles outside of town. Small spread, but nice. Horses mostly. Hear he's a real whiz with horses. I can get you directions."

Alice frowned at learning Dillen had a horse ranch. A man with a home was usually able to wed. Perhaps to a woman to whom he had professed the most tender of emotions and declared the most honorable of intentions. But that was before he learned the truth. Why hadn't she told him sooner?

Because deep in your heart you wanted a man who loved you for yourself and not for your money. She could hardly blame him for leaving her. A lie was a black and evil thing.

She asked the manager if Mr. Roach was married.

"No, ma'am."

She closed her eyes in a vain effort to hide her relief. But the joy was short-lived, for if Dillen had a place of his own and had not even written her, well, that told her all she needed to know. She thanked the manager and he took his leave. Alice poured another cup of tea with a shaking hand.

If there was anything Alice had learned following Dillen's leave-taking, it was that, unlike the other men in her life, Dillen was not lured by her family's fortune. Without that money, what was she? She felt the determination to learn the answer to that question. She had lived a sheltered life quite long enough. Alice was ready to see what she was made of.

She straightened, gathering her resolve for what would come. Giving up the boys would break her heart. But she must honor her friend's dying wish—that her boys be raised by family.

Cody straightened in the chair upon which he knelt. He lowered his fork and lifted his finger.

"Cody, dear, it's not polite to point."

"But, Miss Alice, I see Uncle Dillen, and he looks mad."

Dillen crossed the hotel's elegant lobby but found no sign of Alice, so he headed for the dining room. A fussy-looking gent stationed behind a high pedestal swept him with a disapproving look and his face pinched up as if he'd sucked a dill pickle. Dillen glared and the man spun about and vanished behind the swinging door to the kitchen before Dillen could ask him about Alice. He shrugged and searched the room for Alice. He found her an instant later and he paused in the doorway.

She looked right here, in the elegant surroundings. A refined lady seated at a table draped in white linen so bright it hurt his eyes. The sight made him more aware of his worn, faded dungarees and the smell of horse that emanated from his sheepskin jacket. She belonged here, but he sure the hell did not.

The boys sat facing him, heads down over their plates of pie, their legs tucked beneath them so they could reach the table. Alice sat in profile, and he admired her glossy brown hair looped up into a coronet on top of her head. The style revealed the curve of her slender neck. He'd never seen her hair down, but now discovered that he wanted that more than anything he could think of, apart from seeing her as God made her.

She lifted a fine china teacup to her mouth. Her full lips pursed to sip and Dillen's stomach flipped clean over. His skin went all hot and prickly, and he couldn't breathe until that tiny cup was seated back on its saucer. The woman was like a mule kick to his gut every time he looked at her.

Cody lifted his head, spotted his uncle and then pointed in Dillen's direction.

Alice spoke to Cody and then stilled with her tea suspended for a long moment between her mouth and the table. She lowered her cup, then lifted a hand so her elegant fingers danced over the cameo-and-diamond brooch. As he stalked forward, she released the brooch, clenched her napkin upon her lap before pivoting in her seat to face him. These small gestures were the only indication of her disquiet. But he knew her and was not fooled by her elegant posture and fixed smile. Alice was less than happy to see him.

Who could blame her?

She held his gaze, staring directly at him. One thin brow quirked and her shoulders straightened. The wooden smile of welcome remained, a lie. Only this time he wasn't fooled. He resisted the urge to turn tail. He'd done enough running. Now it was time to settle things, do what was best for the boys. Damn, he felt like such a failure.

Why couldn't Alice be an ordinary sort of woman?

Why did his sister have to go and die when he was holed up in a winter job? Four months, and then what? He didn't know. Another cattle drive? Driving horses?

He didn't want to give his nephews up, but he'd be damned if he'd drag them about from place to place as his father had done with him and Sylvie. Now he was just as rootless as dear old Dad. Children needed a home, and he knew that he couldn't give them one. He had no business even entertaining the notion of keeping them, yet his heart still ached with the impending loss. He didn't understand it. He didn't even know them.

But then he didn't have to. They were Sylvie's. That was enough. He thought of his own father and grimaced.

"Can't do worse than that," he muttered.

Steeling himself for what must be done, he marched across the long runner that bisected the rows of dining tables. This being neither lunch nor dinner, the room was quiet. He passed only one other customer, a gentleman in a clean brown suit whose hat rested, brim up, in the empty seat beside him.

Momentum carried Dillen forward until he rested a hand on the top of the two chairs occupied by his nephews, but his eyes were still on Alice seated before her china teacup.

"You look just the same as the last time I saw you."

Her eyes narrowed at the reference. "Do you mean at the station?"

The corners of his mouth tipped down and he could see from

the glitter in those green eyes that she knew exactly what he had meant.

"I meant in Omaha on Christmas Eve."

Perhaps she was recalling the last thing he'd said to her before his departure from Omaha.

I don't even know you. But it wasn't her lie that had sent him running. It was the truth, and that was a far different thing.

"Appearances can be deceiving," she said. "You above all should know that."

He thought it was this woman, more than appearances, that were deceiving. If only it had not all been a glorious lie. Still, he wouldn't trade his memories of Alice for the truth.

He became aware of the silence and that someone other than Alice was staring. His nephews sat as still as twin fence posts, watching him with the dark brown eyes of his sister. Without their hats, he could see the wide-set eyes fringed with dark lashes and the familiar wavy hair of the Roach family. The resemblance was so strong that he realized, with a pang of pride, that they could easily be mistaken for his. He'd once hoped to be a father, vowing that unlike his own, he would be kind, supportive and present. Now that fate had given him the opportunity, he would be forced to give them up for their own good.

"How's the pie?"

Cody nodded. "Fine, sir. Would you like some?" He pushed the half-eaten pastry in Dillen's direction.

"Cody," said Alice, "what did we say you should call Mr. Roach?"

"Oh." Cody rubbed the back of his neck and then said. "Uncle Dillen, would you like some pie?"

His mouth watered as he shook his head. "That's all right, son. Have at it."

Colin grinned, showing he had a good deal of piecrust stuck to his cheeks. Alice dipped a lace-trimmed handkerchief into her drinking glass and mopped Colin clean. It was a gesture so maternal it made Dillen's stomach drop an inch as the longing gripped him hard and low. She just kept surprising him. Why was she here? Was it only the boys?

Why else? You think just because you missed her every waking moment that she missed you?

"May I join you?" asked Dillen.

Alice motioned to the empty seat. He removed his hat and hung it on the spindle on the chair back, then tucked in beside Alice. He settled in the seat, and for just a moment he pretended he was the head of the household and they were all his. He let the fantasy linger a moment longer before letting it die under an avalanche of reality. He didn't even have the scratch for a haircut, let alone a family.

The waiter arrived and handed Dillen a menu printed on thick cream-colored paper. Every single item on the sheet would have cost him a day's wages. He set the menu aside and then assessed the empty plates, struck with the sudden fear that he'd have to pay for their meal. The shame of not having the funds to cover one lunch nearly drove him from the table. He actually rose when Alice laid a hand on his forearm.

"Where are you going?"

"I—I…" He had no earthly idea. His brain had stopped working the minute he saw that menu.

Dillen stilled as her fingers splayed over his sleeve, and he wished he'd taken off his coat so he could feel her touch. But it didn't matter. Just sitting beside her, smelling her delicate perfume, brought it all back, that night, their kiss. Him being fool enough to think he could ever keep a woman as fine as Alice. Her being fool enough to believe her parents would welcome the likes of him to their family. Her hand slipped back to her lap and her cheeks flushed. Was she thinking of how he'd held her? How he'd told her he loved her?

"Is everything all right, Mr. Roach?" she asked.

"Fine," he lied.

He would rather be back on that crazy three-year-old mustang crow-hopping across the pen than here beside her in this fancy-pants restaurant with those two boys looking to him for answers he didn't have.

The waiter returned and asked what he'd like.

"Nothing," he said.

"Coffee, black," said Alice simultaneously. Then she turned to him. "Have you eaten?"

He hadn't, not since the stale biscuit he'd had with bacon this morning, and it was now closer to dinner than lunch.

"I'm not hungry," he lied again.

Alice made a face. "A ham sandwich with fried potatoes," she said to the waiter.

"I can't stay."

That made her shoulders wilt. But she rallied, her gaze still on the waiter. "Wrap it to go, if you please."

The man nodded and returned the way he had come. She waited until he had vanished to the kitchens before turning to face Dillen.

"You cannot stay?" she asked.

He shook his head.

"What happened at the station?"

"I made a mistake. The telegram you received? That was for a horse breeder. I was asking him to send two horses. Now I've got to go up to Cripple Creek to get the pair because he got the telegram saying I couldn't take them. The one I meant to send to you."

Cody's legs went out from under him and he hit the padded seat hard.

Alice's hand shook, making the teacup rattle on the saucer. "Did you say that you could *not* take them?"

"I just can't take them right now. I need a little time. I'm sorry you came all the way out here."

"Immediate delivery, you said."

"Delivery of the twin Welsh ponies. They are the latest acquisitions for the Harvey spread, and I have to go fetch them now."

Alice's face grew pink as she regarded him for a long silent moment. "Yes, I see. How long will your errand take?"

"Overnight."

"And then you can take them?"

Dillen was silent.

"I see." Alice's gray-green eyes shimmered, and her face looked long and drawn. She rose. Dillen followed her to her feet and retrieved his hat. Alice turned to the boys. "Your uncle and I need a private word. Please stay at the table. Cody, you are in charge."

"Yes, ma'am."

Alice walked to the opposite side of the room, standing before the tall window, each pane frosted from the cold. The afternoon light showed the creamy perfection of her skin. Two pink patches glowed on her cheeks, and Dillen knew that Miss Truett was struggling with her emotions. Dillen felt like a dog as he slunk up before her.

"Mr. Roach, those two boys need you. You are their closest living relative and the only one they have ever met. Mr. Asher's parents predeceased him and they had no other children. Then you send me a telegram to bring these boys immediately and so I have. Now you tell me this is all some dreadful mistake. I need to know, Mr. Roach, what your intentions are toward your nephews' care."

"I want to take them. It's just…" He couldn't bring himself to tell her the truth—that he was a saddle stiff, a carnival hand, a no-account.

"When you conclude your purchase of horses, will you be able to take charge of them?"

He stared at her in mute indecision. He wanted them, but he also wanted what was best for them. He wasn't it.

"Mr. Roach, do you not want them?"

"I want them. Of course I do."

"Is it a matter of time, then? Do you wish me to stay for a few days to allow you to make necessary preparations?"

All the time in this wide world would not be enough for Dillen to provide a home for two youngsters. But Dillen looked down into her large, trusting eyes and saw that Alice really believed he could do it. Her sincerity and confidence took away some of the panic and he reined in his racing heart. Next thing he knew he was nodding yes. *A little more time.* Time for his brother-in-law's great-aunt to reply. Time to find someone who could raise his sister's children, time to disappoint Alice Pinter Truett once more.

"Very well. I'll take a room here and see to the boys. How long will you require for your business?"

"Be back by tomorrow."

"We shall expect to see you then." Alice extended her slender hand, bare now that she was at her meal. Dillen clasped hold. Her skin was smooth and satiny. He used his thumb to stroke the soft skin on the back of her hand. Alice gasped and her green eyes went wide. But she did not pull away. Instead she lifted her free hand and stroked his face, allowing the pads of her fingers to caress the apple of his cheek before traveling over the coarse hairs of his close-cropped beard. Now it was Dillen's turn to go still as her hand came to rest on his chest, her fingers splayed as if to still his thumping heart.

"Come back soon," she whispered, and then withdrew, her hands retreating, her expression changing from wide-eyed need to the deferential demeanor of a proper lady. But for an instant he'd glimpsed her again, the woman he had fallen in love with. The one he had kissed. The passionate, free spirit she had become when she was with him.

Which woman was she?

Dillen watched her walk away. There was no sultry sway of her hips, just the clipped, sedate walk of a woman of means and character. A woman so far above him that he feared he'd just imagined that spark that flew between them like a hot ember jumping from one blazing roof to the next.

But his skin still tingled from her touch and his body shouted for him to advance. Instead he tucked his hat down tight and retreated as fast as his long legs could carry him.

Come back soon, she'd said. *Lord, help me, because she could do so much better than my sorry hide.*

As he reached the train station, he knew he couldn't stay away from her. She was too sweet and he was too hungry. This would end badly for them both. Why the devil had she come here?

Chapter Four

Alice did not see Dillen the following day, nor the day after that.

While she waited for him to conclude his business, she wired her family of her safe arrival, penned her elder brother, Arthur, a letter and did some Christmas shopping for his daughters Harriet, age seven, and Lizzy, age nine. She had already finished her shopping for her younger brother, Edward's, children, though her nieces would hardly notice the gifts since Amelia was only two and Lidia just seven months come December. Alice had always spent Christmas Eve at her grandfather's home, a very elegant affair, the house open for all the right sort of people. Alice never enjoyed this part of the holidays. But afterward they would return to her parents' more modest home and she would exchange gifts with both her brothers and their growing families. Christmas morning was spent attending church with her parents—though she wished she could be at her brother's home in the morning when the girls woke and found what Santa had brought them, but understood that this was a private family time. Knowing so only made her long for a family of her own, for children with whom she could share the joy and innocence of those mornings.

She knew that Colin and Cody believed in Santa with their whole hearts. She managed to distract them with the help of the clerk so she had time to make several purchases for their stockings. The boys left the shop unknowingly carrying their own gifts, which made her smile. They were such good boys. Sylvia would be so proud. She sighed wistfully as Colin and Cody skipped along beside her on the snow-covered road. She needed to get these two to their uncle soon, for she feared that if she waited much longer she might not be able to give them up.

Alice returned to the hotel to inquire at the front desk if there were a message from Mr. Roach. Finding none, she went directly to the telegraph office to inquire there.

"No, ma'am" came the reply from the operator. "Did see him come through town yesterday, though. Had those two ponies. Fine looking pair. Oh, and no word yet from Chicago," he said, smiling and nodding at Colin and Cody who peered up at him as he rested an elbow on the counter. "Going to visit your auntie, are you?" he asked.

Alice felt the tingle of cold as if ice crystals formed beneath her skin. She drew one boy to each side and swallowed back her dread.

Alice lowered her chin. "Pardon?"

"Mr. Roach wrote their great-aunt." His grin dissolved. Perhaps he now recognized from her seething expression or the boys' wide-eyed stares that they had not been privy to this information.

Ben Asher's aunt had died some years back of a stroke. Alice did recall that Ben had two uncles, also deceased. Another possibility struck.

"He said Chicago?"

The telegraph operator drew back from the counter, hesitating now.

Alice patted Colin's back as he clung to her skirts. "Would the name of this relative be McCrery, Ella McCrery?"

"I—I'm not…"

She gave him a scowl, fearing she might need to shout and she hated to shout. She took a step toward the counter, hampered by the clinging children.

He swallowed and then nodded. "Believe that's right, though he said Edna."

Alice drew a breath, praying for calm as her stomach roiled. "To what question did Mr. Roach seek reply?"

The operator's bushy brows rose high on his shiny forehead, but he answered the question. "Whether she could take the boys."

"I see."

She returned to the hotel with her charges, who both had to jog to keep pace.

"Miss Alice?" asked Cody. "What's happening?"

"We have to go see your Uncle Dillen."

"But the man said he doesn't want us."

She didn't know what to say, for she feared Cody's concerns were valid. She looked at these two perfect little boys and wondered how anyone in the world could not want them. Why, she'd give anything to raise them up as her own. She had always loved them, but now that Sylvia was gone, that love had taken root deep inside her.

Alice straightened her spine. She had been put off once too often to make excuses for Dillen. Clearly he was avoiding her and doing all in his power to pack the children off. Alice saw only two choices. She could return to Omaha with the children or she could try one last time to convince Dillen Roach to honor his sister's final request.

"Hush, now, let me think."

Alice forced the anger down. The boys both looked frightened half to death, as if she might just hand them to a stranger. She stilled as she realized that was what she had been preparing to do, for clearly she did not know Dillen any longer. The man she once knew would not shirk his responsibility or ignore his duty to his family.

At the front desk, Alice spoke to the manager.

"How could I arrange transport to the Harvey ranch?"

He gave Alice the directions to the livery and the name of the gentleman to see. "If you've never driven a wagon or sleigh, then hire a driver, as well. And don't set out without a rifle, food and blankets or furs. If you break a runner, you could be stuck for some time."

This bit of advice made Alice's knees wobble, but she reminded herself of her mission. Plus a sleigh ride in the wilderness might be an excellent way to test her mettle.

One hour later, lunched and dressed in their warmest clothing, she and Colin sat in the second seat of a sleigh. Cody preferred to sit with the driver, Mr. Donald Miller, an aged livery hand with a round face, a high forehead and tufted gray hair peeking out from beneath a green knit cap. He held a pipe perpetually clamped between his teeth and his beard was cut in the manner of Puritans, so he reminded Alice of a New England whaling captain. Though the broken blood vessels on his nose and cheeks seemed to indicate that, unlike the Puritan he resembled, Mr. Miller indulged in spirits.

The wind whistled and the runners hissed as the horse trotted in a well-worn groove of packed snow. Despite the hot bricks and blankets, Alice's toes were icy and her cheeks numb. She was saved from inquiring regarding the remaining distance by Cody, who asked the driver that exact question at regular intervals.

According to the last report they were already on the ranch, though it looked no different than the pine forest they had traversed for the past several miles since leaving the town of Blue River Junction. Colin spotted a wooden fence with even split wood planks nailed to upright posts. Alice craned her neck and was rewarded with a glimpse of the sloping peaked roof of a barn. They crested a rise and she realized that what she had assumed was the side of the barn was, in fact, the front. The barn was easily four times as large as she had first imagined. Alice's gaze swept the unbroken expanse of snow that covered the open ground. Pastures, she realized, and beyond them, she spotted a long outbuilding squatting parallel to the barn, and on the top of the next rise the rustic yet expansive log ranch house.

This was not what Alice had expected, but still bore proof that Dillen had managed to achieve his ambitions alone. She closed her eyes at the evidence of his success.

He was not a veterinarian, as he had wished, but owned property and livestock. Alice lifted her head and stared. She was looking at the home he had carved out for himself in a mere two years. A home suitable for a family—perfect, in fact. He clearly had the means to support a wife. And if the curl of blue smoke coming from the chimney of the bunkhouse was any indication, he had hired hands, as well.

If she had not committed a lie of omission when she'd repeatedly failed to tell him who she actually was, would he have stayed? Was it the lie or her that he could not abide?

Alice settled back in her seat feeling suddenly so ill she feared she might lose the little lunch she had managed.

"Here we are," called Miller. "Shall I wait?"

"Yes, most certainly. Please take us to the house."

"Don't see no smoke," said Mr. Miller as he complied.

Alice had to grasp Colin, who seemed to be preparing to leap from the moving sleigh. The instant the horse stopped, Cody was on the long covered porch, his boot heels tapping like a woodpecker on a tree as he charged for the front door. Alice hurried after him, gripping Colin's wrist as he tried to catch up with his older brother.

"Wait up," cried Colin.

"I want to see the horses," called Cody, already lifting his hand to pound on the front door as he sang out, "Uncle Dillen! We've come a-calling!"

Around the side of the building came a lanky older man with a limp. He peered at them with vivid blue eyes and skin as brown and furrowed as a peach pit. His gaunt face was balanced by a thick gray-and-white mustache and his jaw was covered with stubble.

"Can I help you folks?"

"Yes, sir. We would like to see the owner," said Alice.

"Oh, well, I'm Bill Roberts, the foreman. Maybe I can help."

"I'd prefer to speak to the owner."

Roberts pushed back the brim of his battered cowboy hat and wiped his forehead with a gloved hand. "Well, he ain't here. Won't be up this way again until summer."

Her heart sank at this bit of news. Had Dillen left her and the boys behind without a backward glance? "Are you saying that Mr. Roach has relocated?"

"Roach? Oh, no, ma'am. He's here. You must be Miss Truett? He's mentioned you." Roberts extended his hand and Alice clasped it briefly. "He's in the barn with the horses."

"I'd like to see him, please."

"Yes, ma'am. I'll fetch him. Let me just get you and the young'uns inside." He proceeded to bring them into the entrance hall and then to a grand open living area that stretched up two floors and had a fieldstone fireplace with kindling and logs set out for a fire. The room was freezing, and Alice could see her own breath. If possible, it seemed colder inside than out. The room was filled with the work of a taxidermist, and the furniture was shrouded with white sheets to keep off dust. This was no way for a man to live, even if he was a bachelor.

From the walls, dead animals stared blankly as Roberts labored at the hearth a few moments with hands swollen with rheumatism. Alice worried he was not up to the task. She considered offering assistance but feared insulting the man, so she drew the boys in tight, wrapping them between the coat and her body as they all watched and shivered in the cold. At long last he succeeded in striking a match and the flames caught, curling over the dry wood.

"Should warm up directly." He tipped his hat and limped off toward the entrance. A moment later the door clicked shut.

"Look at the moose head!" said Cody, pointing at the trophy above the mantel.

Alice frowned. Had Dillen shot that poor creature or paid good money for a stuffed head?

"And there's a bearskin rug," said Cody, now dancing from one wonder to another. He petted the mountain-goat hide draped on the sofa and knelt to peek under the sheet at the chair fashioned from brown-and-white cowhide and bull horns. Finally he marveled at the chandelier, which was a rustic combination of elk horns and lanterns.

Dillen had all this and still he felt he could not provide a home for these two orphaned boys? The man should be ashamed. The room heated Alice's blood. She had not come seeking a fight, merely some explanation. But her purpose had changed.

Dillen appeared a few moments later smelling of horse and sweat. Even disheveled and flushed, his mere appearance caused her pulse to pound and her heart to race as if she were the one who had just run here from the barn. She stood stupefied as his eyes met hers. For just a moment she forgot why she had come and what she was doing here. Then he looked at the boys and his brow furrowed in obvious displeasure. Cody dropped the front paw of the bearskin rug and straightened as Colin inched closer to her. In that instant, she recalled her mission.

Dillen's generous mouth went tight. He looked less than pleased to see them. It was a new experience for her. Of all the emotions she had secretly hoped her arrival in Blue River Junction would elicit from this man, ire was not among them. In that instant she knew that she should never have come to the ranch. He had made it clear how he felt, and he had explained about the mix-up over the telegrams. He had further asked her to wait and she had, but... Alice's heart sank. She had every reason to believe that he had forgotten her once more. She knew she was forgettable. Alice was too timid to be memorable. It was only her father's acclaim and her mother's money that made her attractive to some. If it were not for Sylvia's boys, she most certainly would have boarded the very next train and departed, tail between her legs. Still, she had hoped that absence had made the heart grow fonder.

Clearly it had not.

"Alice, what in blue blazes? I asked you to wait in town."

"Yes, I know. And we have. But you sent no word."

"So you come all the way out here in the dead of winter? It's dangerous. Alice, why?"

Because I feared you had forgotten me again. Because I am a fool. She said none of this, of course. Instead she ushered the two boys toward the fireplace with a gentle hand on each one's small back, and then retreated to the far side of the room. He followed. She slid one arm into each of the opposite sleeves of the mink as she hugged herself and faced him.

When she spoke her voice was low, for she did not want the boys to hear. "I am sorry to interrupt your work. Certainly it must be difficult to run such a large ranch. But you told me that you have no place suitable for the boys and yet…"

He moved closer. He smelled of the horses and she saw the short dark horsehair that clung to his sheepskin jacket and gloves.

"Yet?" he asked.

"I see you have a large house and the means to care for them here."

Dillen's brow lowered over his dark eyes and his gaze shifted to take in the room before returning to her. He set his teeth together with a snap and Alice hugged herself more closely. The mink ruff brushed her cheeks.

"Are you seeking a housekeeper, perhaps? Is that the delay? Someone to look after the boys while you work?"

"They can't stay here," he said, and glanced to the door as if anxious to see her back.

"It seems a perfectly suitable environment to raise two boys."

"No," he said, with no further explanation.

Her stomach roiled now, and she was quite anxious to leave. But she remembered her promise.

"Mr. Roach, I am aware that you have written to a relative of your sister's husband. I fear that you are, therefore, unwilling to acquiesce to your sister's wishes. I could help you obtain a house-keeper to see to them so they are not underfoot."

"No," he said, glaring now.

She fumed, lowering her chin and matching his cold stare. "Mr. Roach, is it your intention, then, to ignore your sister's dying request?"

"They can't stay here."

"And why not?"

"It's not my house."

Chapter Five

There. He'd said it. Dillen had told her the truth and then watched the shock take her back a step as her mouth dropped open in surprise.

"Not yours?" Alice echoed.

"I don't own it. I never said that I did own it. I'm a hired hand working under Bill Roberts for Alan Harvey. Harvey is the owner. He's a banker. Works in Denver and only comes up here in the summer to enjoy the mountains. All this is a second home. Can you believe that? Calls it his mountain retreat."

"But I thought…" Her words trailed off.

"No. Not mine. That's why they can't stay. I don't have permission to have children here, and even if I got it, I'll not have them living in a bunkhouse, eating beans and bacon. No school out here and no other kids, just work—hard work."

"I see." Alice slipped her arms from her sleeves and extended one hand to him, clasping his wrist. "I've misjudged you."

Yes, he knew she had. He didn't know which was worse, having her think he didn't want his own kin or having her realize he was unable to care for them.

"I'm sorry, Alice. I'm no further ahead than when I left you. I just can't seem to get a foothold."

"I'm sure it must be difficult, all on your own."

Difficult didn't begin to cover it. But he had his pride and would not detail his various financial failures.

"You know, my father was the son of a brewer. He comes from simple roots."

What he knew was that her father was one of the most accomplished and sought-after physicians in Omaha.

"When my mother chose my father, my grandfather was less than pleased with her selection. You see, my father didn't have his license then, just ambitions and intelligence. But she knew what he could become, and she married him against their wishes. It was only after my brother was born that my grandfather relented, paying for my father's schooling. After my father passed the boards, my mother brought him his first patients. You see?"

Dillen had a hard time thinking when she touched him, but he could not understand what the devil she was talking about.

"I don't follow."

"I'm just saying that sometimes a man needs help to establish that foothold."

His expression went sour.

"There is no shame in asking for help."

"There is nothing *but* shame in it. You don't know me at all." He stared at her wide-eyed confusion. How could he make her understand? "I don't take handouts."

Alice felt his arm tense and slid her hand down until she clasped his.

"But we are not discussing *you*. We are discussing what is best for the boys. Perhaps you could wire Mr. Harvey and explain the changes in your domestic responsibilities. He might very well let you occupy this house until he returns."

Dillen chewed on that for a moment. A rich woman would think nothing of such a request. But Mr. Harvey was his employer, not his friend or his social equal. But Harvey was also a father. He might allow it, and Dillen could assure him that he'd take the best of care of this place and secure a new arrangement for his family, God knew what, before his boss's arrival. He let the possibility glimmer before him like moonlight on calm waters before the problems rushed in.

"Do it for their sakes, Dillen," she whispered, and his pride melted away. He glanced to the boys, standing side by side, hands clasped, staring up at the buffalo head mounted above the mantel. He looked to Alice, dropping his voice.

"Even if he went for that, I can't watch over them. I got work and they need tending."

"So your trouble is not a lack of wanting these boys, but a fear that you are not up to the task?"

He stared at her as he wrestled with the truth. "I want them."

Alice smiled. "This is a great relief to me."

"A relief? How do you figure?"

"Well, for a time there, I feared you did not want them and that you were avoiding us."

"Amounts to the same thing."

"Would you be willing to ask Mr. Harvey's permission?"

"Alice…the boys are young. Wanting them isn't enough. They need a mother."

Her eyes twinkled in a way that he recalled, and he found himself staring at her mouth again.

"If it would be of assistance, I could stay for a few weeks, help you and the boys adjust to a new situation. But I must be home with my family for Christmas Eve."

Dillen drew back his hand and shoved it in his pocket. "No."

She gave an exasperated sigh and flapped her arms. "Why not?"

He gave a harsh laugh and met her narrowing green eyes. Still, he told her the truth.

"Alice, you can't run a household."

"And why, pray tell, would you reach that conclusion?"

He knew he should hold back, but he didn't, just charged ahead like the damned fool he was. "You've been pampered and coddled your whole life. You've never rubbed your knuckles raw on a washboard. Why, you don't know the first thing about raising two boys."

"I seemed to have managed until now."

"I'm not talking about ordering room service or tucking up at a table when you are called to tea. I'm talking about real work. The kind you've never done. You walk around in that armor." He motioned to her mink coat and hat and the elegant dress he glimpsed beneath. "You wear gold rings on your fingers and tortoise combs in your hair. What do you know about work?"

"I know how to run a household, Mr. Roach."

"You know how to *manage* a household, not run one. There are no servants here."

"As I am quite aware." Her face was now flushed and her eyes glimmered as she took up the challenge. She actually raised her voice, remembered herself and lowered it to a rasping whisper, which made him straighten up and take notice. "I may lack experience, but I am here and offering you aid. If you won't allow me to help *you,* then please consider what is best for them." She motioned to Colin and Cody, both now studying the stuffed head of a pronghorn antelope mounted between the front windows.

Dillen followed the direction of her gaze and felt his conviction waver. "I can see to these boys and run this house," she assured.

"It won't work," he said, but his words now lacked conviction.

She stared at him, taking his measure and, no doubt, finding him lacking. "You won't know unless you try. I can stay here for three weeks. That will give you time to become acquainted, time for them to become familiar with you and time for you to see if this will work or if they would be better off elsewhere."

He met the accusation in her gaze. "Aunt Alma, for instance?"

She blew out her breath like a dragon spewing fire. "Ben's only living relation is the sister-in-law of his *grandfather* and her name is Ella McCrery. *Ella.* I discussed this with your sister, and Sylvia was of the opinion that her age—she is in her eighties— precluded her from taking on such a responsibility. You were not her only choice, Dillen, but you were her best choice. Like it or not, you now have custody of Sylvia's children and must do what you see fit. Either way, I will have delivered them to you. That ends my duty to my dearest friend. My offer is not for her sake or for yours, but for the boys." She tugged her gloves on more securely. "So, Mr. Roach, will you accept my help or will you not?"

The silence in the room stretched and yawned. Dillen scrubbed his face with both hands and then spoke. "I'll wire Harvey and ask if you three can stay in the ranch house until Christmas."

Her expression held such joy and pride that he swallowed back his trepidation as Alice launched forward into his arms.

"Oh, Mr. Roach. Thank God!"

She squeezed him so tight that he felt the soft curve of her breasts pressed to him and the ridged sheath of her corset against his middle. He didn't know how it happened because one minute she was holding his face in both her gloved hands and the next his arms were about her and he was bending her backward over his arm as he kissed her full on the mouth. She gave a startled cry, which parted her lips and he took advantage again. His body burned as her arms went about his neck and she strained to deepen the kiss. Their tongues danced and she gave a low moan that ripped through him like a spear point. His body grew hot and hard, ready for this woman he could never forget.

He glanced, with his mouth still on Alice's, to judge the distance to the sofa and met the stares of both Colin and Cody. Their mouths gaped and they stood as if witnessing a murder instead of a kiss. Dillen drew back.

"Yuck," said Cody, wiping his own mouth as if he'd been kissed.

Colin repeated his brother's words, "Yeah, yuck."

Alice blinked up at Dillen, a lazy, satisfied smile curling her full lips. She still had one hand looped around his neck and used it to pull him closer. He set her aside and steadied her with a hand at the small of her back, feeling the soft fur of the mink. She swayed as if drunk.

She grinned at him and then turned to glance at the boys. Her eyes popped wide-open and her face flushed bright pink.

"Oh, my," she stammered. "I…" She glanced at him and then back to the children. "I… We had better be getting back. Say goodbye to your uncle, children."

Colin skipped forward and lifted his arms. Dillen glanced to Alice.

"He wants you to pick him up."

"Yeah?" he said and then slid one hand under each armpit and hoisted the child up to eye level. Why, he weighed less than a sack of grain. "What's on your mind, big man?"

Colin leaned forward and planted a kiss on Dillen's cheek, making a popping sound on contact.

"That's the way you're supposta kiss."

Dillen felt an unfamiliar squeezing sensation in his chest, as if someone had hold of his heart.

"That right?"

Dillen nodded. He set Colin's feet on the floor and the boy skipped back to Alice's side. Cody sidled forward with more caution, reminding Dillen of a curious but skittish horse.

Dillen dropped to one knee. "Sorry about the kissing."

Cody made a face.

"You take care of Miss Truett until I come to fetch you."

Cody accepted this responsibility with a nod. "Do I have to kiss you?"

"Naw. Handshake." Dillen extended his hand and Cody seemed relieved to take it.

He watched Cody walk to Alice's side and felt that same ache only this time his gut twisted with his heart. He stared at the threesome, wanting something but uncertain what it was.

"Will you send the telegram to Harvey if I write it out?" he asked.

She agreed and waited while he found paper and wrote to his employer. The man seemed a reasonable sort, but letting his new hand move his family into the boss's house seemed an unlikely outcome.

His family? He stilled and glanced back to Alice. Dillen's chest tightened. He wanted her to stay. He knew his desires didn't mean staying was best for the boys. Lingering at the ranch would just postpone the inevitable day when she reached the conclusion that he was not father material and that she couldn't run a household. But if he could put off that moment, keep her here with him a little longer, then he was willing to let her send the damned wire.

Chapter Six

Alice spent the ride home mulling over the meaning of Dillen's kiss and her wild and unladylike reaction. If he had no feelings for her, why would he kiss her with such abandon? It confused her while simultaneously sparking new hope. Finally both the wintery chill and distance cooled her ardor and she took hold of herself. She wasn't going to allow him to hurt her again, was she?

Despite her trepidation, she did send the telegram to Dillen's employer immediately upon return to town and added one of her own, explaining who she was, who her father was and who her maternal grandfather was. Since her grandfather owned a sizable stake in the railroad and his name appeared often in the newspapers, she thought Mr. Harvey might recognize the name and this might help Dillen's cause.

She did not wait for Mr. Harvey's reply, as it was already past dark and she and the boys were wilting from hunger.

They went back to the hotel for a hearty meal, but worries dampened her appetite. She sipped her tea as she turned the problem over in her mind. Despite her bravado, Alice had little practical experience cleaning, though she was an excellent cook. To fill the gaps in skill, she had a secret weapon. Before her journey here, she had purchased a copy of *Mrs. Beeton's Book of Household Management* and had pored over the tome at every opportunity.

Still, reading was not doing and this troubled her.

Dillen's words played again in her mind. *You don't know the first thing about raising two boys.*

She didn't.

The next morning, Alice woke with a headache, but managed to get the boys dressed and breakfasted before setting off for services in a drafty unfamiliar church. She missed the Latin, but thought it better that the boys understood what was said and hoped they took some comfort in knowing their parents were safe in God's hands.

After services, she was approached by Mrs. Louise Pellet, who was the niece of Mr. Harvey's foreman, Bill Roberts. Louise Pellet was sturdy and curvy with clean clothing of a simple style, and she wore her hair drawn up in a no-nonsense bun. The woman's demeanor shouted practicality, and her expression showed the clear-eyed gaze of intelligence. She was expecting Dillen and her uncle for Sunday supper and invited Alice and the boys to join them at her boardinghouse. Alice was happy to accept, and they walked together through the town, Mrs. Pellet's boys quickly befriending Cody and Colin.

Once at her home, Louise ushered them into the parlor, but before Alice even had the boys out of their coats, Mrs. Pellet's four younger children tumbled in, asking if Colin and Cody would like to see their snow fort behind the house. Alice admired Mrs. Pellet's natural, no-nonsense style with her children as she sent them off with coats buttoned and mittens on. Her hostess had an innate warmth so absent in Alice's own mother. Mrs. Pellet turned and caught Alice staring.

"Something wrong?" asked her hostess.

"You seem so confident with them."

"The children?" She laughed. "I remember when my first was born. Lord have mercy. I was so scared I'd do something wrong. And I did, of course. Live and learn. But she came out all right. Isn't that right, Lizzy?"

Behind them came the clatter of silverware as a young woman set the table in the adjacent dining room. She stepped into the doorway and introductions were made.

Mrs. Pellet smiled proudly. "Could run the place herself. Her husband will be a lucky man. This one doesn't want to sit in church with me anymore. Not when she can sit with her intended."

Lizzy flushed and then returned to her work.

"So, Mrs. Truett, any word from Mr. Harvey?" asked Mrs. Pellet.

Alice took a moment to recover from her shock. She had no idea how Mrs. Pellet knew this, but was impressed, as she had only sent the wire last evening.

"Ah, it's Miss Truett," she corrected. "And no, I'm afraid the offices are closed today."

"Oh, but I have a special connection." She turned to Lizzy. "Isn't that right, my girl?" Louise Pellet beamed at Alice. "Tommy is one of the operators. That's Lizzy's beau."

And that explained that.

"Yes, well, I'll be seeing to the boys' care in the short term."

"So you'll stay through the winter?" asked Mrs. Pellet.

"No, unfortunately, I'll be returning to my family for the holidays."

"Oh, that's a shame. I'm sure the boys will miss you. When will you be back?"

"Well, I'm not certain," said Alice. "My responsibility was only to bring the boys to their uncle."

"You've gone a sight farther than that. Offering to see them situated. But have you thought what will happen after you make those three a home and then disappear?"

Alice felt her breathing catch. "I have no claim on them, nor has Mr. Roach asked for my assistance past the holidays."

"Is that so? So you two never…" She let her words trail off. Mrs. Pellet was a very perceptive woman.

Alice felt her face heat. "Well, we did see each other, but that was some time ago."

"And his sister sent you out here, to him."

"To bring her boys to him, yes."

Mrs. Pellet's smile was knowing. "Might be mistaken. Would explain why he works so hard, though."

Alice shook her head in bafflement. "I don't follow."

"Uncle Bill told me that Dillen seemed real focused on earning money. Won't say why. He thought Dillen owed a debt, but now I'm thinking that reason is you. Wouldn't be the first time a man was intimidated by a gal's fortune."

"I wouldn't intimidate anyone." But his words ricocheted in her mind. *You don't understand me at all.*

Mrs. Pellet snorted. "Dillen is a working man. You wear a diamond brooch." She pointed to the cameo at Alice's collar. "You've got fine clothes, a fine vocabulary and a sort of carriage that might make you a little difficult for some men to approach."

"Difficult? In what way?"

Mrs. Pellet ignored her question. "Still, you surely love those boys. That's plain. Plus, you brung them all the way out here. That's gotta count for something."

Alice continued to stare at the spotless carpet, thinking of what he'd said before leaving her behind. *It would not work between us. No future.* Those words collided with the ones he had spoken to her only days ago. Alice twisted the lace that protruded beyond her fawn-colored cashmere bodice.

"He kissed me at the ranch," she said, touching her fingers to her bottom lip.

Mrs. Pellet's brow lifted. "That so? Suppose he wants you but just can't figure how to make that happen. Maybe you can think of something. Those little boys sure need a mother. And likely he can't picture you keeping house."

"He already alluded to that. Laughed, actually."

A smile flickered on the landlady's lips, but she tamed it and met Alice's earnest stare. "No, Miss Truett, you sure are not cut from broadcloth. Satin and lace, real French lace, maybe."

"And why should my attire be of concern?"

"Roach is an ordinary man. A good man, and that's rare enough, but he's ordinary in his roots." Mrs. Pellet lifted one eyebrow at her in speculation. "If you want him to see you as ordinary, you got to act ordinary."

"How?"

"Start with that hairstyle and your fancy clothes. Stop using words like *alluded* and *attire*."

"I see."

"You want him to forget you're a lady? See you as a wife? Then you've got to show him you can tend those boys. And that underneath all those petticoats you're a flesh-and-blood woman."

Dillen looked surprised to see Alice seated at Mrs. Pellet's table. Would he have come to see her and the boys if they were not invited to share Sunday supper?

She felt a new tension between them as they took their places at the table. Dillen seemed distracted. Had he also lost sleep over his decision to ask his employer if she and the boys could stay on his property?

She straightened as something occurred to her. Could Mr. Harvey dismiss Dillen over such a thing?

Mrs. Pellet had seated Alice beside Dillen, something that would never have occurred at her mother's table. Cody also sat next to Dillen, who helped him carve up his ham. Did Dillen realize he had the same easy confidence with the boys as Mrs. Pellet had with hers? Colin sat to Alice's right and only spilled his milk once and was not the only child to do so, much to her relief.

The table was so crowded and the exchanges so lively that Alice had trouble following the discussions. She'd never seen such a raucous, happy family. The quiet conversation of her own family's dinners quite paled by comparison. Alice thought of returning to their table and of all the years and years of sitting in that quiet room. It frightened her more than any challenge she might face at the ranch. She could do this, because the alternative was returning to her parents' home permanently.

She had to remind herself that Dillen had only agreed to let her stay for the boys' sake, not for his.

In all the commotion, no one noticed when Dillen's leg lolled against hers. She straightened, and then remembered Mrs. Pellet's words. Make him see her as an ordinary woman. But how did she do that? She glanced across the table at Lizzy and Tommy, seeing them holding hands. Alice moved her hand from her napkin and reached until her fingers brushed Dillen's muscular thigh. This time it was Dillen who straightened. Then he turned to her and smiled, but his eyes blazed with heat. A moment later his hand covered hers.

The boys remembered their manners and thanked their hostess before their departure. Dillen helped Alice on with her fur coat and walked them to the hotel. There he hesitated outside the entrance. Was he thinking of kissing her good-night?

Oh, she hoped so.

Alice glanced nervously about and then saw the boys shifting from side to side, anxious no doubt to be out of the cold.

"I hope we hear one way or the other real soon," he said. Then he touched the brim of his hat and turned to go. Alice had to resist the urge to call after him.

Instead she took the boys inside and retreated to their hotel room. That night, when she lay in bed, her head filled with possible ways to get Dillen to recognize her as capable and also approachable. Mrs. Pellet said to show Dillen that beneath her petticoats she was a flesh-and-blood woman. Did Mrs. Pellet mean what Alice thought she meant? She flushed at the possibility and felt a nervous, gnawing worry that if she made some advance, Dillen might rebuff her soundly. But then she recalled his hand covering hers. It gave her hope.

If she could show him that she could see to the boys and live a simpler life, would that make him want her again?

On Monday, Lizzy found Alice and the boys at breakfast and told her that her Tommy had set off for the ranch to deliver Mr. Harvey's answer to Dillen's wire.

"He said yes." She beamed and clapped her hands.

Alice now had the experience of getting what she wanted and being frightened half to death. Could she do it? Could she care for them all on her own out there in the wilderness?

What if they got hurt or sick?

She glanced at the boys, who looked to her with anxious expressions. She plastered a confident smile on her lips and nodded.

"Well, that is very good news, Lizzy. Thank you for the information."

After breakfast, Alice went to Mrs. Pellet to seek advice on supplies and spent the following two days obtaining what she lacked in the way of foodstuffs and made several adjustments in her wardrobe, leaving much behind at Mrs. Pellet's and supplementing her existing attire with several necessities that were lacking.

She planned to set out on Wednesday, but the sleigh was too small, so Alice had to hire a wagon, which then had to be set on runners to carry her, the boys and her supplies out to the ranch house. She suffered the delay by making some arrangements with the bank to hold her valuables. Just after lunch on Thursday, they were finally on their way.

They set out under crystal-blue skies. Several inches of new white powder had fallen overnight and the world looked brilliant and the air snapped with freshness as they left town. The boys began the journey tucked beneath a blanket in the back, but were too excited to stay put, and to keep them from mischief she enter-

tained them with Christmas carols, singing the ones they knew
and teaching them some they did not. Even Mr. Gulliver, their
driver, joined along, his voice a wobbly baritone that occasionally strayed from the tune.

The horses trotted along, adding the jingle of sleigh bells to
the music, and it was no wonder that both Dillen and Mr. Roberts
were waiting for them as they drew into the yard.

The boys tumbled out first, and Dillen came forward to offer
her a hand.

"No furs?" he asked.

She bounced down before him. Alice had exchanged her furs
for a woolen shawl and wore a simple woolen bodice and skirts
with no hoops or bustle whatsoever. Her jewelry remained behind
in a bank safe. She felt lighter, freer, and she beamed her happiness at seeing Dillen again.

"We heard that you received a wire," she said.

Dillen glanced in the wagon and then back to her. "That Tommy
is going to get himself fired, yakking like a woman."

"Perhaps so."

Roberts limped forward, putting a hand on each of the children's heads. "Boys, let's get your gear unloaded."

By midafternoon all her supplies and necessary possessions
were stacked in the living room and Mr. Gulliver had left them.
Dillen seemed glad to see her but somewhat reserved, rubbing
his neck as he looked at the pile of gear. She feared she'd overwhelmed him again and shifted uncomfortably as she considered
this latest misstep.

"I've got chores in the barn, getting those two horses trained,
but I'll be back in a bit to make you dinner."

Make her dinner?

Mrs. Pellet was correct, Alice realized. He did not even think
her capable of fixing a meal.

"What time will you be in?" she asked.

He glanced at the mantel clock, which read three in the afternoon.

"Around six, I think."

"Would you like the boys' help or would they be underfoot?"

Both Colin and Cody went totally still, and she could see them fairly vibrating with excitement and anticipation at the possibility of seeing the horses. They all knew Dillen's reputation in town for being a fine horseman and were mad with desire to learn to ride.

Dillen hesitated and then glanced to Roberts, who nodded.

"They can come with me," said Dillen. "Give you time to rest after the ride out here."

Did he really think she would be going to her room for a nap? If he did, then he'd be wildly disappointed. Alice had used her time with Mrs. Pellet to good effect, recording some simpler recipes. But she still wasn't sure how to prove she had desires like any other woman.

Alice threw back the shawl that had covered her head.

Dillen frowned as he studied her. "You look different."

She smiled, wondering if it was the simpler chignon that he noticed, or her lack of jewelry. "Do I? I feel different. Perhaps it is the mountain air. It seems to agree with me."

Dillen's brow remained wrinkled as he nodded, and then shepherded the boys toward the front door.

"You rest now," Dillen said.

She smiled as they headed out in the direction of the barn. The moment the latch clicked shut, she broke into a frenzy of motion, unpacking the boxes and setting up her kitchen before launching into meal preparation. Something quick, delicious and memorable. Something that would make Dillen Roach reconsider his opinion of Miss Alice Pinter Truett.

Chapter Seven

Dillen took the boys to the barn, wondering with each step if he'd just made the worst mistake of his life. He'd asked Mr. Harvey if his nephews could stay until after he got these horses trained and delivered. Even mentioned Alice and her willingness to help out until the holiday. He'd never expected his boss to say, *Sure! Move the woman and kids into my personal residence.* But Harvey had said yes and now Dillen was just stuck.

He had horses to train, a ranch to run, two boys underfoot and the temptation of Alice so close that he swore he could smell her perfume clear out here in the open. Dillen leaned forward and sniffed Colin's collar, finding Alice's scent. Had the boy spent some of the ride nestled up against Alice's body? Dillen scowled.

"What?" asked Colin.

"Nothin'," said Dillen.

At least he had one other option. Mr. Gulliver had delivered more than the boys, Alice and her gear today. He'd also delivered a reply to his wire.

Great-aunt Ethel had agreed to take his boys. But with Alice staying until Christmas, he could put off that decision until the holiday. He shoved the folded paper deep into his coat pocket. This was what he wanted, wasn't it? What was best for the boys. They why did he feel so blue?

"Uncle Dillen?" said Cody.

Dillen forced a smile and rubbed his gloved hands together in anticipation.

"You two know anything about horses?"

His question met with silence.

"Riding?"

Cody's eyes shifted and he looked uncomfortable. "I want to learn to ride."

"That so?" Dillen scratched his head. He'd have to get in a

training session with the twin ponies and then saddle up Dasher. If he didn't have to cook dinner, too, he might manage. Steak and eggs, he decided. Fast and filling. "Follow me, boys."

Once inside the barn, his nephews were surprisingly quiet and stayed out of the way as he led the two ponies from their stalls.

Dillen talked as he worked, showing the boys how to brush them and saddle them, pointing out the parts of the horse, describing the care of the horses' hooves as he cleaned and inspected each leg.

The boys sat on the fence rail as he worked the two ponies round and round in the ring on lunge lines. Though the ring was snow covered, Dillen had added sand to the outer perimeter, and the ponies trotted, walked and turned on command. They did so well that he tried them with no line for the first time, using only the long whip to tap them when needed. As it happened, he didn't need it as the pair already knew the verbal signals and could walk, stop, trot and turn on command.

When they returned to the barn, Dillen only had to remind the boys once to stay clear of the ponies' hindquarters. He didn't let them curry or brush the ponies. Just didn't trust the green horses around his nephews. But when he brought out Dasher, he let the boys pet him and showed them how to feed a horse a sugar cube without losing a digit. Both Colin and Cody were brave, taking to Dasher like trout to a brook. Cody even managed to lift Dasher's saddle, though Dillen couldn't believe his eyes. The two boys seemed eager to please. It twisted Dillen's heart.

There was so much of his sister in them. They had manners, smarts, and Colin seemed to have a sense of humor judging from his attempts to comb his hair with the currycomb and making his brother burst out laughing.

He took them each before him in turn as he walked and trotted with Dasher around the ring. At first they clung to the saddle horn, but soon they were moving with the saddle and holding on with their strong, short legs. He dismounted and set Cody behind Colin, then led Dasher around the circle.

"Did you know that this horse was in the circus?" He didn't say that he had been, as he wasn't especially proud of that nine months of his life. The promised fame and fortune had not materialized—

or the fortune part had not, but that job had gotten him this position when Harvey had seen what he and Dasher could do.

"Really?" piped Colin. "Does he do tricks? Can he walk on his hind legs?"

"Sure. Want to see?"

Cody looked concerned, and Dillen realized he thought his uncle meant with the two of them mounted up. Cody did not object. But he did wrap his arms about his little brother and grip the saddle horn with both hands.

"Yes!" shouted Colin.

Dasher's ears twitched and he turned one to listen to the new, tiny riders. Still, his mount was calm and acted the perfect gentleman.

Dillen pulled the boys down and set them on the fence rail. Then he began some of his act. Dasher should have been out of practice, but he picked up the routine in midperformance as if they had never stopped entertaining. Dasher stole Dillen's hat and tossed it on the ground, stealing it again as Dillen reached to retrieve it. Then he placed it roughly on his master's head. The boys roared with laughter. His foreman, Bill Roberts, limped over and leaned against the rails, talking to the boys as Dasher trotted away with Dillen seeming to be chasing his errant horse. When the horse made an abrupt rehearsed stop, Dillen ran into Dasher's hindquarters. Then he put a foot in the stirrup the wrong way and mounted up backward on his horse's withers just before the saddle. Dillen turned toward the front and Dasher took him around at a trot, then stopped and lowered his head so Dillen slid down his neck to the ground. From there they changed from opponents to a well-oiled machine, with Dasher keeping up a steady trot as Dillen mounted and dismounted using the frozen ground to vault back up from each side of the saddle. The light was fading when he dismounted and had the horse walk a few steps on his hind legs. Finally, he motioned for Dasher to drop down on one foreleg to take a bow. The boys clapped and Roberts whistled.

Cody's exuberance bubbled over. "I want to be just like you when I grow up, Uncle Dillen!"

"No, you don't," he said, a little too gruffly, he realized, judging from his nephew's quivering chin. "You could do a lot better than me."

Back in the barn, he let Cody remove Dasher's bridle and saddle blanket. Roberts smiled at the boys and then at Dillen.

"That was some fine, fancy riding," said his foreman. Then to the boys he said, "Nice to have you two here. My boys are all raised up and off on their own."

Dillen hadn't realized Bill had children.

Both boys brushed as much of the horse as they could reach, and Dasher stood like a benign giant.

"He's the smartest horse in the world!" said Colin.

"It's training, isn't it?" said Cody. "You use hand signals."

Dillen nodded, pleased at Cody's observations. "For some of it. Some parts he's just got memorized. Good horse, Dasher." Dillen patted his mount's shoulder. It was full dark when the four of them headed to the house. He thought he heard Colin's stomach growling.

Dillen hoped that Alice had entertained herself. They didn't have books or a piano. She was likely bored already. He glanced at the chimney, relieved to see that she'd managed to keep the fire going.

When he opened the door he smelled food and his mouth started to water. His first thought was that she'd hired a cook, but surely he'd have seen the arrival of a wagon.

"Hello, the house," called Bill. "Something sure smells good."

Alice appeared from the dining room, her cheeks flushed. She wore a plain sage-green dress with no bustle or doodads. It was simpler even than the black skirts and bodice she wore when accompanying her father on house calls. Everything about her seemed more relaxed. Wisps of fine brown hair had escaped their moorings, cascading down the sides of her face, making her look young and healthy and so tempting. Dillen had to fix his feet to keep from dragging her up against him.

"Wash up, boys," she said to Colin and Cody. "The sink is in the kitchen."

"What smells so good?" asked Bill, limping by Alice on his way past the boys.

"Beef in a red wine sauce over egg noodles," said Alice.

Dillen stared at her in fascination, as if seeing her for the very first time.

"Where'd you get supper?" he asked.

She laughed and stroked his cheek. The sparkle in her green eyes, the curling of her lips and the warmth of her fingers trailing over his cold skin worked like a magnet to metal shavings. He actually bucked forward, drawn in as she spoke.

"I made it, silly." She turned and headed through the empty dining room toward the kitchen. "You smell like horse, Dillen. Soap is on the sink."

He trailed after her exactly like Dasher had followed him around the ring, but unlike Dasher, Dillen was interested in much more than a pat on the chest and a bucket of grain. After supervising their washing up, Alice directed them to sit at the large kitchen table and served them the best meal Dillen had ever eaten. That included the one-dollar steak he'd had at that fancy hotel in Dodge City the fall he'd worked a cattle drive.

She'd even managed a bread pudding for dessert that was riddled with streaks of brown sugar and plump raisins.

"That sure was a fine meal, Miss Truett," said Bill Roberts. "So happy you could come and stay awhile."

"Thank you, Mr. Roberts. Would you care for more coffee?"

He lifted his cup and she poured. She seemed content and comfortable in this kitchen, thought Dillen, as if she belonged here. It was an adjustment for him, seeing her out of her glittery bangles. She reminded him of the woman he'd first met, the one that was a lie, or was it? She actually seemed more at ease now than in her fancy duds. Maybe the elegant, wealthy woman was the lie.

Ridiculous—wasn't it? He knew she was kind, educated, refined. He knew from seeing her work as her father's assistant that she was not squeamish and that they shared a love for animals, riding and music, and that she could sing like an angel. Still, she seemed suddenly a stranger and at the same time more approachable.

"Dillen, are you all right?"

He snapped out of his woolgathering. Alice Truett had a bright future and could likely do far better than his mangy hide. Why hadn't she?

Stop it, he admonished. She was here to do a friend a favor because she was a fine Christian woman. Not because she wanted him. His mind flicked back to that kiss. Maybe she did want him. But that only showed one tiny blind spot in her good judgment. He'd be a scoundrel to take advantage of her.

"Dillen, is there anything else I can offer you?"

There sure the hell was, but he couldn't say it out loud.

"Nothing. Thanks," he managed. "Fine meal, that."

She beamed. "Thank you."

Gosh, she was a beauty, especially when she smiled.

Roberts rose. "Let's go tuck in by that hearth. Dillen, go get your fiddle."

"Oh, no. Alice doesn't want to hear my fiddling."

She pressed her hands together. "Yes, I do. Bring it, please."

He left her to go get his father's fiddle, and when he returned, Roberts was smoking by the fire, telling the boys about an Indian attack that had happened years ago, though whether in Bill's memory or his imagination was unclear. Alice was nowhere to be seen.

"Alice?" he asked, laying his fiddle on the mantel.

Bill thumbed toward the back of the house. "Chased us out of her kitchen."

Dillen headed through the dining room and found Alice drying the last of the dishes.

"Need a hand?" he asked.

She startled and then smiled, returning the plates to the cupboards. "All finished."

He approached, seeming unable to keep his distance from this woman. "I didn't know you could cook."

"I'd imagine there are many things you don't know about me." She reached behind her back and untied her apron, ducking out of the collar and setting it aside before brushing off her skirts.

"I've never seen you in a dress like that before," he said.

"It's new."

He frowned. Of course it was. Likely she bought it, perhaps an entire wardrobe for her little rustic adventure.

Alice's brow knit as if she recognized the misstep. "Do you like it?" She lifted the skirts and turned this way and that. Here was the Alice he recalled. Charming, bubbly and full of unreasonable optimism where he was concerned. She'd overestimated everything about him, especially his prospects.

"Yes," he said truthfully, stepping in, looping an arm behind her back even as he told himself to leave her be.

She rested her hands on his chest and smiled up at him. For just a moment he pretended that she was his, that those boys were their children and she was a mother instead of a lady of means.

"Thank you for taking such good care of them," he whispered.

"You're welcome." Her hand lifted and stroked the rough stubble at his jaw. She cast him a winning smile. "I saw your performance. You are a trick rider!"

He stiffened. "How?"

She motioned toward the window above the sink. The world beyond was now dark, but he realized she would have a fine view of the riding ring from here. The fact that she'd seen his shenanigans did not please him.

He did not share her delight. Rather he felt a wash of shame. A man might have to dig ditches for a living or dress like a clown to put food on the table, but it didn't make him proud.

Dillen released Alice and stepped away. "I did a stint with the circus."

"Really?" She still seemed fascinated, but her smile now looked brittle.

"Yeah." He rubbed his neck. "Want to…" He motioned his head toward the living room.

"Oh, yes."

For the next hour, Dillen played and Alice sang. Bill even sang a tune or two and the boys joined in on anything they knew. It was a magical evening. But afterward Dillen forced himself to remember that despite her wardrobe change, Alice was still a lady and he was still a saddle tramp.

Chapter Eight

$\sim\!\!\infty\!\!\sim$

Alice rose from her chair and eyed the boys, who correctly judged her intent and groaned in unison.

"Bedtime," she said. The house had running water in the kitchen, but the privy was out back and she saw no chamber pots under the beds. "Privy first," she said, gathering the boys' coats.

"I want Uncle Dillen to take us," said Cody.

He absorbed this news with a tiny snort. Then he laid aside his fiddle and drew on his coat. He headed out the door with a lantern, Cody over one shoulder and Colin over the other. Both boys were shrieking as they vanished into the curtain of snow.

Alice drew her shawl about her and realized the snow was coming down hard now. Dillen had to plow his way across the yard. When they reappeared, she took her turn and when she reached the relative warmth of the kitchen she shook the snow from her skirts.

Hands and faces were washed in the large sink using the hot water from the reserve on the stove. Dillen banked the coals and Alice filled the water tank so there would be hot water in the morning.

Once back in the living room, Alice spoke to the boys.

"Say good-night to Mr. Roberts and thank him for his stories."

They did, in chorus.

"Can I help you tuck them in?" asked Dillen.

She could not keep from smiling as she nodded her consent. Her throat chose that moment to constrict with emotion as she realized that he was beginning to act like a father.

They headed up the main stairs together. Bill sat closest to the fire, packing tobacco into his pipe.

"You mind?" he asked, lifting the pipe.

Alice shook her head. It wasn't her house after all, but she appreciated the request.

Dillen gave the boys a piggyback up the stairs, and as a result they were too excited to lie down. They bounced on the beds before she finally got them settled.

At last, she had them kneeling beside their beds to say their prayers. Tonight they both asked God to bless not only their parents, Alice and Uncle Dillen, but also Mr. Roberts and Dasher. Alice saw Dillen drop his chin to his chest. She also heard him repeat *amen* along with the boys. They lifted their heads and looked to Dillen. He stood in silence for a moment and then gave a curt nod of approval. Alice released a breath.

"Colin, Cody, you settle down, 'cause I'm going to tell you how I met Alice."

The promise worked like magic. Both boys nestled back into the feather pillows at the promise of a story and drew the covers up to their chins.

He told how their mother used to be a companion for an old woman who was ill and so she called the doctor a lot. She had met Alice, the doctor's assistant. He related how they became friends. He explained the way Alice used to come to the house. She had cared for their grandmother when she'd gotten sick.

"We thought Alice was a nurse. We didn't know she was a princess in disguise and that her grandfather was a king who owned half the railroad that carried them out there."

Colin loved trains and removed his thumb from his mouth to sigh. "Gosh."

"When your mother got married to your father, Alice was her maid of honor. I was the best man, so we danced at the wedding." He glanced to Alice. "Remember?"

As if she could ever forget. It was the first time he'd ever held her in his arms. There had been many a night when she'd thought of that dance and the start of their relationship when the world was nothing but possibilities. Her mother had married a professional man, so Alice saw no obstacles between Dillen and her. After all, Dillen was the son of a banker with an acceptance to attend a university. She smiled at the memory. "You looked very dashing."

"And Alice was as pretty as a rose," he said to the boys. "Later, when you were born, Cody, Alice held you at the baptism. She and I are your godparents."

"What about me?" asked Colin.

"Well, that was two years later."

Two years, and everything had changed for Dillen and Sylvie. Their father had abandoned them under the cloud of scandal.

Dillen went on. "But yes, we stood up in that church for you, too."

"And promised," said Alice, "to see you both raised properly."

Dillen gave her a long look and then nodded. "Yep. We sure did."

"And that is what we shall do," she whispered, stroking a hand over Colin's feathery hair. His eyelids drooped now, but Cody struggled against sleep.

Dillen looked troubled again. Was he wondering where he and the boys would live? She wondered, too. She could offer help, but knew from her last attempts that Dillen was too proud to take her money. Would he take it for the boys' sakes?

"Are we going to live here now?" he asked.

"For a while."

"I like it here," said Cody.

"Why's that?" asked his uncle.

"'Cause it's got chimneys. Lots of them."

Dillen's brow wrinkled and he cocked his head at the odd answer.

"Uncle Dillen, if we don't have any chimneys, how will Santa find us?"

Dillen's mouth went grim at this question.

Cody didn't notice past the yawn. They had been through a full day, riding out here, spending much of the afternoon outside in the barn and then enjoying their musical evening. She looked to Colin, who was already puffing out steady breaths, his thick eyelashes brushing his cheeks. Alice felt the tightness in her chest every time she saw them sleeping. Was it longing or love? She didn't know.

Alice just tucked Cody in tight and kissed his forehead. "He'll find you here, lambkin."

Cody sighed and closed his eyes.

Dillen stood, hands in the back pockets of his dungarees. Alice turned down the wick on the lantern but left the lamp on the table beside the bed.

Dillen followed her out into the hallway.

"Why did you tell them that?" he asked, his voice strained but still a whisper.

"What?"

"That Santa would come here. Alice, I don't have money to buy them toys."

"Then make them some."

He thought about that for a moment. "I've never made a toy before."

"But I know you can work wood. I saw the cradle you made for Cody. It was beautiful."

Dillen rubbed his neck.

"Well, don't fret. I bought them a few little toys and candies for their stockings. We'll manage."

His expression turned sad again. "Alice, you can't keep buying them things. When you're gone, it will be even harder on them."

He said it as a fait accompli. She was going. But if he would only ask her, she'd stay forever.

"They are just a few little items." She dropped her chin and stared at her hands, realizing they were scratched and nicked from all her work in the house.

"And new black suits and shoes and hats and coats. I know Sylvie and Ben never bought those things," said Dillen.

"I just…" She lifted her chin. "Who else am I going to spend it on?"

That took him back. He cocked his head. "I don't know."

"You won't let me help you. You made that very clear when I tried. But at least let me help the boys."

"You are helping. You cleaned this house up and saw us all fed. Best meal I ever had. I'm just saying there's other ways to help." He rested a hand on her shoulder, his fingers caressing her neck.

It was so hard not to draw her in and kiss her. She'd let him. He saw it in her eyes.

"I know that. I just… I'm trying not to make mistakes. To do my best for them, and I don't really know what I'm doing half the time." She felt defeated and let her shoulders sag, a momentary lapse in her generally perfect posture.

His hand left her, and she almost whimpered at her grief at the loss of his touch. But then he used his knuckles to lift her chin, bringing her gaze up to meet his.

"You'll never convince me of that." He grinned. "You look like you know exactly."

"I don't," she admitted, feeling the sudden need to get this off her chest. She motioned him down the hall, farther from the open door of the boys' room, and lifted a finger to halt him before retreating a few steps into her own room. She returned with *Mrs. Beeton's Book of Household Management,* offering it in two hands. "I've been using this."

He accepted the well-worn volume and thumbed through the dog-eared pages.

"Didn't figure you'd know your way around a kitchen. You learned all you been doing from this?" He held up the heavy book.

"Some. But not the food preparation or mothering. I've been cooking for years, and mothering is akin to nursing, I think."

He extended the book and she returned the volume to the table just inside her room.

"Your mom wasn't much of a—what'd that book call it—a household manager?"

"No. As you correctly surmised, she directs, plans menus and goes over the accounts with the housekeeper."

"What about mothering? She do any of that?"

She couldn't hold his searching gaze and for a moment considered changing the topic or outright lying. But she knew what her lie of omission had cost her before. So she buckled down and prepared to answer him. She hoped he wouldn't show her any pity. It was too ridiculous. She'd had every advantage that money could buy and yet, she felt so uncertain.

"I had a nurse and a nanny and a governess. Later, I had teachers and tutors. Some days I did not see my mother. On occasion she would come into the nursery dressed in her finery before she and father went out for dinner or to some function. She had her charities and social responsibilities and…" Her words fell off.

He blinked at her as if she'd just grown a second nose.

She turned away. "Oh, I shouldn't have told you. Those boys just lost their mother, and I'm complaining about the stupidest things."

He grasped her by both shoulders and pulled her back against his body. The contact was solid and reassuring, but it made her heart rate soar and her stomach flutter.

"They did lose a mother, a damned fine one. But at least they *had* a mother."

"So did I. She loves me. I know she does. But she is a very exacting sort of person and she does not like loud noises and messes."

Children, he thought. *She's saying she didn't like children or, specifically, her own daughter.* Alice continued on, sounding apologetic.

"I know she only wants what is best for me." Alice leaned on Dillen as if drawing strength from his touch. At last, she turned in his arms and gazed up at those big dark eyes.

"She also tended to use bribery and threats. So your comment about buying things strikes deep. Please believe me, Dillen, I have done my best to avoid such tactics with the boys."

"Better than using a belt, I reckon."

Alice's eyes went wide at this admission, and he immediately regretted mentioning it.

"Your mother used a belt on you?"

"My father. When he was around, which wasn't often."

"You and I never spoke about what happened, but I know there was talk."

Dillen gave a mirthless laugh. "I'd expect so. Man embezzles that kind of money and runs off."

"Sylvia also told me that he abandoned you."

He drew back. Had Sylvie told her all of it? That the bastard had found another woman, a mistress, stolen thousands of dollars from the bank he'd managed and run. According to the detectives who had come round investigating the crime, his father not only had a mistress but had fathered three children by her. Then he had cut and run. Left them and taken his new family West. Dillen had been midway through his first year at the university. He'd dropped out and gone to work. What else could he do? His mother and sister had needed him.

"She told me that once she was married, she offered to take your mother in so you could go back to school."

But Sylvie was a newlywed then and his mother had been so frail, the scandal killing her as surely as a cancer. In the end it was her heart, according to Alice's father. His mother had not lived through the year.

"Did she also tell you those were lean years for her? Ben could barely support them. He was starting a business." Then his mother was gone and Sylvie was expecting and there was no money for the university.

"It was very noble," said Alice.

It had nearly killed him. He'd given up his career and somehow he'd known that he would lose Alice, too, and that was before he'd known who she really was. They had courted before he'd gone to the university. Back when he'd been a man with a future with a past unsullied by his father's shame. Dillen found it hard, but he met her eyes. "Sylvie went to work, too. You helped her get a job nursing at the hospital."

"Yes." Alice lowered her gaze. Did she know how much that money had meant to a young mother whose husband's business had yet to succeed?

"You never told her who you really were."

"But we were friends. I would do anything for her. Sylvia knew me better than my own family, I believe. We both liked the hospital and helping people. My mother didn't approve of my choice to work with my father and tried to get me to quit. Later she resorted to bribery. But threats and bribery will only carry one so far. My mother learned that again quite recently."

"What do you mean?"

"She forbade me from bringing the boys to you. She said that it was improper for me to travel unescorted and that caring for two boys was unseemly for an unmarried woman." Boarding that train had been an act of outright defiance and it had made her feel grown up and terrified all at once. Alice had half expected her grandfather to turn the train around. "It wasn't the first time she's tried to keep me from acting against her wishes."

"No?" His eyes glittered dangerously in the darkened hallway.

"When she discovered who you were, she forbade me to see you. I would have defied her then, too, but…"

The sentence trailed off. Did he know what she had left unsaid? She would have defied her then, too, but he'd left her before she had the chance.

"You never told me that."

"No. I didn't. I only wanted to help you succeed. To help you return to the university and earn that veterinary license you so wanted. I never meant to deceive you by allowing you to continue believing I was only in my father's employ."

Her smile faltered.

"You were Sylvia's friend for more than four years, but she never knew who you really were. When we were courting, you never told me, either. Why? Why'd you make me think I could have you and then snatch it all back?"

Alice stiffened. "That was never my intention. Before I met you, I had been conversing with my father about, well, a disappointment, and my father said that I…" She twisted her index finger as if she meant to unscrew it. "That if I was bored with rich, useless men, I should look beyond Mama's social set, which I did. He's the one who encouraged me to work with him at the hospital. And I liked it. No, I loved it, because for the first time in my life I had something meaningful to occupy me and I was just like anyone else."

"So…what? This was all some kind of game, seeing how the other half lived?"

"No. It wasn't."

"Charity work, then? A great lady washing wounds and tending the sick. Just the acts of a good Christian? Must have been some laugh, when you invited me to meet your folks. That place was so big. I thought maybe it was some kind of hospital. Imagine my surprise when I see that it is your home." He scrubbed his broad hand over his mouth.

"My grandfather's. We always had Christmas Eve dinner there."

"You and a hundred of his closest friends?" He had tried for humor but the bite of betrayal colored his words.

Alice lowered her chin, looking small and contrite. "They weren't my friends."

He'd always thought she had played some cruel joke on him, but now he wondered.

"I had to attend, and I'd been trying to find a time when you could meet both my parents. You see, they have had some difficulties and seldom appear together any longer."

He did not know that. Had they separated? Dillen looked at Alice with new eyes, seeing the hot pink shame splashed across her cheeks.

"You asked to meet them and you seemed to think I was putting you off, but truly, it was a challenging request."

Dillen cast his mind back to that night. Her mother's cold expression. Her father's warm one. Then he thought of Alice.

He lightly grasped her elbows. She lifted her chin and met his gaze.

"I remember what you were wearing. White lace, miles of it. You were all tied up and buttoned up. Fussy and fancy with a bustle out to there. You looked so fine that I didn't recognize you at first. You remember? Looked right past you and asked the butler for you, thinking all the while I had the wrong place, and then he motioned to you and I about fell on the floor 'cause you looked so different. Like a stranger." He gave a laugh that sounded raw and painful.

"Dillen, I never meant to play you for a fool."

His brows lowered and he tucked his chin as if preparing to take a punch in the jaw. "You should have warned me, Alice."

"I was afraid you wouldn't come. You said you wanted to speak to my father. I so wanted you to."

"I had no right to speak to him. Not after I realized... Why, Alice?"

"I was afraid of losing you. If you knew I was his daughter or who my grandfather was... In the end my lie did make me lose you anyway." She rested her hands on his chest. "I've regretted that lie every day since you left. I've lain awake wondering if you would ever forgive me."

"You think I left because of that?"

She heard the incredulity in his voice, for she shifted from side to side. "Well, I did. But now I'm not sure what to think." She searched his face for answers and found only a grim poker face.

"You told me you had feelings for me, Dillen. That you wanted to ask for my hand. Then you broke all ties. You never wrote. What was I to think?"

"I didn't leave because of the lie."

"Then why?"

"I left because, well, hell, it doesn't matter now."

Her fingers curled around the flannel of his shirt, and she tugged as if trying to bring him closer. He didn't move but she did, lifting onto her toes.

"What do you mean? Of course it matters! Dillen, you tell me this instant why you left. Was there another woman?"

His snort was not a laugh, exactly. In fact, his expression held no mirth whatsoever. She thought she saw only pain now reflected in his eyes.

"Tell me, please!" she begged.

He looked away, and for a moment she did not think he would answer. When he spoke, he still averted his eyes as if looking at her was too difficult.

"I left so I could make my fortune. My sister was doing better financially. She took in my mother. I planned to earn a boat full of money and then ask for your hand. I was going to prove to your grandfather and your mother that I was the best choice, better than all those rich men swarming you like honeybees. Didn't quite work out like I figured, though."

"You what?"

He glanced back. His expression reminded her of the night he'd said goodbye. "Stupid, right? I thought if I just had enough money your parents might welcome me into your family. That money was the ticket into your world. I've learned two things since. Money isn't that easy to come by, and a sow's ear is a sow's ear no matter how much silk you sew over it."

"You are not a sow's ear!" She said that too loudly and clamped a hand over her mouth, glancing back toward the boys' bedroom. They listened a moment and heard no stirring. But they moved to the top of the stairs to put more distance between the sleeping boys and their conversation.

"You," Alice said, "are a wonder with horses and will make a fine veterinarian someday."

He gave a joyless laugh. "That's just a pipe dream."

"But it's not."

He held up a hand to stop her.

"You are helping with the boys, Alice. Don't think I'm not appreciative. But in less than a month, you'll be in Omaha and I'll be here." With that, he turned and descended the stairs.

Chapter Nine

Alice hurried downstairs after Dillen.

Mr. Roberts was already at the door, shrugging on his heavy coat. "See you tomorrow, Miss Alice. Thanks again for the fine meal."

Dillen didn't even bother to put his coat on, just squeezed it between his two big, capable hands. He half turned but did not really look at her. "Good night, Alice."

The door opened and a blast of cold air reached all the way to her heart. Alice watched them retreat toward the bunkhouse, driven back inside by the cold. She pressed her hands to the door and wondered at what Dillen had said. It hadn't been her dishonesty. It hadn't been the lie.

It had been her money that had driven them apart. Her wealth had created some insurmountable obstacle that he could never match. If he would not accept her help to go to school or start a business, then she must prove to him that she didn't need the money to be happy.

But even if she did that, even if she convinced him that she did not require her parents' blessing, what about the boys? She had managed to care for them up until now. But what if they were sick, or injured? How long until they recognized that all her knowledge and wisdom came from a book?

That question kept her awake a good deal of the night. In the morning she felt positively fuzzy headed with fatigue. But she had the boys up and dressed before the men returned to her kitchen for breakfast. She knew from the lantern glow that they were feeding the horses and mucking stalls. Despite her hope to have a moment alone with Dillen, she did not manage that day or the next. Dillen and Mr. Roberts came to the house for meals and to take the boys for part of the afternoon. On Sunday morning, Alice sat with the boys in the back of the large wooden sleigh, their feet on warm bricks and their bodies tucked under a real buffalo skin. Dillen drove the two-horse team and Mr. Roberts smoked his pipe and pointed out hazards that Dillen seemed to have noticed before the foreman.

Alice began to see what Dillen had tried to tell her and what Mrs. Pellet had worried over. Taking care of the ranch, horses and Mr. Roberts was more than a full-time job. Add two boys to the mix and something would have to give. Could she really manage such a task indefinitely? In addition, she recognized this was not really a home. They stayed on the charity of Mr. Harvey, and she found that did not sit well with her. She began to understand Dillen's refusal to accept her help. But she wasn't seeking to give charity. It was different, wasn't it?

She didn't know.

How could she convince Dillen to let her secure a home for the boys? More important, how could she convince her parents? What if they really did cut off her source of income? Would Dillen be able to support them all?

The best thing to do was convince Dillen to get his degree in veterinary sciences and then convince her parents that he would be a professional man. That way, the boys could stay with her as Dillen attended school and...

She was getting ahead of herself again. Dillen had said that he had left because of the money. She did not really know if he still harbored tender feelings for her. That, she decided, was the first step.

The boys wiggled some in church, but were very devout during prayers. They seemed to be asking God's favor quite diligently, and Alice assumed they spoke to Him about their parents or perhaps *to* their parents. She did not pry, but did worry. She seemed to be doing that more often since she'd taken on the responsibility of ferrying the boys to their uncle.

They shared a meal with Mr. Roberts's niece, Louise Pellet, and Alice was happy to have a woman with whom to speak, if only for a little while.

The temperature had dropped, and the ride back to the ranch was a cold one. Dillen had the fires roaring shortly after their arrival, and Alice made hot coffee for the men and broth for the boys.

The men went to check on the horses and the boys followed along, looking like two miniature versions of the cowboys.

That evening, they all gathered by the fire to try out the pop-corn popper Mr. Roberts had unearthed. The process required a lot of shaking to keep the kernels from burning and a lot of gig-gling from the boys as the nuggets exploded inside the tin box.

Alice felt the days ticking away and her chances to reunite with Dillen waning. She had done what she could to show him that she was capable and she had offered help in caring for the boys, which had only seemed to further injure Dillen's pride.

So here she was, eating popcorn and listening to the music that vibrated from the strings of Dillen's fiddle as she tapped her toes and sang along. Their voices blended perfectly, just as they always did. Couldn't they blend their lives the same way? She'd missed this, missed him, though she hadn't even left yet. What else could she do to impress upon him that she wanted to remain here?

Why had she told him she needed to return to her family for the holidays, when the truth was no one needed her? Instead of en-couraging him to pursue her, it had only caused an artificial dead-line that she could not rescind without losing face. But Christmas was for family, wasn't it? And she should go home to hers. Alice looked from Dillen to the boys and felt like weeping.

They finished the popular song "Home on the Range" and Dil-len took requests for Christmas carols. The boys called one upon the next as their uncle considered them all.

"What about you, Bill? You have a favorite?"

"Well, I've always been partial to 'O Holy Night.'"

Dillen nodded, looking relaxed now. Was it the food or the company or the fiddle that made him seem so at ease?

"You two know the words?" asked Dillen.

"Yes, sir," said Cody.

"Okay, then. All yours."

Dillen began to play and the boys sang on cue. Alice pressed a hand to her heart. The Asher brothers had beautiful voices, as sweet and pure as springwater. She smiled and listened, feeling the stab of regret as she considered her approaching leave-taking.

Might it be for the best? Dillen had bonded with the boys and they to him. Perhaps he wanted her gone. Perhaps her visit was an imposition and he would be relieved to see her back. But then she recalled that kiss. He certainly had not kissed her like a man who felt nothing for her. She knew that because she'd been kissed by at least three men who fit that situation exactly. All three men had been passionate about her wealth, but less so about her person. In one case she'd found a gentleman caller trying on one of her hats, which disturbed her greatly, though she was not certain why.

She watched Dillen as he drew the bow and winked at her as he finished the last verse at a slower cadence. She broke into applause as they finished.

Dillen set aside his fiddle. "Boys, I hate to tell you this, but it's past your bedtime."

The two gave heartfelt cries of anguish as if he were sending them out into the cold instead of to their comfortable beds—Harvey's beds.

Mr. Roberts chimed in. "None of that. Santa only brings gifts to good boys."

The whining halted instantly as the two glanced about as if expecting to see Santa at the window. There was no further argument as Dillen rose from his seat. Together he and Alice climbed the stairs toward the boys' bedroom.

Alice stood and extended her hand to Colin.

"I'll take them," said Dillen. "Best learn how."

The boys cheered as he threw one over each shoulder and carried them up the stairs.

Alice watched Dillen until he disappeared from sight.

"Oh, no, you don't," she whispered. "You are not going to figure out how to do without me again."

Alice decided then and there that before she boarded that train, she would discover if Mr. Dillen Roach still harbored any tender feelings for her. That would require her to take bold action, unladylike action. There might be consequences, but she would rather return home knowing that she had lost her heart than to live her life with this nagging uncertainty.

Over the next several days, Dillen worked the Welsh ponies as Colin and Cody played beyond the fence.

The ponies were growing accustomed to the feel of the reins

on their necks but were not yet aware that this rein contact was an instruction as to which way to go. They were smart horses and learning fast, so he was sure they'd figure it out soon.

He'd set up a sawhorse and nailed a set of steer horns on the front so Cody could practice with a lariat. He'd told them briefly about his time riding north with the herds out of Texas. Now Cody swung that rope again and again, trying to get it to open and close at just the right moment. Had it been a real steer, he was quite sure the critter would be blind or addled from all the blows. But the boy was persistent. Reminded Dillen of his sister. That thought put a hitch in his step. He sniffed and wiped his face on his sleeve, then walked the horses over to the rail, tied them off and slipped between two slats to join the pair of boys.

Cody swung the rope, threw and tugged. He'd managed to capture one horn. Colin clapped and then ran to release the rope.

"You did it, Cody! You got him." He dropped the lariat and Cody reeled it in, looping the lanyard just as Dillen had shown him. The boy needed some gloves and a hat. Dillen stilled. He needed many things. Dillen could buy the clothes. But what about the rest? He didn't want Cody and Colin to turn into saddle bums like him. He took the rope from Cody.

"That's enough now. You ought to be learning from books. That will take you a sight further than a rope."

The pride left Cody's face and Dillen felt out of his element again. He wanted better for his boys than what he had. *His...boys.*

No, they should go to great-aunt what's her name. He imagined them in that musty house with teacups rattling and a piano to dust. He stared at the two, cheeks flushed, vapor coming from their mouths with each breath.

"You like it here?" he asked.

They both nodded.

"Miss your folks?"

Another nod.

"Yeah, me, too." He slipped back into the ring. "Come on, let's get these two settled."

Colin crested the top of the fence, his little face now close to eye level.

"You got them sugar cubes?" asked Dillen.

They reached into their trouser pockets and held out the treat. "Okay, then. Like I showed you."

The boys bravely held out their palms to the ponies, thumbs tucked tight to their hand to prevent an accidental nip. The sugar was sucked away by the pair.

"That's right," said Dillen, and smiled.

"Can you teach us to ride?"

Cody shushed his brother, but then turned his large hopeful eyes on his uncle.

"Maybe," said Dillen. "Take some time."

"We got time."

They didn't. Not if great-aunt whats-is took them. He knew that the boys needed a home, but boys could live rough for a little while, just until he could get his legs under him and settle someplace permanent. If he ever did find such a place. In the meantime, did he really think to drag these boys around from town to town with his saddle? Maybe he could keep them until spring. He had this job until then. If they were going to stay, he'd need to see to their schooling and feed them. The impossibility of it all closed in on him. He wondered if he might convince Alice to stay, too.

Maybe, just maybe, Alice was enough of a Christian to come back here after her elegant Christmas holiday and look after the boys while he searched for full-time, steady work. She might do it for the boys' sake. He could stomach that much help. What he couldn't stomach was talk of taking her money. He wasn't the fortune hunter her mother had accused him of being.

Just a little while more, and then he'd let her go. Damn, this time he feared her leaving would kill something inside him.

"Will you teach us?" asked Cody.

"I'll think on it."

They trailed him to the next stall. Cody climbed up on the lip of the stall to watch him tend to Temptation's overlong front hooves. Colin's head appeared beside his brother's. Dillen slid his hand down the horse's leg encouraging him to lift his hoof. There was a shout and a thud. He straightened.

Beside the stall rail, Colin lay motionless on the ground.

Chapter Ten

Alice set the kitchen to rights and took a smoked ham from her larder for supper. She was humming a hymn from church and peeling potatoes when the front door banged open and Dillen bellowed her name. She dropped the potato into the sink as a chill of apprehension straightened her spine. Dillen's voice was always calm, steady. But now it held an unfamiliar note of hysteria. She knew it was one of the boys. Something terrible had happened.

She lifted her skirts and ran toward the front of the house.

Dillen carried Colin in his arms, the boy's form still and limp as a rag doll.

"What happened?" she asked, fearing she would not even hear the answer over the deafening drumroll of her own heartbeat.

How many times had she helped her father care for an injured child? How many times had she seen the terror on the face of a parent? Now that same terror consumed her, making her skin tingle as a spiny ball of fear lodged in her throat.

"He fell into the stall with Temptation," said Dillen. His face was as pale as snow and his eyes seemed huge.

"Was he kicked?"

"No. I...I..."

"Put him there." Alice pointed at the big rough-hewn dining room table. "Is he breathing?"

"No. No!" Dillen laid Colin down and turned to Alice. "I don't think so."

Colin's eyes were wide-open, but his face was blue.

"Coat!" said Alice.

Dillen tore the child's coat open with one mighty rip, sending buttons flying, and then pressed a hand to the child's forehead. "He was gasping at first, and then he stopped breathing."

"Was he eating something?" Alice tore off the coat, searching for some injury and finding none. Colin's eyelids drooped. He was fainting. She sat him up and checked his ribs for a fracture. Then she opened his mouth and looked inside. There was something white deep in his throat.

She sat him up and pounded on his back. The object flew across the table and skittered to the floor. A heartbeat later, Colin drew a great rasping breath. His color changed on the next breath. On the third, he started to wail. Alice scooped him up in her arms and held him close, rubbing his back. She sat down as the fear that had carried her left in a rush. She closed her eyes to better absorb the wave of dizziness.

When she opened them, it was to meet Cody's frightened face. She extended one arm and he ran to her. She pulled him in for a hug, too.

"He's all right now. Nothing to worry about."

Dillen stooped and lifted the object from the floor. "Sugar cube," he said, and leaned against the table as if he, too, needed support.

Bill limped in, arriving as quickly as he could manage.

"Is he all right?" he asked.

Dillen held out the sugar. "Nearly choked to death on this."

Bill lifted the sugar to examine it.

"Big enough to block the windpipe, I guess. Knew a boy that once died choking on a tin whistle. Closed his throat quicker than diphtheria."

Alice and Dillen exchanged looks of horror. Colin's sobs diminished and he snuggled closer to Alice. Cody chastised his brother.

"That sugar is for the horses!"

"I kn-n-now," sniffled Colin.

"That's enough now, Cody," said Alice. "Go and fetch your brother some water." Alice stroked the damp hair back from Colin's forehead. "You know it isn't safe to play with something in your mouth. We talked about that when I gave you those lemon drops."

"Yes, ma'am."

"I'll expect you to be more careful in the future. Now apologize to your uncle. You scared him half to death." She did not mention that her own heart still batted about her ribs like a rubber ball.

"I'm sorry, Uncle Dillen. I know that sugar was for the horses."

Instead of scolding the child, Dillen pulled Colin out of Alice's arms and hugged him, burying his face in the child's neck. Alice gaped as she saw that Dillen was crying. That sight undid her, bringing the burn of tears to her own eyes. But as Cody arrived with the water, holding the glass in two hands, Alice wiped her eyes and accepted the offering.

Dillen released Colin, whose hair stood up on top like a rooster, and his eyes were red rimmed and she had never seen a more beautiful sight.

"Drink some water, son," said Dillen.

Alice stilled. He'd called him *son* and somehow she knew that Dillen wanted only what was best for the boys.

Colin drank in loud thirsty gulps as Cody helped hold the glass.

Dillen met her gaze and spoke in a quiet tone, meant only for her. "It's too dangerous for them here."

All Dillen's hopes had died today with one lump of sugar.

After another fine meal and an hour's leisure while they listened to Alice reading aloud from *Treasure Island,* Dillen sat with Bill by the fire as Alice put the boys to bed.

He sat staring at the top log, half-consumed by the flames, blackened and glowing orange in places. His body rested, but his mind would not. Colin seemed to have already forgotten how close he had come to death. Meanwhile, Dillen would never forget.

Up until this afternoon, Dillen thought he might just be able to keep the boys. With Alice here, this was almost like a real home. He had to remind himself that it was all make-believe.

For heaven sakes, he didn't know how to be a father. All he had ever learned from his own dad was how *not* to be a father. Loving them wasn't enough to keep them safe.

If Alice had not been here, Colin would have died today. He knew it, and the powerlessness consumed him.

Alice settled beside him. "You look miles away."

Bill roused with a snort and glanced about. "Boys asleep?"

Alice nodded.

"Well, I'm off to bed. Got to trim those hooves tomorrow." He shuffled toward the door and retrieved his coat. Dillen rose and turned to follow, but Alice clasped his hand and tugged. He glanced back at her. She lifted her brows and stared up at him as if expecting him to read her mind.

He turned to Bill. "I'll be right along."

Roberts hesitated, then shrugged. "Okay."

The door opened and Roberts stepped out. The cold air slithered across the floor as the door shut behind him.

Dillen lifted their joined hands and kissed Alice's knuckles. She blushed and then pulled him down to sit beside her on the sofa. Dillen glanced toward the door, feeling the need to leave before he did something they would regret. Then he turned toward Alice and found her smile warmer than the fire.

"You saved Colin's life today," he said.

"We both did. You ran him in here so fast, there was still time."

"I didn't know what to do, Alice. Still don't. If you hadn't been here..."

She squeezed his hand. "I was."

"But soon you'll be gone. I'll have them all to myself." He slumped back on the sofa. "It happened so fast. One minute he was hanging on the stall rail and the next..." Dillen dragged both hands through his hair.

"We made a good team."

"I'm sending them to their great-aunt."

"Oh, Dillen, no. They love it here and you are so good with them. You had a scare. Your reservations are completely understandable. But you can do this."

"It's more than just what happened to Colin. There have been times when I had to sleep outdoors. You understand? I didn't have a roof over my head."

"If you get your license to treat large animals, then you could afford a home."

"That's not likely. Not now."

"You could do it. You're smart enough."

He exhaled away his frustration, and she knew what he left unsaid. It took more than intelligence to get through a university. It also took time and money.

"Never gonna happen, Alice."

"But..."

"No. I've got those two boys to look after now. Do what is best."

"You had a scare today. It is no reason to do something rash."

"It isn't rash. I've been thinking. Doing nothing *but* thinking of what's best for them. That's what Sylvie wanted. What was best. But she didn't know. I never told her how hard my life was…is. If she knew, she never would have picked me. But I wasn't honest. I only told her about the good stuff. I never thought it would do any harm. I just didn't want her worrying. But now it's past time I grow up and face facts. I need a job, a stable one that's in one place."

"I could help."

He shook his head, rejecting any help she might offer, for he knew that her kind of help meant money.

Alice reminded herself to proceed with caution. Dillen was a proud man. She loved that about him. But he was stubborn, too. Not easily swayed once he had made up his mind.

"I told you before that when my parents met, my father was not a physician."

Dillen gave her a cautious look.

"He was a brewer's son with ambitions to become a physician. My mother convinced her father that my dad would be a great doctor, the finest in Omaha, and he really was. My dad was still in medical school when they became engaged. He didn't pay for his schooling. His father did. And both my grandfathers helped them with their first home. You see, they didn't do it all alone. Their family helped them start."

"I'm not expecting any help from my father. He's dead to me."

"No less than he deserves," she said. "But *I* expect help from my parents."

"I'll not be a bought man, Alice, if that is what you're saying."

"Neither are you an island." She slid her hand along his arm, up and back over the flannel.

"I can't get enough of you, Alice."

"That's good, Dillen. Because this is the real me, the inside me. This is what's underneath all those manners, lessons and corsets. I never showed anyone that before. I was choking to death, just as Colin was. Losing myself one day at a time to the prison of that wealth and the dreadful responsibility to marry well. I don't want it. That's why I chose you."

Dillen stilled at that. "You just said you picked me because I'm a failure."

"No. I picked you because you are the first man who ever needed me for me, not for my family name or my fortune or my connections. You only wanted me. With you I could see a life of purpose, one where I was valued for myself. I knew you cared for me but I was fearful that once you learned about the money you would want that more than you wanted me."

"That could never happen."

"I know! But that was why I kept it from you. And now I realize that I feared the wrong thing. My wealth has not made you choose me because of it—it has made me lose you because of it."

"I don't understand."

"The men, my suitors. The ones who only wanted me for my fortune. I never let them in, none but you…. I showed you and…I won't hold back anymore. I want you to know another secret I kept from you then." It was time to say what she'd never had a chance to tell him before, to be brave enough to put everything on the line and pray it was enough, but still the words stuck in her throat. His eyes held caution as he stared down at her. "It was no game. I fell in love with you, Dillen."

"You loved me?"

She nodded, gazing up at him. "I never stopped loving you, and I need you more now than ever. I should have told you then."

"I love you, too, Alice."

She gave a little cry and then leaned forward as if to kiss him on the cheek.

The hell with that, he thought and turned his head, kissing her full on the mouth.

Her lips met his with the burn of longing and the sweetness of a promise finally fulfilled. She leaned forward until she pressed against his hard muscular body, melding to him. Dillen hesitated just a moment before gathering her up in his arms. At last, she thought, she would show him how she felt.

Chapter Eleven

She loved him. And she wanted him. The truth spurred Dillen to near madness. Nothing else mattered. Nothing but Alice.

He splayed his fingers about her waist, kissing those yielding lips. His body roared with need as he pulled her in. They slipped from the sofa together and onto the bear rug before the fire. She stretched out before him. He eased down beside her, nuzzling her neck as he kissed the shell of her ear. Dillen breathed in her sweet fragrance, growing drunk from the scent. Alice's proximity worked on him like an opiate. She reached to unbutton his shirt, surprising him with her boldness.

This woman had always been more than she appeared. She was beautiful. Other men saw it, but she wouldn't have them because she only wanted him. That truth roared through him with the need.

Alice slipped her hands to either side of his torso and then upward, kneading the heavy muscles of his chest. For just a moment he had the impression that *she* was seducing him.

He released the top button of her blouse and she worked from the bottom until the garment parted like the sea, revealing her pale skin and the sheer camisole that accentuated the slope of her breasts. He used his knuckles to stroke that long inviting slope, finding her skin incredibly soft. Her eyes fluttered closed and she sighed. He kissed her exposed neck and worked down, slipping the straps of her underthings over her shoulders. Alice was naked to the waist. How many lonely nights had he dreamed of this sight? He took just one moment to marvel at her form. She was the most beautiful woman in the world, he realized, and he was the luckiest man. He kissed her collarbone as she gasped and clung to him. He closed over the peak of her breast, drawing and teasing the sensitive flesh with his mouth and tongue. She shuddered and moaned his name, exciting him past all caution. Dillen drew back to blow on the damp skin, watching her nipple draw tighter as she sucked in a breath.

Her big green eyes snapped open and pinned him. She rose up, turning to face him and slipped one knee between his legs. She rubbed against his aroused flesh and his thoughts turned from her pleasure to his. With an expertise that should have shamed him, he had Alice's skirts up and her bloomers open. In the past, he had found the slit in the fabric that separated the two legs of a lady's undergarments more than ample to accomplish his goal, but now he wanted to see her as God made her, and that would require her consent. He patted the pocket of his blue jeans, feeling the square packet of the French preventative made out of vulcanized rubber. He had begun carrying one of the paper envelopes since Alice's arrival at the ranch. He was a dog, he knew it, and he should be ashamed. But instead he was inspired to be the lover she wanted. God, he'd do anything to please her, anything to make her happy even for just one night. But he cared too much about her to make her suffer. No one would know. Dillen would see that she did not endure the scandal of an unwed mother for her lapse in good judgment where he was concerned.

He lowered her to the floor, kissing her breasts, and then scaled her one kiss at a time until he reached her mouth. She met him with greedy kisses. The small mewling sounds of desire drove him to distraction. He reached beneath her skirts to release her bloomers, drawing them down and over her stockings and then the carefully laced shoes. Suddenly he wanted to see her feet, feel those heels dig into his back as she urged him on. Dillen slipped his hands up her velvety inner thighs and separated her legs. Alice wrapped her arms about his neck and drew him down for more sweet kisses as his fingers danced over her most private places. She was slippery wet as he toyed with her folds, parting her and titillating her needy, swollen flesh. She arched and clung and called out his name. He hushed her and she nodded her understanding as she glanced to the stairs above where his nephews slept. Alice bit her bottom lip and moaned as he continued to flick and rub and tease.

He knew he should pull back, withdraw and leave her here, but she was wet and wanting and he had what she needed to satisfy her. Dillen unfastened his buckle and then the rivets holding his jeans closed.

He watched her face as he released his engorged penis from

the denim restraints, fully expecting her to scream or run or skidder backward across the floor. Her rejection was what he needed to turn back.

But Alice was nothing if not unconventional. Threats and bribes, she had said. Neither worked on her because she was strong willed and knew what she wanted. Even if he questioned her judgment, he admired her tenacity as she reached out for him.

She enclosed her fingers about him and slid her hand from base to swollen tip. His eyes dropped shut and he groaned. So she did it again, using both hands this time. One of her delicate fingers caressed his balls, making him jump and twitch like a trout on a hook. But this was a hook he never wanted to escape. He cupped his hand over hers and showed her the motion, mimicking the loving rhythm. Then he reached down to find the pocket of his jeans and withdrew the rubber, quickly tugging it from its packet. He captured her hands, drawing them away from his engorged flesh.

She glanced at the circle of rubber and a tiny line creased her forehead between her brows.

"Do you know what this is?" he asked.

"I've heard of them. But never seen one."

"It will protect you."

She smiled and he kissed her mouth. She used her nails to score the flesh of his belly and chest, then dipped to take one of his nipples in her mouth. Sweet Mary, he'd never felt the like. He dropped back to the rug for a moment, savoring the sensations that tingled outward in all directions. Then she drew back and blew, just as he had done. Alice was nothing if not a fast learner.

He wanted her safe, but he wanted to feel her just once before he sheathed himself in the rubber. He urged Alice back, so they lay side by side. Then he lifted one of her legs over his hips and rolled toward her until her bottom pressed against his groin. Then he slid himself along the long, wet cleft of her slippery folds. Alice nestled closer and pressed her warm, taut bottom against him, increasing the friction. He had not intended to go farther, but she smelled so sweet and her flesh was slick with need. He rolled her to her back and found his place between her spreading legs. Alice stared up at him, her face a contradiction of need and anxiety. He tried for a smile but feared it was more grimace as he positioned himself to slide home. He started slowly, telling himself to use control, even as he gripped the rubber in his fist that was planted beside her head. He had no restraint where Alice was concerned. She loved him and he loved her. For the moment, that was enough.

When he felt the resistance he slowed, and then slipped his opposite hand around the back of her neck. The slim column of her throat seemed so pale and her flesh so fragile. He gripped her, held her as he thrust, breaking the membrane that marked her purity. Alice stifled a cry by placing a hand over her own mouth. Her startled eyes stared up at him. He lowered his forehead to hers, and breathed deep of the air scented with woodsmoke, kerosene and Alice.

"Shh," he whispered. "It's your first time. It won't hurt again. Rest a minute."

He needed to pause. Had to rein in the impulse to thrust deep again and again. Dillen gripped the rubber tighter and then slowly withdrew. He was slick with the wetness of her body and streaked with blood. Still, he did as he intended, slipping the rubber over his head and rolling it over his erect flesh.

"Dillen?" she whispered, her fingers seeking him, reaching down between them and stroking his stomach and chest until he thought he'd go mad.

He dropped over her, kissing her mouth and then moving to her ear. He kept his mouth on her lovely flesh, wishing the night could last a lifetime and knowing even that would not be long enough.

Alice began to writhe against him, lifting her hips and making a mewling sound of need. He moved to her breasts again as his fingers danced over her most sensitive places, stroking her thighs and then the flesh between her thighs. Dillen rubbed and thrust and titillated until Alice thrashed and bucked. Only then did he ease back inside her. The rubber helped. He realized that the deadening of sensation was, for him, a very good thing. He thrust quick and smooth, setting a deliberate rhythm as she lifted up to meet each stroke. Still, he kissed her neck and whispered encouragement as his fingers rubbed the tiny nub of sensation between her legs.

He was getting closer and thought he might need to pull back again, for he was determined that Alice would experience her own climax before he found his. But he did not realize just how near she was. One moment she jolted against him, eager for all he could give and the next she stiffened, arching up and pressing her breasts tight to his chest. He covered her mouth with his, deadening her cries of release. She moaned and her body went slack. He held her close as he thrust again, bringing another cry from her as he reached his own ecstasy. They fell back against the rug as their bodies slackened, his flesh going soft inside her. He gathered himself and the rubber, drawing back. She reached a now-clumsy hand and missed then tried again. Persistent, he thought, and dragged a large sheepskin rug from the ottoman beside the fire, tossing it over them. Alice cuddled against him, and he held her close. He slipped the used rubber into his pocket and let his head fall back on the bearskin.

"That was wonderful," she whispered as she stroked the coarse curly hair that covered his chest.

"Yes."

Her breathing deepened. But she muttered against him, "I never knew it would be like this. I thought you loved with your heart. Now I know it's so much more."

He smiled, proud to have given her the gift of a pleasure she had not even known existed.

They dozed. He woke when she shivered and pulled her close. Dillen opened his eyes to see hers already open.

"What?" he asked.

"I think we should get a Christmas tree tomorrow."

"Yes?" He drew lazy circles on her shoulder, savoring the feel of her satiny skin.

"For the boys." She rolled to her side, slipping one foot up his leg and then down again.

"Hmm," he said, changing his stroke to run up and down her spine. Alice was finely made, like his fiddle, all interesting hollows and enticing curves.

Alice laughed, a sound of pure joy. "I cannot wait to see them on Christmas morning."

He stiffened. Alice wasn't going to be here on Christmas morning. She was going to be with her family in Omaha.

Alice lifted her chin and gave him a silly, drunken smile.

What the hell had he just done?

* * *

Alice felt the change in his body first. He went from lethargy to tight-coiled muscles without appearing to move. But she perceived it and saw the change in the tense lines bracketing his full mouth.

"What?" he muttered, pressing a broad hand across his forehead.

"Christmas morning, the boys. I'm anxious to see them come down those stairs."

He sat up, forcing her to do the same. She suddenly became aware of the space between them.

"You'll be in Omaha."

"Of course not. I'm staying here with you and the boys."

"But..." Dillen's confused expression struck at her like an arrow. He glanced toward his coat and the door as if already planning to leave her again.

"Dillen. You just told me you loved me. We just..." She covered her mouth as shame burned at her cheeks. What had been the physical embodiment of love to her had been—what?—a lust-filled interlude to him? Alice drew the fleece to her body, hugging it like a pillow as she shook her head.

He reached out for her, clasping her shoulders. She dropped her chin so that she did not have to see his anxious eyes and worried expression. Whatever he said now, she was certain she would not like it.

"Alice, this doesn't change anything. You still need to go back. I still need to find a new job."

"And the boys?"

He didn't answer, but when she raised her gaze, she saw the pain in his eyes.

"And then you'll send for me?"

She forced herself to look, to witness his rejection. The room seemed suddenly freezing, but not as cold as his words.

"Those boys need a home and they need a mama. Someone used to hard living and doing without. Alice, you aren't made for that kind of life. You don't know how hard it can be."

Had he just told her that he planned to marry another woman?

"You said you loved me."

"And I always will. But it doesn't change what I have to do."

"Let me help you, please."

"We've been over that. Alice, you don't know what it's like to have nothing. I hope you never have to find out."

"I'd have you. I'd have the boys."

He turned away, drawing up his blue jeans and fastening his belt. He'd already decided, already made up his mind before any of this ever happened. And still he took all she had to give. But not her money. Not her help. Those he would never accept.

"So you'll send me away? Send the boys to Chicago?"

"Maybe, if times get lean."

He was pulling further and further back, she could feel it, and he hadn't moved a muscle. She launched herself at him, clinging to his back as she encircled him with her arms. "Then let me take them with me to Omaha."

He peeled her away and thrust her crumpled blouse and camisole at her. "Is that what my sister wanted? Did she ask you to raise them or bring them to me?"

She ignored her clothing and clasped his forearm with both hands. Her voice cracked. "Dillen?"

"Let me go, Alice." She didn't, so he looked away. "Cover yourself."

Shame made her cheeks glow with heat. Her fingers slipped from his arm and she accepted the garments, clasping them to herself like a frightened child clutches a favorite blanket.

He shrugged into his shirt and left it flapping open. Then he stood and retrieved his coat and hat from a peg beside Mr. Harvey's door.

"I thought you wanted me," she whispered.

"I've always wanted you. But it's not enough, Alice."

Dillen stood and headed for the door, pausing only to place his hat on his head and draw on his coat. Then he left her.

Alice crawled to the couch, still clutching her blouse and underthings as she watched Dillen run away again. The humiliation scalded her skin and burned her throat.

The pain of his rejection strangled her words, making them a weak whisper. "Wait."

But he didn't even look back as he bolted out the door. A moment later she heard the latch click.

"Wait," she whispered, the pain closing her throat.

She had her answer. Whatever feelings he had, they were not deep enough. It was time for her to accept the truth. He did not want her to stay.

Chapter Twelve

Dillen went back to the bunkhouse to find Bill snoring away. He buttoned his shirt, lingering to remember the feel of Alice pressed against him. He washed his face in water so cold the top layer was slush and he added another log to the stove. He hadn't meant to bang the stove door closed, but he did, and Bill snorted himself awake and launched into his familiar phlegmy cough.

"Back so soon?" he said.

"Guess so," said Dillen.

"Never took you for a fool." He rolled to his side. "Until now."

Dillen ignored the gibe. It took only a moment to strip out of his jeans and into his long underwear to sleep. But sleep eluded him. Finally he kicked off his blanket, stepped into his clothing, coat and boots. Then he headed out into the cold. He padded through new snow toward the barn, seeking the quiet comfort of the horses. The animals' gentle breathing and warm, earthy smell always calmed him and helped him think. He shoved his hands in his pockets, finding a used rubber in one and the damned telegram still in the other. He drew out the wire and read it again.

This time his reaction was not sorrow, but anger. He didn't want to lose Cody and Colin, and he didn't think some old woman could do a better job raising Sylvie's boys than he could. Alice had reminded him that just because his father had been a first-class shit didn't mean he couldn't do different. And damned if he wouldn't. He could do a sight better. Damned if he'd send them off. He'd raise them as his sister had wanted.

He scratched under Dasher's chin and then tugged playfully at his soft, furry lower lip. "She said she loved me."

His horse said nothing.

"Can you believe that? Me."

The horse's eyelids drooped and closed. Dillen wrapped a horse blanket around his shoulders and settled on the hay in Dasher's stall to think. Instead he dozed.

He woke shivering, wrapped in a horse blanket, wondering if Alice was really willing to take the step down to be his wife. Did she understand all she would lose in choosing him? Would she still have him if he wouldn't accept her money? What if her parents disowned her for marrying him? What if he couldn't make her happy? He didn't think he could live without her. But he knew full well she could live without him. And that truth had stopped him every time he'd considered going back to her.

This time, though, there were the boys to consider. It gave him an excuse to try, even fearing she would tire of the hardships, or worse, become dissatisfied with him. He pushed back his hat and thought long and hard. He knew what he wanted, but chances were good he'd never keep her.

He stood, stiff and heartsore. Dasher rested his front foot, his eyes closed in sleep. He didn't open them when Dillen let himself out of the stall, lowering the latch behind him. Dillen thought of what Alice had told him about her father. How her mother had married him before he was a great doctor. How he'd accepted help to begin his practice and buy their first home. Her father was a respected professional man and he'd used his wife's money to start that practice. Dillen stilled as he realized that her father was the bigger man. He'd made his own way but still had the self-confidence to take what his wife offered. Was Dillen willing to do the same? Or would he let his pride cost him Alice Truett again?

"No, damn it. I sure won't. I won't let her go again." Dillen stood and headed out of the barn, aiming for the house. He paused midway to the building. It was still the middle of the night. The only lamp burning was in the boys' front room. Alice's room was dark.

Before he went to Alice, he had business. He needed to wire Great-aunt Ethel and tell her that he was keeping his boys and he needed to cut down a Christmas tree. Then he would get down on his knees beside that tree and beg Alice to marry him.

"Wake up, Dasher. We need to ride."

Dillen hit Blue River Junction after sunup. The telegram got sent and then Dillen headed back to the ranch in deep, heavy snow. Without a track and sled, it was slow going. He finally left the main road for the pine forest where the snow was less deep.

He needed to find that Christmas tree for Alice and the boys.

After her humiliation, Alice returned to her room and packed her belongings through a blur of tears. If she could have done so, she would have left that very minute.

Instead she had tried and failed to sleep, stumbling from her bed as the sky turned gray. She had determined to leave with as much dignity as possible, knowing that she had left all she had on the floor beside the hearth. Her last, best, most desperate attempt to hold a man who would not be held. She had found a man who was independent, self-sufficient and knew how to work. But he preferred to do without, or at least without her.

She placed the wrapped gifts she had picked for the boys on the mantel and then went to find Dillen. There was no use in waiting another day. But Dillen was not in the bunkhouse. Mr. Roberts was as surprised as she was to see his empty bed.

"Do you think he would leave without telling you?" asked Alice.

"Naw," said Roberts. "He left his saddlebags and gear in the bunkhouse. He'll be back."

But the morning wore away and he did not come back. Alice asked Mr. Roberts to take her to town. She fed him and the boys and then bundled Cody and Colin beside her in the sleigh with her trunks and satchels. They drove through a heavy wet snow that stuck to the rooftops, making the town look like a village in a snow globe. It would be a white Christmas here, though likely not in Omaha.

Alice's first stop was the home of Roberts's niece, where she arranged for Mrs. Pellet to look after the boys until Dillen came for them. She put on her traveling clothing. The corsets squeezed her. The cashmere dress and sable-trimmed coat felt strange, as if they belonged to someone else.

She stared at herself in the oval mirror in Mrs. Pellet's best guest room. Outwardly she looked exactly like the woman who had arrived in Blue River Junction with two orphans in tow. But she was not the same.

She had felt alive here, and now the old numbness seeped through her. Soon her heart would cool, like a cup of tea left too long at the table. Passion would bleed away and there would be nothing left but this lovely, expensive shell.

Alice studied her pristine kid-gloved hands, her fingers interlocked before the row of faceted glass buttons on her flat, corseted stomach.

She would be well provided for, surrounded by and covered with things, the very things that had kept Dillen from her. How she hated them. Alice withdrew the pearl hatpin from the crown of her lush velvet and felted wool chapeau and threw it violently at the mirror. It ricocheted like a bullet off a rock canyon. Next, she unfastened her cameo brooch that was set with a small diamond and held it tight in her fist. Then she flung the finely carved shell toward the wall where it struck hard before falling to the floor.

She had removed her watch, complete with ruby fob and chain, and was swinging it over her head to create more velocity when Mrs. Pellet entered and stopped her.

Alice clutched at the woman who had everything she lacked—a home, a husband and children—and she wept.

Louise rocked her slowly as if Alice were a child. At last, Alice had cried herself dry. Mrs. Pellet retrieved the cameo and hatpin. Alice replaced the pins, one to her hat and one to her collar. Then she withdrew a dog-eared tome. She set her copy of *Mrs. Beeton's Book of Household Management* gently on the bedside table, resting two fingers on the cover for just a moment.

At last she stood and wiped away the twin rivers of her tears, the moisture quickly absorbed by her black leather gloves.

Mr. Roberts called from the entranceway. A few minutes later he transported her luggage to the station and checked on the schedule.

Alice ate lunch with the boys but barely touched her food. Mrs. Pellet tried to cheer her, but to no avail. Alice had failed and now faced the grim reality of a loveless, suitable marriage to one of the many dandies, or the lonely life of a wealthy spinster. In the short term, she would spend Christmas Eve in her grandparents' palatial home and Christmas morning in church, missing again the joy-filled morning her brothers shared with their families. Their happiness now served only to emphasize her misery.

"Did you tell him you love him?" asked Mrs. Pellet.

"I did, and I offered myself."

This shocked Mrs. Pellet.

Alice lowered her head. That he'd turned her down was obvious.

"Oh, my," said Mrs. Pellet, and then, "You're too good for him," which made Alice cry.

She cried again when Colin presented her with her Christmas gift. Mr. Roberts had helped the boys carve cedar shavings and then used white yarn and a blanket stitch to sew them into a red bandanna fashioned in the shape of a heart.

"It's a satchel," said Cody.

"To make your socks smell nice," added Colin.

She hugged and kissed them both and let her heart break when they told her they didn't want her to go. How she wished she could scoop them up and take them home with her. These two could fill the empty places in her heart, and with them she would have a life to be grateful for. But Sylvia had asked her to bring them to her brother. She had done so, and it was time to go.

The boys waved goodbye from the window of Mrs. Pellet's home as Mr. Roberts drove her to the station. There she stopped to send a wire with her new arrival information to her father. Roberts spoke to the operator, who revealed that Dillen had sent a reply to Chicago this very morning; the operator didn't know what he'd said, but he did know that Roach had arrived before business hours and awakened his assistant by pounding on the door.

Alice's mood sank still further. The boys would be going East to their great-great-aunt. She knew that Dillen would have made a wonderful father, but the decision was not hers. All she could do was tell Mr. Roberts that she was more than willing to take the boys temporarily or to adopt them if Dillen found he could not care for them.

The train whistle sounded low and mournful. Alice checked her hatpins and pressed two fingers to the ornate shell cameo at her throat. Then she lifted her traveling case and stepped from the depot to the platform. There was no one to kiss her goodbye.

She managed to hold back the sobs, but not the tears. She glanced over her shoulder for Dillen and then propelled herself into the car, taking her seat beside the window. She was still searching for one last look at him as the whistle blew and the train inched from the station.

Chapter Thirteen

Dillen reached the ranch dragging a ten-foot pine behind Dasher. But he found the house empty. Further searching led him to discover the sleigh, Bill Roberts, Alice and the boys all gone. The accumulation had covered their tracks, but now that he was looking, he realized they were heading for town. He sliced the rope holding the tree, turned about and met Bill right at the edge of town coming back empty.

"Where's Alice and the boys? Shopping again?"

Roberts gave him a hard look. "If you made indecent proposals to that woman, I swear I'll climb down off this sled and bust open your nose."

A chill went through Dillen as he realized something was very wrong.

"Bill, where is she? Where are the boys?"

"The boys are at my niece's and Alice is on a train for Denver with a connection to Omaha. What the Sam Hill did you do to that woman to send her packing?"

Dillen heard the train whistle. "She's on board?"

Roberts nodded.

Dillen lifted his reins.

"Where you going? It's too late. Train's gone!"

Dillen pressed his heels into Dasher's sides and his horse erupted into a gallop.

He had to stop Alice. But first he had to stop a train.

Dasher was a fast horse and the tracks were clear of most of the snow. Dillen rode like blue blazes and caught the train before it had traveled too far outside Blue River Junction. Now he had to get on board and convince the engineer to hit the brake. Riding at a gallop, he passed the caboose and the three passenger cars. When he reached the engine, he used his trick-riding skills and stood on the saddle until he had both hands on the rails that flanked the ladder to the engine. Then he stepped aboard and watched Dasher veer off at a trot. *Good horse,* he thought, swinging up into the engine and drawing his pistol.

"Stop this train," he shouted.

The engineer and the fireman, still holding his shovel of coal, both turned in unison. The engineer raised his hands as his eyes widened. The fireman gripped the handle of his shovel, judged Dillen out of range and set it aside.

"Stop it, now!" he ordered.

The engineer swallowed. "I gotta signal the brakeman. He's in the caboose."

"Do it, then," growled Dillen.

The man reached for the whistle and let out a series of blasts. A moment later Dillen heard the brakes squeal. The engineer reached for the engine brake. The steel tracks and steel wheels shrieked as the train slowed.

"I hope to hell you know what you're doing, boyo," said the grizzled engineer.

Dillen was already off the engine and running along the tracks.

Alice marched behind the conductor along the raised rail bed. The snow had begun in earnest now, and it stood in bright contrast to the long black sable fur on her cuffs and collar. Had the conductor not mentioned a wild-eyed cowboy named Roach, she would have most assuredly remained in the passenger car. Instead she strode into battle, afraid that she would not have the luxury of an exit that did not involve further tears. She thought again of last night's debacle and her cheeks heated in shame. Dillen did not want her, but apparently he wanted something, for stopping a train was no small matter and bore certain unpleasant consequences.

According to the conductor, Mr. Roach had used a pistol and a fast horse to convince the engineer to delay their travel. She approached the steaming engine and saw him hanging from the car, staring back at her through the fast-falling snow.

"Alice?"

"Mr. Roach, what is the meaning of this?"

Now that he had her here, he seemed quite speechless. She

glanced about at the movement to her left and discovered that Dasher had found his master and was attempting to scale the steep embankment to reach him. Both the engineer and the fireman stared at her. She hated being the center of attention and considered retreat. But something in Dillen's eyes pinned her to the spot.

"I came for you," he said.

"You're going to jail," said the conductor to Dillen.

Dillen bared his teeth. "Hush up, you."

The situation teetered from precarious to perilous. Alice knew Dillen was an excellent shot. She also knew he had never aimed a pistol at a man before. What on earth had driven him to such folly? Her heart fluttered with hope that it was her leaving.

The fireman chimed in. "He said you was his wife and you abandoned your kids and all."

"He what?" Alice gave the man a scathing look and he dropped his gaze. She then turned her attention to Dillen, who held the engineer and fireman at gunpoint. "Your pardon, sir," said Alice to the engineer. "Do you know my grandfather, Mr. John W. Pinter?"

The engineer's eyes went round, the fireman dropped his shovel and the conductor began to choke. Apparently they all knew Mr. John W. Pinter, or at least they knew his name.

"Boys," said the engineer, "if anything happens to that little lady, we're all fired."

The fireman lifted his shovel and Dillen struck him on the head with the butt end of his pistol, hard enough to send him staggering back as he dropped the coal shovel in favor of clutching his head.

"Stop!" shouted Alice.

All three men and one weary horse turned their attention to her.

"I would like to speak to Mr. Roach in private, please. I'm sure my grandfather will be very grateful for your consideration."

"But he's armed," said the conductor.

She turned to Dillen. "Put it away."

He did.

"Now follow me." Alice made her way along the track, stopping before the cowcatcher of the enormous snorting iron horse. Both Dillen and Dasher trailed her.

"I'm sorry about last night," he said.

Not half as sorry as she was. "You made your regret fairly obvious, Mr. Roach." Alice lifted her stubborn chin and stared past him to the rivets securing the front panel of the engine.

"And I'm sorry I left you last night and that I left you in Omaha."

Alice met his gaze, seeing her own grief reflected back at her. Snow accumulated on the wide brim of his worn, stained hat and filled the notch in the crown. She wanted to tell him that he did not need to stop a train to tell her he found her lacking and unsuitable as both wife and mother. Instead she said nothing, using all her energy not to weep in front of him.

Dillen rubbed his neck. "I always figured you'd be better off without hitching yourself to my sorry carcass. I've accepted that I'm not ever going to be able to make the kind of money your granddad has."

"I never expected you to."

"You still don't understand."

Alice brushed the snow that clung, sticky and wet, to the lace veil of her wool hat. "I'm trying, but, Dillen, if you love me, why let me go again?"

"Alice, why can't you see? You want me to accept your help."

"Yes!"

"But you never needed mine."

"What?"

"I didn't just leave because of the money."

Why, then? Her stomach heaved at the possibilities, and she clasped both hands across her middle, forbidding herself the humiliation of being unwell before him.

"Oh, Alice, how do I make you understand? If you'd ever come to me ragged or needy, just once... If there was one single thing I could give you that you didn't already have... But there's nothing I've got that you need."

She stared in horror for a moment.

"I want you. But I need a woman who needs me, too."

Alice realized that this entire time all he wanted, all he needed, was the same thing that she did—to be essential to him.

"But you have *everything* I need in this world."

His face showed disbelief, for what could he have that she could not buy?

"I need you to give me a home to call our own. I need you to give me love in the long cold nights. And I need you to give me children to adore. I don't want an empty palace. I don't want things. I'm sick to death of things. All I need in this world, Dillen Roach, is your arms around me and the love in your heart."

Dillen stared at her in wonder. Her heart hammered as she waited for him to speak or to act. Was it enough? But for a long moment he just stood as the snow drifted silently down upon them from above. Then he opened his arms to her. Alice stepped forward happily.

"I can give you those things."

She nodded, her tears wetting his sheepskin jacket. "And I'll take them all, gladly."

"I love you, Alice. Please don't go."

"Never," she whispered.

Alice closed her eyes as the sorrow melted from her heart with the snow on her cheeks until she felt only the warmth of his embrace and the joy welling inside her like a hot spring.

Chapter Fourteen

Alice had taken note of the names of the engineer and his fellows before she departed with Dillen, riding double on Dasher. Had she really tried to throw away her grandmother's cameo brooch in Mrs. Pellet's home? Yes, she had, because all this time she thought it was those things, those wretched, glittering alluring things that had kept Dillen from her these two long years, when all the time it had been her inability to let Dillen help her. The need to be needed. We all have it. Why hadn't she seen that her armor of wealth had made him think he wasn't fundamental to her happiness?

Dillen stopped at Mrs. Pellet's home to pick up the boys. Alice longed to linger in the cheerful parlor. It was already festooned with evergreen swag and garlands accented with bright red bows. Beside the window was a Christmas tree that stood ready for the woman of the house to decorate after her children were tucked safely into their beds. The boys rushed to Alice in welcome, and their exuberance filled her heart to brimming.

Mrs. Pellet ushered out her family and drew closed the two pocket doors, leaving Alice and Dillen with Cody and Colin. Dillen did most of the talking, explaining to the boys that he planned to marry Alice and that they would be a family from here on out.

"What do we call you?" Cody asked Alice, ever the practical one.

"Well, I am not going to try to replace your mother. She was my dearest friend and I loved her very much. So I will understand if you wish to continue to call me Alice. If you ever wish to refer to me as your mother, I would be honored."

Dillen glanced at Colin. "You have any questions, little man?"

"Where will we live?"

Dillen took that one. "We'll stay in the ranch house until the thaw." He glanced toward Alice. "After that we'll be looking for a spread of our own."

The snow was now falling so heavily that Dillen rented a sleigh from the livery, leaving Dasher safe and snug in a stall. They arranged to return for the sleigh after they completed their business.

The first was the telegraph office, where Dillen sent a message to Alice's father asking for his daughter's hand. Alice was fearful that her father would not recall Dillen or would deny his request because her mother *did* recall him.

Dillen took them to dinner while they waited, and the reply arrived as the boys were finishing their pumpkin pie. Cody, at least, seemed to sense the importance of this moment, for he lowered his fork and watched Dillen with anxious eyes.

Alice laced her fingers together beneath the white tablecloth and prayed as Dillen scanned the message and then grinned. The breath left her and her head dipped for a moment as she sagged with relief.

"Read it, Uncle Dillen," demanded Cody.

"'Permission granted. Stop. Take good care of my precious girl. Stop. Will inform Mother of your plans. Stop. Fremont Truett.'"

"Guess we'd better go find a preacher," said Dillen.

"Now?" asked Alice.

"Heck yes, now. When you've waited as long as I have to wed the gal you love, the wedding can't come soon enough."

Alice longed to kiss him, but refrained from public displays of affection and settled for squeezing his hand under the table.

The church was Presbyterian instead of Episcopalian, but Alice did not care. Reverend Middleton was gracious in his agreement to marry them on short notice just prior to the Christmas Eve service. And that was how Alice Pinter Truett, heiress to a considerable fortune, wearing a simple dove-gray dress and with no adornment save a borrowed veil, wed Dillen Roach, a man of considerable pride and integrity. In her hand she carried a prayer book, and in her heart she carried love and hope.

The little church was full to bursting with the members of the congregation. Bathed in soft candlelight and decorated with sprigs of evergreen, the interior glowed with the enchantment of Christmas services. Alice could not think of a more lovely setting to exchange her vows, and Dillen told her that he had never seen a more beautiful bride. With the simple exchange of words, a kiss and two signatures, they were married. In that moment, four people became a family and one wandering cowboy set down roots deep and strong.

Alice believed in him, and that gave him the confidence to accept what she offered: her help, her heart and her courage.

He was the luckiest cowboy alive.

Something hit the bed with enough force to bring Dillen upright. The next jolt struck him square in the chest as Cody joined Colin on the bed Dillen now shared with his wife, Alice.

Alice groaned and her eyes fluttered open as Cody slipped into the gap between them. Dillen peered at the gray light filtering through the window above the half curtains. Pellets of ice struck the pane, and the room was cold enough for him to see his breath.

"Wake up!" said Colin, nudging Alice. "It's Christmas! Santa came! He came!"

Alice had been up late decorating the tree and filling the nosegay ornaments with treats. Dillen had busied himself whittling a slingshot for Cody and painting the hobbyhorse he'd already finished for Colin.

Then he'd kept her up even longer. A grin broadened across his face.

"All right, I'm up. Come on, boys. Let's get the fire started and give Alice some privacy."

Colin swung onto his back and Cody led the charge from the room. Dillen glanced back to Alice.

"Do you think Santa brought you anything?"

"I already have everything I ever wanted."

"Still, Saint Nick wouldn't forget you."

Dillen had the fire started and the coffee on before Alice appeared, her hair in a loose braid and wearing a simple blue woolen dress that was as relaxed and pretty as its owner. The boys dug into their stockings as she started a breakfast of eggs and ham. Cody and Colin ran from the hearth to the kitchen to show her the caramels and the peppermint and sassafras sticks that Santa had brought them. The bounty continued as she set the table and sliced the bread, the stockings disgorging licorice whips, jacks for Colin and a sack of marbles for Cody. Alice insisted they eat before they indulged in the treats Santa had provided, but when the boys took their places, there was a distinct smell of licorice at the table. Dillen bowed his head and gave thanks. Everyone echoed his amen and Alice was quite horrified at how fast the food vanished and festivities commenced.

Dillen kept the fire blazing as the boys opened their gifts. Both Colin and Cody feigned appreciation for the knickers and jackets, showed minimal interest in the hosiery, but the riding boots were a great success. Cody was in ecstasy over the slingshot, which Alice worried was a horrendous idea. Both she and Dillen extracted promises from Cody that he would not shoot either his little brother or any songbirds. Colin proved a great horseman on his new hobbyhorse, which he rode all about the house wearing new boots.

Alice placed the goose that Dillen had provided in the oven with potatoes and onions. Mr. Roberts arrived to give the boys each a handful of lead soldiers that looked as ancient as the foreman. He stayed long enough to have a cup of coffee and admire what Santa had brought. Then he was off to the home of his niece for Christmas dinner.

After Mr. Roberts's departure, Alice settled in her chair. The boys approached, hands behind them, and Alice's smile broadened as she glimpsed the bundle past Cody's narrow body.

"We made you a present," said Cody.

Alice protested. "You already gave me my gift, my lovely satchel."

"It's for the tree," said Colin. "For the top."

"Don't tell her that!" growled Cody as he quickly handed over a gift wrapped in one of the dish towels.

"For me?" Alice kissed them both on their foreheads and then drew back the edges. "Whatever can it be?"

"It's an angel," said Colin.

Cody groaned and glanced to Dillen, who just smiled and shook his head.

Alice drew back the cloth to reveal a carved wooden angel with white feather wings. "Oh, she is beautiful!"

Dillen came to stand beside her, one hand on her shoulder. "A tree topper," he said. "I tried to make one like the one I saw on your tree at your grandfather's home, except there's no gilding and the head isn't porcelain and it's goose feathers."

"We glued them on!" said Colin, bouncing now with excitement.

"It is the most beautiful angel I have ever seen." She kissed the boys and then her husband. "Please put it on the top of our tree."

"We can get another someday," said Dillen. "A store-bought one."

"No. That angel shall top every tree from here forward. Our first tree."

Dillen grinned in pleasure as he took the ornament and lifted it into place, using the wire he'd fastened to the back to secure it to the fir tree.

Alice stood by his side, admiring their angel. "Angels are usually blond," she said.

"My angel is one of a kind, and she's got light brown hair." He gave her a squeeze and dropped a kiss on her head.

The boys stared up at the angel as if mesmerized. Alice broke the spell.

"And now I think it is time for a little music. Cody, the fiddle, if you please."

Cody scrambled to retrieve the fiddle from the corner table beside the sofa. Dillen tuned his fiddle and rosined up his bow as Alice settled the boys beside her on the sofa.

"What song would you like?" asked Dillen.

"Boys?" said Alice, deferring to them.

"You pick, Mama," said Cody. It was the first time he had called her that and her reaction surprised her. She burst into tears and hugged the boys as she stared up at her husband, who seemed on the verge of tears himself.

"Oh, I can only think of one carol to sing right now. What about 'Joy to the World'?"

Dillen lifted his fiddle and bow. Next their voices filled the little ranch house with music and her heart with gladness. Alice was home for Christmas after all.

* * * * *

DANCE WITH
A COWBOY

KATHRYN ALBRIGHT

Dear Reader,

I am delighted to bring you Kathleen and Garrett's story that takes place in the backcountry of Southern California—one of my favorite places. They've each had their disappointments and regrets and truly deserve a "happily ever after," if only they can forgive the hurts of the past. Perhaps, in this season of miracles, they can. After all, love is the greatest gift.

A big thank-you to my agent, Mary Sue Seymour of The Seymour Agency, and to Harlequin editors Linda Fildew and Charlotte Mursell. You are each a treasure on this publishing journey.

I love to hear from my readers. You can find me online at www.kathrynalbright.com, Facebook and Goodreads. Stop by and say hi.

Merry Christmas!

Kathryn Albright

DEDICATION

This story is dedicated to my first critique group—
Maggie, Nina, Barb and Cheryl.
I couldn't have come this far without you.
Thanks for always being there!

Look for
The Gunslinger and the Heiress
Coming January 2015

Chapter One

Southern California, 1882

Garrett Sheridan latched the gate after the last of the Corriente steers pushed through into the small holding yard. Sweat dripped down his temple and veered toward his eye, the salt stinging as he squinted. He swiped the moisture with his arm and then resettled his hat. Temperatures might be in the fifties but he'd worked up a lather getting the small herd up the Old Slide Trail to the enclosure behind Ham's butcher shop.

Next to him, Eduardo tilted forward in his saddle, the expression of anticipation on his face making him look younger than his twenty years.

"*Gracias,* Eduardo." Garrett tugged off his leather gloves, dragged the folded wad of money from inside his vest and counted out a third of the vaquero's earnings. The rest, Eduardo had insisted when he hired on, should go directly to his mother. Garrett counted that out, too, and tucked it in his hip pocket. "Daybreak Monday."

A wide grin split across Eduardo's face. He reined his mount away from the corral and took off at an easy lope down the main road toward the saloon and an evening of gaming and drinking with his friends from the surrounding ranches. He'd find his way to his parents' home by morning.

Garrett might have only eight years on Eduardo, but he couldn't remember the last time he'd felt that carefree.

He stroked Blue's neck and then led him to the water trough. While the horse drank his fill, Paul Ham stepped from his shop. They'd already negotiated the price per head on the cattle, so Garrett figured this was more a social call—and he had an idea what it might be about. Still, he waited for Paul to get past the idle talk of the weather, knowing the real issue would come soon enough.

"Saw smoke out your way."

"Took down a dead tree at Gully's Creek. Burned the rotted part."

"Got a few good memories of that spot."

He didn't need a trip down memory lane—not today. "Nearly lost a steer. A dead branch came down with that last storm."

"Guess you had to do it, then, but it still won't seem the same."

That was the idea. That tree had witnessed a lot. He'd had enough of the reminders, although he wouldn't admit that to Paul… or anybody.

Paul studied him for a moment. "You hear the news about Kathleen?"

Even after five long years, hearing her name still had the power to chase any other thought from his mind. He wished that weren't the case.

"Seems it's common knowledge." Common for everyone but his family. It was a bur under his saddle. Kathleen hadn't sent word to the ranch to let his folks—or him—know she'd returned to Clear Springs. He took a deep breath, steeling himself for more questions.

"You seen her?"

"Not yet. I'll stop by Molly's today." Ma had learned of it when she hosted the ladies' quilting group. Then she had told Pa, and they'd both informed Garrett it was his duty to bring Kathleen on out to the ranch. She had no business paying for her room and board when a perfectly good room lay vacant there. Besides, Ma was fair itching to help with her child—a thing Garrett had difficulty believing even now. He was an *uncle*.

"She took that opening at Becker's."

Garrett nodded. He hadn't heard that.

"Christmas Dance is in a few weeks. Maybe you can talk her into coming. I wouldn't mind a turn around the floor with her." A smirk appeared. "Lucy Mae's planning to go."

Garrett grunted. Lucy Mae had set her sights on him for last year's party, and in a moment of weakness he'd agreed to go with her. Luckily, a sick calf had needed him more than Lucy Mae and he'd ended up staying at the ranch. After that, Lucy had made it known that he was something of a scoundrel. "Likely I'll be there. You know how Ma looks forward to it every year."

"Women." Paul snickered. "They're tamin' the countryside. In a friendly way, if you know what I mean."

Garrett shook Paul's hand, and then gathered Blue's reins and headed down Main Street. At the crossroad, he took a right, passed two tall clapboard houses and then stopped in front of a small log home. Señora Nuñez bent over her clay oven in the side yard, removing bread. In a routine that had become familiar to them both, Garrett gave her Eduardo's earnings, refused her invitation to stay for dinner and thanked her for the thick slice of warm bread with a slab of cheese that she pressed into his hands.

He turned back toward the main road and Becker's Bakery. Half of him couldn't wait to see Kathleen again. He felt it deep inside, the old charge of excitement he'd tamped down and controlled for as long as he could remember. Had she changed? It'd help immensely if she'd grown fat and ugly over the past five years. The other half, the half that had spurred him into torching that old tree…that part of him wanted her to stay far, far away.

But most of all he had to know…why had she come back? This town held nothing but bad memories for her. He'd lived with those same memories—the ground rumbling, the explosion and then the air choking with dust as it billowed from the mine. And right in the thick of it, his brother, Josh.

The bells over the door tinkled twice as more customers entered the shop. Kathleen looked up from the dough she'd just shaped into a fat braid. A tall woman she didn't recognize stood contemplating the baked-goods display while a man behind her waited his turn. The town had changed since she'd lived here. The discovery of gold had new people moving in. Yet some things remained the same, and she relished seeing those people she remembered as they stopped in the bakery.

"Kathleen! Remember to knead that another ten times!" Sue Becker called out from the register.

She sighed as she contemplated destroying her artwork. The dough had become sticky again. Sprinkling flour over the mound and onto the board, she shoved the heels of her hands into the center of the dough and pushed it away from her. Ten times! Her hands and arms ached from a week of kneading and slicing and stirring. She blew out a breath, hoping to displace a fallen lock of blond hair that obscured her vision without using the back of her hand. Although why that mattered she didn't know. She was already covered in flour from topknot to toe.

She separated the dough into two loaves, braiding both of them into a pleasing design. She would take one loaf to her aunt's for supper. She smiled as she thought of the woman's condition for watching Lily during the day. Soft warm bread…and company of an evening so that the night didn't tarry so long. Of course, Kathleen would have none of that. Molly had turned her home into a boardinghouse in the years since her husband had passed away and Kathleen would pay for her keep just as anyone else would.

She set the earthenware trays with the loaves on an iron rack over the oven. An hour to rise and they'd be ready for baking. As she lowered her arms and dusted the flour from her apron, she realized the chatter in the bakery had ceased. What was more, Sue and the tall woman looked from her to someone in the shadowed corner with more interest than seemed warranted.

The figure stepped into the light and for a second Josh, her husband, stood before her. The breath ceased to move in her lungs. That build…those powerful shoulders. It could be him. It could… but that was impossible. Josh had been gone these past five years.

"Hello, Kathleen."

Her breath caught. The voice was Josh's. But…no…Josh was dead. There had been a funeral…a body…badly scarred.

The man removed his well-worn Stetson.

Garrett.

She let out her breath as recognition set in. Josh's brother. Older by two years, but still the same lanky build and light brown hair. Everything the same except for his eyes. Josh's eyes had been brown where Garrett's were sea-green—the color of a wave with the sun shining through.

Her own eyes burned. She stood frozen, barely breathing. The turbulence inside of her took her by surprise. She hadn't an inkling that coming face-to-face with him after all these years would matter. She thought she had matured—moved beyond her past.

"Garrett," she murmured, and felt like she was sixteen again and standing before him in the Satterlys' barn. It had to be that he was a familiar face. That was all. Nothing more.

She stepped up to the counter. "How are you? I…I planned to visit once I got settled." Hopefully, her words weren't a lie. She just needed to bolster her courage before confronting the Sheridans en masse.

He nodded, his gaze glued to hers. She couldn't tell if he believed her. "You're looking well," he finally said. "How is…?"

"Lily." She frowned slightly at supplying the information. Didn't he remember? "She's fine."

"Oh, for goodness sake," Sue said. "Kathleen, you've been working hard all day with Christmas coming and all. The shop won't fall apart if you take a short break and visit for a spell."

The shop might not fall apart, but she sure could. She knew she owed the Sheridans an explanation. They were family—Lily's family—not hers. Never hers. Maybe it was best to get this over with. She knew Garrett slightly better than his parents, although that knowledge wouldn't make the conversation any easier.

"Thank you, Sue." She reached behind her waist and untied her apron. Removing the loop over her head, she hung it on a peg by the window and then washed her hands in a pan of tepid water on the stove. With a quick check of her hair, she tied on her straw bonnet, grabbed her cloak and stepped from behind the counter. "I won't be long."

Garrett held the door open and followed her out into the late-afternoon light that filtered through the pines. They stood for a moment, staring at each other. He was taller than she remembered… taller than Josh. And where Josh's nose had tilted up in a friendly fashion, Garrett's was straight as a knife's blade. He didn't say a word, just turned and started down the boardwalk.

She supposed walking—and talking—would be easier than standing still and looking at each other in an awkward attempt at normality. Although her legs ached from standing all day, she fell into step. They headed away from the mill. The sound of the saw's constant whirring lessened even as the buzz of nervous energy inside her began to build. Their footsteps grew louder on the boards, emphasizing their lack of conversation.

At the corner he stopped.

"We could sit." He tilted his chin toward the bench in front of the hotel.

"I'd like that." Stilted. Proper.

They crossed the street and he waited while she settled herself. He didn't sit, but leaned against the post that supported the small overhang to the hotel's front entrance. To anyone passing by it looked like a casual meeting, but the sharpness of his gaze belied that. She drew in a deep breath, filling her lungs with the scent of the crisp mountain air. "I've missed the smell of the pines. It's different on the coast. Salt in the air. Brine."

He raised his chin slightly in acknowledgment. Small lines fanned out at the corners of his eyes, yet she doubted with Garrett that the lines were from laughing.

"So you're back."

She nodded, pasted on a bright smile.

"Alone?"

"With my daughter."

"Josh's daughter," he murmured. The lines deepened between his dark brows. "You named her Lily?"

"After my grandmother." He should know this; she'd sent a note after the birth. "She is five now."

"Why did you come back?"

It was more a challenge than a question. She'd been asked the same thing half a dozen times since her return, but now the answer sounded too simple, even to her own ears. "I wanted Lily to grow up here."

He seemed to turn her words over in his mind.

She stiffened her spine. She wasn't about to blurt out all that had really gone on—the snide comments questioning Lily's parentage. The suggestive glances and remarks from men who thought she was lonely. Her parents' constant disappointment in her, in Lily.

"The memories are still here," he said.

Meaning Josh. Those memories. She relaxed slightly. "I have good memories from growing up here—the schoolhouse, swimming in the lake. It's a good place to raise a child."

Again, he seemed to consider her answer, looking past the surface of her words. He'd always done that, even when they'd been younger. Her gaze drifted to his lips, remembering her very first kiss and how sweet and gentle it had been. So different from his brother. She frowned, upset at the comparison. She'd come here to move on with her life, not to dwell in the past.

She stood, gathered her shawl closer around her and moved to the edge of the porch. "I'd better go. Sue is in a tizzy getting ready for the season."

He straightened and moved away from the post. "I'll walk you back."

Always the gentleman. He hadn't changed in that regard.

"It's not necessary. I'll see myself back to the bakery." She started down the steps to the street.

"When can I see Lily?"

She stopped. She'd been expecting the request, but she wasn't ready to share her daughter. "Another time."

"I don't get into town very often. I can wait until you're done working."

"No!" It came out fast—unthinkingly—without tact.

His eyes narrowed. "Do you want to explain why not?"

"I need to prepare her first."

"Prepare her! What the heck for?"

She raised her chin. "Other than my great-aunt Molly, Lily has no idea she has relatives here." Before he could say another word, she turned and hurried away.

She hadn't told Lily anything about his side of the family!

Garrett kept Kathleen in his sights while she crossed the road, holding the hem of her blue dress out of the mud as she dodged a flatbed wagon. Wispy blond curls escaped from under her hat and whipped across her cheeks, pink from the cool air.

All peaches and creamy skin—even prettier than he remembered her. His dreams hadn't done her justice. And trim, like she'd been before Lily. He could probably span her waist with his hands. The only things big on her were her blue eyes—the color of cornflowers. Next to her he felt gangly…and too awkward for the wooden bench she'd sat upon. She disappeared into the bakery without looking back.

Her answers to his questions had raised more questions. He

hadn't come close to suggesting she move out to the ranch like his mother wanted. Yet…she'd come back. Maybe, just maybe, things could be put right.

A burst of belly-aching laughter emanated from inside the saloon. Kathleen would be at least another hour at the bakery. He stepped off the porch and headed toward the Rawhide Emporium. A game of darts would while away the time until she was free. He couldn't go back to the ranch without at least setting eyes on Lily. Family looked after family. How many times had he heard that over the years from his folks? That was all there was to it in their way of thinking. And he agreed.

All the way up until it had gotten his brother killed.

Chapter Two

Through the bakery's front window, Kathleen watched Garrett head to the saloon in his long, achingly familiar stride. He'd changed over the course of five years. Leaner, tougher, quieter. She put him from her mind—not an easy task—and turned back to helping Sue for the remainder of the afternoon.

At closing time, Sue flung her scarf over her head and tied a knot under her chin. "You get home to that daughter of yours, now. I don't want you working so hard that you give up in a week."

"Then I probably shouldn't have started the week after Thanksgiving."

Sue grinned. "Good for me, though. My busiest time of year." Her eyes twinkled as she closed the door behind her.

Kathleen finished washing out the bowls, eggbeaters and measuring cups they'd used that day and then wiped off the counter. She wrapped the loaf of bread in brown paper and tucked it under her arm and then turned down the lantern until the flame sputtered out. When she stepped from the shop, stars winked in the darkening sky. The streets were empty except for two men sitting on the upended barrels outside the saloon, smoking their rolled cigarettes. Light from a few establishments—the saloon, the restaurant and the hotel—brightened the otherwise black street.

She tried to lock the door with her free hand, but without success. There had to be a trick to it.

"Let me." Garrett yanked the door shut so that the lock aligned, then turned the key and handed it back to her.

His presence should have startled her, but a strange intuition had enveloped her ever since their earlier meeting. "Don't you have a ranch to run?"

He stayed at her side as she walked across the road. "My father can handle the ranch."

"Oh." She felt a stab of conscience. She hadn't asked after his folks earlier. "How are your parents?"

"The same. Guess you'll find out now that you're back. They'll want to see you…to see Lily. You're family."

"No, Garrett. I'm not."

He frowned. "You married Josh."

"And he's dead. That pretty much dissolves any family ties, don't you think?" It was a harsh thing to say—and so unlike her. She wasn't sure where it had come from, but somewhere deep inside her it had thrust its way to the surface.

He stopped walking. His face hardened and the air between them chilled a good ten degrees.

She should apologize for her outburst, but she couldn't. Barbara and Brent Sheridan had been furious about the shotgun wedding. Although they had never said anything outright, their opinion of her had always been clear. She had lived on their ranch for a few short weeks after the wedding and although they'd been polite, they'd never opened up to her. Even Josh had noticed.

"It's been a long day. I don't want to stand here and argue." She didn't have the time or the energy, not with a pile of mending waiting for her after supper. "What do you want, Garrett?"

"I told you earlier. I want to see Lily."

"And you received my answer. Not today." She started for Molly's again.

"I don't get away from the ranch all that much. It'll be a while before I come this way again."

Panic set in. Lily would be at the door the moment Kathleen opened it and they were nearly there. She stopped walking and faced him. "Look. Coming here has been a huge upheaval in her life…and in mine. Please, just let this go for now."

He searched her face and for the first time she thought she glimpsed concern in his eyes. "All right. For now, I'll wait."

She breathed a sigh of relief.

"But in return, once you've talked to her, promise to bring Lily out to the ranch. My folks want to meet her. Show her a bit of her heritage."

The thought of facing the Sheridans made her stomach clench, but Garrett didn't look as though he was going to budge unless she acknowledged her part in this bargain.

"Very well."

"This week." He backed into the shadows.

She didn't answer, but turned and opened the door. With a cry of delight, Lily ran from the kitchen and hugged Kathleen about her hips.

"You're home! You're home! What's that?" Lily asked, eyeing her package of bread.

"A present for Molly and you." Kathleen glanced out into the yard. The night had swallowed Garrett, but she sensed he was still there—watching. She entered the house and shut the door.

Later that night, with her basket of darning supplies held snug against her waist, Kathleen took one more peek at Lily burrowed into her blankets and then closed the bedroom door. She headed for the parlor and sat in the bentwood rocker beside the hearth. She might not keep her eyes open long enough to finish the mending, but she needed a quiet moment. Darning egg and needle in hand, she glanced at her great-aunt, who dozed in the chair across from her. Her gray hair frizzled out from her head in disarray and a big yawn escaped her attempt to stifle it. Her knitting lay untouched in her lap.

"Garrett Sheridan came by today," Kathleen said.

Molly roused and peered over her spectacles.

"He wants to see Lily."

"I'm sure his family will want to help you in any way that they can."

"That's what worries me. In the past whenever I've accepted help, it has come with unspoken expectations. It's better if I manage on my own."

Molly picked up her knitting needles. "Garrett's a good man. Salt of the earth. He's done a lot of improvements to the ranch. Kept it going after Josh passed."

"Next thing you'll be saying is that I should be happy that he is Lily's uncle." On hearing the sarcastic tone in her words, she sighed. "I'm sorry. I know you are friends with the Sheridans."

"You could have ended up with a lesser man with that title. That's for sure. So why is it bothering you?"

"It's not… It isn't."

Molly raised her brows. "Could have fooled me. You wouldn't be thinking on him so hard if everything was fine and dandy."

You're family now.

The words echoed through Kathleen's mind. What, exactly, did that mean? Josh had insisted on telling his parents about the pregnancy by himself. Afterward he'd stopped by and nearly put his fist through the door in utter frustration when he knocked. The Sheridans hadn't taken the news well. During the wedding she'd felt the disapproval beneath their polite words. It was in their worried glances, the flash of a tight smile. It was the same with her father and mother. Josh hadn't measured up. She hadn't measured up. Her wedding day should have been a day to remember, but instead it was a day ripe with regrets on all sides. All sides but one. Garrett hadn't even been there.

"Did I ever tell you who gave me my first kiss?"

Molly's look of puzzlement confirmed she hadn't.

"Garrett Sheridan."

"Well, now," Molly murmured, adjusting her spectacles. "How did that come about?"

"It was a silly game of truth or dare in Satterly's barn. Lucy Mae and the Bartlett twins dared me to kiss one of the boys. There wasn't much to choose from—Billy Jenkins, Patrick Onnus and Russell Lakes. Garrett was whistling outside. He'd come to fix the door latch and didn't know we were inside."

"And…?" Molly prodded.

"I was sixteen—and a bit impulsive. I walked past the others and out to Garrett, told him I hoped he didn't mind, and then stood on my tiptoes and kissed him."

Molly chuckled. "On a dare, then! Doesn't that beat all."

"Yes," Kathleen murmured, holding in the rest of the memory. Garrett had surprised her. He'd kissed her back. What she had thought would be a gentle peck had been, oh, so much more. Magical. Even now the memory could make her blush when she dwelled on it.

Afterward she'd been in the clouds with a moon-size infatuation. She'd maneuvered a time or two to talk to him, but he'd never taken the hint or asked her out. And knowing how her father felt about the Sheridans, she never invited him to the house. It was Josh who'd made her realize the kiss hadn't meant the same to Garrett. Josh had teased her and said Garrett thought that she was just a silly young girl. At the time his words had hurt. Funny how a year later, Josh had courted her so earnestly that she'd succumbed to *his* charms. All because of those sonnets…

She pressed her lips together, pushing the memory back to the past where it belonged. "The Sheridans… It was awkward after we married. They were distant. I'd hoped…" She'd hoped they would accept her but it hadn't happened. She sighed. "If that's 'family', then I want nothing from them."

Molly leaned forward in her chair. "That doesn't sound like Barbara and Brent."

"They didn't even acknowledge Lily's birth. As far as Lily and I are concerned, we owe them nothing."

"Well, child, I just don't understand. The Sheridans are founding members of the church here. It doesn't seem possible that they'd treat you like that."

"Maybe that's why. I ruined their perfect son, their perfect world. Josh wouldn't have taken that job at the mine if it hadn't been for me and a baby on the way." She set down her needle and woolen yarn. "Lily's all I have. I may have to live with my parents' disapproval—and with the Sheridans', too, for that matter, but I don't want that for her. I left home to get away from that."

"Well, you're going to run into them from time to time. You can't live in a small town and avoid bumping into people."

"I don't want Lily seeing them if I'm not present."

Concern lit Molly's features, but then she settled back into her chair and began knitting, her needles clicking. After a moment she spoke. "Very well. You have to follow your conscience."

"I'll manage on my own." She had Molly to help her—and her job at the bakery. She didn't want things to be this way, but Lily's happiness was too important. She would protect her daughter at all costs. And Garrett Sheridan would just have to accept that.

Chapter Three

Garrett readjusted the gelding's hoof and squeezed it securely between his knees. Grabbing a nail from his back pocket, he positioned it on the iron shoe and hammered it into place. He repeated the process five more times and then dropped the horse's leg. "There. See how that feels."

He straightened and stretched his back.

"Digger throw a shoe?" his father asked as he entered the stable and hooked a rope over the last stall's post head. Brent Sheridan was solid, trim and serious—a man other men in the area respected and most of the women admired.

Garrett nodded in answer to his question.

"Did you check the others?"

"They're fine."

"You were late getting home last night."

"Paul has a new buyer out toward Banner. We could use an additional three steer next trip."

His father grunted. "That's good news."

Garrett grabbed a rag from the corner and sat on the old trunk. He hiked his saddle over his knee and applied a generous smearing of saddle soap to the tired leather, then concentrated on rubbing it in, paying attention to a particularly worn area in the seat. When he realized his father was observing his every move, he relaxed his hold on the saddle. "She's back."

"And the baby?"

"Lily's five now."

Brent Sheridan nodded slowly. "Did you see her?"

"From a distance. Dark hair. Dark eyes."

Pain flashed crossed his father's face. "Like Josh. A granddaughter, fancy that. Been raising boys for so long I'm not sure what I'll do with a little girl around the place."

He'd best let his pa know what had happened. He couldn't

quite put his finger on what was going on with Kathleen, but something was off. She was different, guarded now. "Kathleen's changed some."

"Well… losing a husband, having a baby…those things take their toll."

"She's not all fired up to let Lily meet us."

His father pulled off his leather gloves. "Think it has anything to do with Sadie?"

Garrett shook his head. "Can't tell." Sadie had left town after Josh's death. She'd insisted that nothing had happened between them. It hadn't mattered what she said. People knew where Josh had spent his last night, and it wasn't with his wife.

Pa sighed. "Josh sure made a mess of things at the end."

"Kathleen's been through enough. I don't want her to find out."

"Same here, son, but we can't muzzle the entire town."

"I can try."

"The way Kathleen's acting… Could be she just needs to feel a bit more welcome."

"I hope it's that simple. Right now she doesn't even want us *near* Lily."

"That's not gonna sit well with your ma. However, I guess we can hold off a few more days."

Ma would bust at the seams if she had to wait. She'd already refigured her annual trip to San Diego in order to buy a few girl-suitable Christmas presents.

When Pa left, Garrett applied more saddle soap to the leather. His thoughts drifted back to Kathleen, remembering the one time she'd sat in this saddle. It had been new then. He was nineteen and mending the fence along the west edge of the property when he'd heard chatter down by Gully's Creek. Hot and sweaty and in need of a break, he'd chucked his gloves and wandered over for a look.

He'd found Kathleen with two of her friends under the old oak, barefoot and wading in the shallow water, their pinafores hiked up to their thighs. They'd been all of fourteen and in that silly giggling stage going on about whatever girls of that age talk about. When they'd caught sight of him they'd shrieked. Kathleen had stepped forward, slipped on a submerged rock and twisted her ankle. She'd sat down hard, getting her clothes soaked up to her waist. Her face had reddened to the color of a jalapeño. He figured it was from embarrassment, but she didn't act embarrassed when he'd come closer and scooped her up. It was only as he'd deposited her on the bank that he'd realized she was actually spitting angry. For some reason that had made him chuckle. Which had made her punch him. He'd caught her fist and told her to quit acting like a child.

The other girls had buzzed around as he'd checked the damage to her ankle. It hadn't been broken as far as he could tell. There was no swelling. But he'd figured she shouldn't put any weight on it. He had told her as much, picked her up again and sat her on his horse. He'd been about to climb up behind her when he'd noticed how her soaking cotton dress clung to her—everywhere. Where she'd once been as straight as a pine, suddenly curves were making themselves known. He'd averted his eyes, grabbed the reins and walked his horse to town without looking back. Her two friends had chattered on, oblivious to the fact that Kathleen was in a lot of pain. Any other time he would have blocked out their noise, but that day he was grateful for it. It had helped keep his mind off what he shouldn't have been thinking on—Kathleen's soft, smooth calf and the fact he'd run his rough, steer-herding fingers all over that slippery skin.

That was the day he had started waiting for her to grow up. Three years he'd waited, and it had only taken one impulsive act to lose her to his brother.

Kathleen dried the last baking pan with a swift wipe of a towel and set the pan above the large stove. "We've run out of honey and cinnamon."

"I'm not surprised with all the extra baking I'm doing," Sue said. "You'll need to stop by Gilliam's and order more. Actually, if you head over now you'll catch Eileen before she closes. Make sure her brother delivers it first thing tomorrow."

"Then I'll see you in the morning." Kathleen donned her dark blue cloak. Usually the days remained warm enough for a heavy shawl, but as the end of the year approached, the evenings had taken on a stiffer chill.

More than once Sue had mentioned that Kathleen's arrival

had come at the most opportune moment for the both of them. Sue's daughter, who usually helped in the bakery, had married and moved to Yuma only one month before. Sue had been lonely without her daughter and tied down without any relief at the bakery. Kathleen's appearance had remedied both problems.

On her way to Gilliam's, she circumvented the stagecoach as it turned into the livery. No passengers today, but she'd seen the driver hand off a packet of mail to Eileen's father. The dry-goods store housed the U.S. post office in town. It was nothing compared to the grand post office in San Diego. There, stone columns made for an impressive facade, while inside four clerks waited to serve the customers. Knowing that, she'd still take Clear Springs any day over the city. People knew her here and she knew many of them. Here, everything was familiar.

She found Eileen in the back, removing the brown paper wrapping from three new bolts of fabric. Eileen was a petite brunette with a round face and china-doll features. She unearthed the necessary supplies and set them on the counter. "I'll tack this onto Sue's bill and see it gets over to the bakery in the morning."

"Thanks." Kathleen turned toward the door.

"What's all goin' on over at Molly's?"

Kathleen stopped. "Nothing I know of. Why do you ask?"

"Just wondered what Garrett Sheridan is up to. He's not one to come to town. Especially since—" She stopped abruptly and a bit of red crept up her neck at her collar. "Sorry. I shouldn't be so nosy."

Garrett was at Molly's? Had something happened? Concern for Lily surfaced immediately. "Thank you, Eileen." Kathleen dashed through the door and flew down the road, around the corner and up the short hill to the boardinghouse. She burst into the parlor, short of breath and flushed despite the cold air against her cheeks.

"Lily? Lily!"

"In here!" Molly called from the kitchen.

Kathleen rushed toward the back of the house and found Lily kneeling on a chair at the table, mashing a bowl full of boiled potatoes. She checked down the hall, and then out the back window. "Where's Garrett?"

Molly glanced up from the baked chicken she'd just removed

from the oven and waved a dish towel. "Left hours ago. Sure was a surprise to see him."

"What was he doing here?"

Molly shrugged. "Just started in on the front steps—replacing that rotten board that's been sagging more of late." She turned back to her task at the carving board. "He was here for the better part of the afternoon. Never came inside. Took the coffee I offered then was gone before I chanced to look out again."

"Is he coming back?"

"Oh, he finished that job. I doubt we will see him here again."

Molly's words didn't reassure her. Kathleen had asked him to wait. Was this his less-than-subtle way of prodding her? It had only been five days.

Lily emitted a melodramatic sigh. "Am I done yet?"

Kathleen eyed the lumpy mashed potatoes in the bowl. "They look perfect." She wiped her daughter's hands with a towel and determined to put Garrett Sheridan from her mind for the evening. Not an easy task, since he'd been popping into her thoughts frequently since their conversation.

Garrett held on to the fence post while Eduardo used his foot to tamp down the dirt at its base. It had been a week since he'd been in to town, yet Kathleen had occupied every corner of his mind since then. Hard manual labor seemed to be the only relief—and it offered very little at that.

The flash of red leather caught his attention.

"New boots?"

Eduardo grinned. "The ladies like them."

"I bet that's what they notice." His ranch hand was a smooth talker. Eduardo and Josh had been cut of the same easygoing attitude when it came to women. Josh could spin a tale or tell a joke easier than he could set a post or break a colt. For Garrett, things were just the opposite. Maybe he should take some pointers from him. It might set his practical nature on edge, but hadn't Kathleen already done that just by coming back? Kathleen again. The woman unsettled him. Seemed she was never far from his thoughts. He just wanted there to be some peace between them, and maybe a little trust. All right…he wanted a lot of trust.

Trust starts with being truthful.

He shut out the thought. No point in dragging up painful memories. If she didn't know certain things, he wasn't going to be the one to tell her. She seemed to be putting the past behind her. Coming here, taking a job—she was moving on.

Could he?

He gripped the small roll of barbed wire and stretched it from the old post to the new replacement they'd just planted. Looping it twice, he used his pliers to twist it against itself and lock it in place. He tested the tension, feeling the same tautness inside himself. Kathleen had had more than a week to ride out to the ranch, and she hadn't come or sent a word.

"This will hold back a stampede," Eduardo said. "East forty next?"

"I'm heading into town." Garrett all but growled the words. If she wouldn't come out, the least he could do was make sure she was comfortable at Molly's. He hadn't thought much beyond that other than he hoped he'd get a glimpse of her even if it meant she'd scold him when he did. Seeing her still did crazy things to him inside.

In town, he stopped at Harley's Hardware and Tack to pick up a few supplies and then made another stop at the sawmill to have a few planks of lumber delivered. When he and Eduardo reached Molly's, they ground tied their mounts behind the cabin and Eduardo followed Garrett into the shed. An hour later, they were both atop the outhouse, battling with the stubborn branches of a pine and the rank odor that rose through the hole they were repairing.

"Señora Birdwell asked you to fix this?" Eduardo asked after prying up the last of the rotten boards.

"Molly? Ask for help?" Garrett shook his head. "That will never happen. Ma mentioned there was a steady drip last time she was here for quilting. I'll hand the new wood up to you." He had already descended the ladder and grabbed the first board when he caught sight of Lily.

He'd have known her anywhere. Her eyes and her coloring were his brother's. So much so that it caused an ache in his chest. She had long chestnut hair, pulled back into two braids and tied with ribbons, and held a rag doll that looked to have been her constant companion for years. He hesitated, gripping the board between them like a shield. When she continued to stand there, watching him with her wide brown eyes, he nodded. "How do, Miss Lily."

She stared back.

"Boss?"

Eduardo's voice jolted him. "Miss Lily, this here is my ranch hand, Mr. Nuñez. Eduardo, this is Miss Lily."

Eduardo tilted his hat to the girl and winked, which earned him her first response—a small fleeting smile.

"Figures," Garrett mumbled. He pushed the board up to Eduardo and then climbed the ladder to help secure it with nail and hammer. They continued working, and after a while Molly called and Lily went inside the house. Every now and then Garrett would check the window and find her nose pressed up against the glass, watching him.

"Muy linda," Eduardo commented. "But she doesn't talk much."

"She doesn't know me." *But she will.* He owed it to Josh to be there for his daughter whether Kathleen wanted him to be or not.

Chapter Four

"Folks asked after you at church service today," Molly said as she emerged from the pantry carrying an earthenware bowl filled with potatoes, carrots and onions. "It would do Lily good to meet some children her age. You used to run around the churchyard—all pigtails and petticoats a-flying. You certainly had your share of fun and mischief."

Kathleen smiled, remembering. "It's been a long time since then."

Molly set the bowl on the kitchen table. "She'll be going to school in less than a year. It might make the transition easier on her."

Kathleen started in peeling and quartering the vegetables. Maybe it *was* time. "All right. I'll take her to the Christmas Eve service. It will be a good beginning for her."

Molly smiled, pleased, and then cocked her head. "What's that I hear?"

A rhythmic whoosh and thud came from outside. Kathleen glimpsed through the gingham curtains and stopped short.

Garrett. Again.

"Well, I declare!" Molly said, plopping her fists on her ample hips. "Can't turn around without him bein' here anymore." She stepped outside.

Kathleen untied her apron and slipped it over the back of a chair. She had a thing or two to say to him, too. She might not have done as she'd said—she hadn't dropped in at the ranch—but he hadn't kept his word, either—not exactly.

He swung the ax high overhead and struck the small log, splitting it cleanly down the middle. In the short time he'd been there, he'd managed to chop several hearth-size logs into smaller pieces of firewood.

"I know I needed wood," Molly called out. "But I don't recall asking you to do that, Garrett Sheridan."

"Your wood bin is low."

"That it is. But I won't have you breaking the Sabbath for me." Her eyes twinkled as she spoke. "You're still in your finest Sunday clothes, too."

"Cold weather on the way. I might not have another opportunity." He took a moment to shed his coat and roll up his shirtsleeves, revealing muscular forearms. Most likely his entire body was like that—having been raised on a ranch. Kathleen's cheeks warmed. She'd like to blame her fanciful thoughts on the fact he looked a bit like Josh, but she knew that wasn't it. She'd always felt something special for Garrett—even before that kiss.

A brisk knock sounded on the front door, releasing Kathleen from her reverie. She left Molly to deal with Garrett and headed through the parlor to the door.

"I'm here to see my granddaughter."

Her jaw dropped open as Barbara Sheridan swept into the room and deposited her cloak over the back of a chair. Never the frilly type, she was dressed in a white button-down blouse covered with a forest-green silk bodice. A blue plaid scarf belted the waist of her dark green skirt. Her dark upswept hair had streaks of gray through it now, but that made her look even more forbidding than years ago. Suddenly, however, her regal stance softened.

Kathleen followed her line of vision. Lily had walked into the room.

"What a surprise, Barbara," Molly said, entering behind Lily. "Especially since I just spoke with you at the service."

"I realize I haven't been invited…and that this is a bit awkward…" Discomfort crossed her face. It was the first time Kathleen had ever seen the woman unsure of herself.

"…but I couldn't leave town without meeting my granddaughter. It's time, don't you think?" She tugged off her gloves. Waited.

Lily hid deeper in the folds of Kathleen's skirt.

Barbara's chin went up a notch and her gaze slid to Kathleen. "You look well. How nice to see you after all this time."

The words, stiff and formal, did little to ease the tension in the room. Outside, Garrett continued chopping wood. Sheridans.

She squeezed her daughter's shoulder. "Lily? This is your grand-mother. You have two. My mother, Grandmother McCrory, lives in the house by the sea. This is your father's mother, Grandmother Sheridan."

Slowly, Lily stepped from the folds of her skirt.

Barbara gasped. "Oh…my…" and again, "Oh." She looked up at Kathleen and then back at Lily. "She has the Sheridan eyes. There's no doubt about it."

Kathleen tensed. Was she searching Lily to make sure of her birthright?

"I'm sorry. That came out all wrong. I'm just so…surprised. And, and…stunned. She is the image of Josh when he was young. Will she come to me?"

At the request, Lily clung tighter to Kathleen's skirt.

Barbara's shoulders slumped. "I'm not here to frighten you. I've waited a long time to finally get to meet you, Lily."

The sight made Kathleen uncomfortable enough to rethink her reaction. Perhaps Barbara felt as awkward with this as she did. Kathleen crouched down and brushed the hair away from Lily's face. "I see Josh every time I look at her," she admitted softly. "Lily? Honey? Please…greet your grandmother as we practiced."

Lily gripped the sides of her pinafore, put one foot behind the other, and dipped into a quick, wobbly curtsy. "Hello, Grand-mother Sheridan."

The older woman smiled, and with it her angular face lost its forbidding expression. "Hello, Lily. I…I have something for you. A present." She held out the package.

Lily's eyes widened, and after a quick look at Kathleen to make sure it was all right, took the package and tore off the paper. It was a carving—no bigger than Lily's hand—in red-toned manzanita. A horse…no…a foal lying down.

"This is a likeness of Dixie. She was born at our ranch this past spring."

Of course it would have something to do with the ranch. Bar-bara Sheridan thought, slept and breathed the ranch that had been in her family for three generations. One more reason she'd never been able to accept that her son had chosen a "townie" like Kath-leen. Kathleen knew nothing about ranching.

Lily accepted the gift, a perplexed look on her face.

"Perhaps a doll would have been more appropriate. I've had so little experience with girls." Barbara pressed her thin lips together. "I have something for you, too." She withdrew a small book from her satchel.

The volume of sonnets. Kathleen's stomach clenched. A myriad of conflicting emotions swept through her. Along with Lily, this book represented her time with Josh. She took the ribbon-tied book and held it gingerly.

"I found it among Josh's things last year," Barbara said. "I hadn't been able to look through them in all that time. Losing him…" Her voice trailed off.

Kathleen held herself rigid, frozen to the spot. Inside, her chest ached. Of course Barbara Sheridan had grieved—just as Kathleen had. But she had also hated the idea that Josh married her. That Josh had *had* to marry her. Kathleen stiffened her spine. "Thank you, Mrs. Sheridan."

"Please, call me…"

Kathleen braced herself. There was no way she'd call this woman mother.

"Barbara. I hope you'll come by the ranch. Brent and I…" Her voice trailed off for a moment. Then she took a big breath and squared her shoulders. "You're welcome there anytime."

Welcome was not the feeling she'd gotten.

"We have room for you…even to stay if you would like?"

"Thank you for the offer. It's…kind of you." She stumbled over the words. "But I'm comfortable here. This arrangement suits Aunt Molly and Lily as much as it suits me."

Barbara Sheridan pressed her lips together. "Then I'll be going."

The woman left as quickly as she'd barged in. Momentarily stunned with the turbulence the woman had stirred up in her wake, Kathleen barely noticed Lily tugging on her hand. "Read this, Mama. Is it a good story?"

She smoothed her fingers over the embossed title. Josh's book.

"It's not a story. It's a book of poems."

He'd given it to her at the beginning of their courtship. At the time, it had turned her head to think he thought of her the way those poems of love professed. She'd been naive, trusting and so very foolish. Love wasn't like that. Could never be as pure and selfless as the flowery words made it out to be. How could she have believed such ridiculous words? She took a deep breath. At least she was smarter now…wiser. She flipped through the pages to the beginning.

For Kathleen McCrory
With affection
JGS

Josh Grover Sheridan… She'd learned soon enough after the wedding that he thought the sonnets were silly. None of the words of love in that book had meant a thing to him. She'd wanted so badly to believe in them that her own romantic foolishness had clouded the truth. The knowledge was bitter to face. Lily was the only good thing to come from all that foolishness.

"I have a better idea," she answered her daughter, and closed the book. "How about I read from *Alice's Adventures in Wonderland?*"

Her daughter's quick smile was the only response she needed. The thwack of blade against wood as Garrett wielded his ax outside reminded her she wanted a word with him. "Run and get the book. I need to speak with Mr. Sheridan for just a moment."

Kathleen peered through the window. Garrett buried the ax in a log and walked over to the water pump. Giving the handle several strong jerks, a steady stream of liquid surged into the bucket. He cupped his hands and, filling them, splashed water on his face and the back of his neck. She shivered at the thought of the ice-cold water this time of year.

"Here," Molly said, slapping a towel in her hand. "Give him that and ask him to dinner. It's only proper after all the work he's done around here. I've got to get more carrots from the root cellar." She trundled off to do just that.

First Barbara Sheridan and now Garrett. Kathleen was beginning to wonder if Molly was maneuvering all of them. She threw on her shawl, her motions tight with frustration, and opened the door.

He stood ready to knock. His look of surprise mirrored hers, no doubt. Quickly he lowered his fist. He'd unbuttoned the top of his collar. Water glistened in the tanned V of his neck, drawing her gaze. A whisper of interest skittered through her and centered in her abdomen. Ignoring it, she met his eyes. "Do you always help Molly with these things?"

"No." He took the towel from her and wiped his neck and face.

He'd shaved that morning—likely for church. The usual day's growth of beard that darkened his jaw and made him look older, tougher than his twenty-eight years was gone, and smooth skin begged her touch. The urge took her by surprise. Perturbed by her wayward thoughts, she looped her fingers behind her back.

"Then does this have something to do with getting on my good side?"

He raised a brow. "Your good side?"

Was he being sarcastic, or did he not even realize his helping around the place put a debt on her she didn't want? "What is it about you Sheridans? First you, then your mother."

"Ma's here?" He stepped close and glanced over her shoulder into the kitchen. His expression froze when his gaze landed on the book of sonnets on the table. Something flashed across his face. Did he recognize it? Had Josh mentioned it to him? Could he have laughed about her naïveté right along with Josh? Brothers did that sort of thing. Yet she couldn't picture Garrett being that cynical. She picked it up and pressed it against her breast. Despite her feelings regarding the small volume, it was tangible evidence that Josh had, at one time, desired her. And for that, the book was special.

"Your mother just left."

"I figured she might stop by. She's been pacing around the ranch ever since she learned you were in town." He stepped back, looked her up and down. "You okay?"

Startled, she glanced up at him. She hadn't expected his concern. "Yes. Yes, I am. She was…cordial."

"She only wants to be a part of Lily's life. A part of yours."

"She wasn't interested before." Long ago the bitterness inside had hardened into a tight knot. "She didn't even acknowledge Lily's birth. Not that I expected presents or a visit."

"But you did expect something."

She nodded, for a moment too upset to speak. "A note, perhaps? I sent an announcement. I thought…"

"She never received it."

Through her anger, his words registered. "What?"

"She never received it," Garrett repeated, slowly, deliberately.

Kathleen hadn't considered that. "I gave it to Franklin, my brother-in-law. He posted it."

"Maybe he did, but it never arrived." Garrett shrugged into his leather jacket. "When we didn't hear any word, I rode out to check on you and Lily."

"You came by?"

"Ma figured you had the baby in June. I stopped by your father's new store. He wasn't pleased to see me. Said you'd moved on from that part of your life. It was your sister, working that day, who told me where to find you. You had Lily on a blanket in the shade next to the house. You were weeding in the side garden."

Her world spun with his revelation. "Why didn't you say anything?"

"What was there to say? You were where you wanted to be. You hadn't contacted my side of the family. I figured you wanted it that way."

He didn't look at her while he spoke, and that was how she knew she had hurt him—or if not Garrett, then his mother. She felt sick inside. Here she'd been holding a grudge against the Sheridans for years.

"I take it your father didn't tell you."

"No." Father had always been envious of the Sheridans and their ranch. Her connection, and Lily's, to the family had been one of the reasons for his move to the coast. It was one way he could hold power over them. "I didn't know."

He shrugged lightly. "Doesn't matter now."

But it did. It explained so much more than he realized. She stepped toward him and placed her hand on his bare forearm. He had to know it wasn't her doing. "I'm so sorry, Garrett. It shouldn't have happened like that."

The furrow between his brows smoothed and his gaze locked on hers. For a moment something fragile and sweet pulsed between them. Warmth radiated from his skin. She let go. Blushed.

"You ask him yet, Kathleen?" Molly entered the room.

"Ask me what?"

It struck her then that she'd been reluctant to do Molly's bidding. She'd had enough of the Sheridans that week to last her a good long while. But something had changed. Now she could imagine Garrett sitting across the table from her, and it didn't seem nearly so uncomfortable. "She wants to know if you would like to have Sunday dinner with us."

He contemplated the question, his sea-green eyes searching her own. Again she noticed the brief splaying of lines in the corners. Five years had done that to him. What did her face reveal about her?

"Well," Molly said. "What's it going to be?"

He looked up, breaking the spell, and tipped his hat to her aunt. "Thanks just the same, ma'am. Like you said before, I've got things to attend to at the ranch."

Kathleen had thought for sure he'd stay. It'd be his chance to visit with Lily. The confusion must have shown on her face.

"You're not ready."

"Of course we're ready. Molly keeps a boardinghouse. She's always ready for extra guests at her table." Still perplexed, she followed him to his horse.

He shrugged into his coat. "That's not what I mean, Kathleen."

"Then what?"

He mounted and looked down at her. "It's you I want the invitation from. Not Molly. I'll wait."

Chapter Five

Garrett paced outside the bakery. Seemed Kathleen stayed longer every night. The holidays had everybody in a frenzied state. Even the animals could sense the difference. Finally the light from the kerosene lantern dimmed and then went out. When she stepped onto the boardwalk, she didn't seem surprised to see him. Maybe she was beginning to accept his presence in her life. He hoped so... even if all it meant was he could help out with Lily. Josh would have wanted that. Garrett didn't for one minute think she'd let him into her life if it wasn't for her daughter. That door had closed long ago and now there were too many secrets that stood in the way.

Her eyes drooped with fatigue. He'd offer to carry the cake she held, but with his lack of grace he'd likely ruin it. Instead he took her scarf, which was looped over her forearm, and slipped it over her head and around her neck in the way he'd seen her place it. When his fingers skimmed her throat and jaw for a second, a tingling sensation raced up his arm. He swallowed, trying to ignore it. Instead he concentrated on the fact that her acceptance of his touch was a testament to her exhaustion—and that was all.

He took the key from her hand and locked the bakery. "You're tired."

"I started early. Judge Perry is having a party tonight. I've already carried over two large platters."

"This the last?"

She nodded, then smiled up at him. And he found he just couldn't let her carry that load.

"Let me." Carefully he took the platter from her and they started down the boardwalk. "My folks will be there."

"The largest ranch in the area? They should have a voice in whatever plans are being hatched." She looked over his suit. "You must be going, as well."

"We share equally in the decisions." He hesitated, unsure if

Kathleen was ready to hear his next thought. "You could come, too."

She shook her head. "I haven't seen Lily all day."

Her dedication to her daughter—it warmed him from the inside out. He'd heard comments—people thinking she was crazy and not a good mother because she'd left her family and a world of support to come here and take a job. Something had happened to spur her to make that choice. He hoped someday to learn the reason. For now, he realized she'd completely missed his subtle hint. Whatever happened on the ranch would affect Lily.

The tinny sounds of the piano spilled out of the saloon. Some raw language, too.

"I'm glad Lily didn't hear that," she murmured.

"I wish you hadn't," he muttered.

The corners of her mouth tilted up. "I knew what I was coming back to, Garrett. Clear Springs has its rough edges, but all in all, it's home—more home to me than on the coast."

Another expletive burst from inside the saloon.

"I'd like to muzzle that Russell," Garrett growled. "He shows up at quittin' time like a lot of the miners. If he's smart, he eats something at the restaurant for supper before stopping in the saloon. Can't figure out how he makes it to work the next day."

"It's hard to believe the change in him since school. He barely acknowledges me now."

"He changed a lot after—" he stopped talking, suddenly aware they were getting mighty close to talking about Josh. Too close. Russell had been the last man with his brother. He had tried to stop Josh, who'd still been drunk and angry from the night before, from setting off the dynamite.

They walked the rest of the way in silence.

Through the windows of Judge Perry's house, a kaleidoscope of colors dazzled and tantalized those passing by. Wreaths of holly hung on both sides of the entry door, and candles, their flames dancing, lit each front window. Garrett knocked on the door, and it wasn't a minute before Lucy ushered them into the dining room. Carefully, Kathleen took the large tray from his arms and set it on the table under the chandelier.

"Thank you, Mrs. Sheridan."

"Now, Lucy. Judge Perry's maid or not, you've known me since Miss Alport's class. Just Kathleen is fine. The house looks lovely for the party. So festive."

Lucy grinned and relaxed. "I gave it my best, whether the mine owners will notice or not. It's a regular forest fire in here when they all get to smokin' those big cigars. Don't know why they like the smelly things."

Garrett cleared his throat.

"Course, Garrett, you and your parents ain't like the rest of them." She leaned toward Kathleen and lowered her voice. "Besides, Saturday will be much more fun with the dance and all. Alan is playing his fiddle. Are you going?"

She asked innocently—a bit too innocently.

"I'm not sure. I'll have to see about Lily."

"Oh, there's plenty of folks who'll keep an eye out for her. Lots of families bring their young'uns." She cocked her head slightly. "Has Garrett asked you?"

"Lucy..." His warning fell on deaf ears.

"Just to let you know," Lucy continued, "he asked me last year and then gave some flibbertigibbet excuse as to why he couldn't make it at the last minute. Sick cow or some such thing—as if that doesn't happen all the time on a ranch."

"It wasn't like that, Lucy."

"Sure it was. Just wanted to warn Kathleen about your character. For me, I wouldn't go with you if you asked me three times whilst you stood on your head."

Kathleen pressed her lips tight, but still a small smile wiggled through. "Your warning is duly noted, although there is no need for worry on my account. If I go at all, it will be with Molly and Lily."

Being a punching bag between these two women was about as uncomfortable as Garrett cared to get. When a knock sounded at the front door, he breathed a sigh of relief. The first of the company had arrived.

"I need to get that...." Lucy moved toward the parlor.

"Garrett's staying, but I'll let myself out the back," Kathleen said. "Don't worry about me."

Garrett opened the swinging door between the kitchen and the dining room for her. "I'll see you home first."

"I thought I heard a familiar voice! Miss Kathleen? A nice surprise, indeed!" A tall man dressed in a dark gray suit and silver sateen vest strode in from the parlor.

She turned around. "Mr. Spencer! What brings you to town?"

Garrett's gut tightened. The familiarity Kathleen used in addressing the man… How did they know each other? Mr. Spencer was a few years older than him—a good ten years older than Kathleen—and well-known for the progressive improvements he'd put into his mining operation.

"The judge's party, of course. And I certainly didn't expect to find you so far from home." He looked from her to Garrett.

"Oh. Excuse me. May I present Garrett Sheridan. Mr. Sheridan, this is Mr. Andrew Spencer…a friend of my father's."

They shook hands and Andrew said, "Just the man I hoped to see tonight. I want to discuss the boundary lines between your ranch and my property."

"We'll talk as soon as I return from escorting Mrs. Sheridan home."

"Mrs. Sheridan?" Mr. Spencer glanced about the room. "My sources didn't mention that you were married."

Kathleen's face flushed. "He means me, Andrew. Garrett is Lily's uncle."

"Oh…oh, I see."

Garrett did, too, as relief came to Spencer's face. Something twisted inside. Garrett drew in a slow, steady breath.

"But…surely you are staying for the party?" Andrew asked.

"No. I just came by to drop off a few things."

"Then will you save me a dance at your family's annual New Year's party?"

"I'm afraid I won't be there. Merry Christmas, Andrew." She smiled apologetically and then slipped through the doors and headed toward the back.

Garrett nodded to Mr. Spencer and followed Kathleen as an ominous, sinking sensation flooded through him. He'd recognized that feeling in his gut—jealousy. He didn't want to feel that way again. He'd told himself it was about looking out for her. About looking out for Lily. All this was for Josh—because Josh couldn't be there.

Ten steps from the judge's back door, the words burst from him. "How well do you know Spencer?"

"What do you mean?"

"He didn't even realize that you were a Sheridan. How the heck did your father introduce you once Lily came along? The Widow Kathleen?"

The shock on her face should have warned him. He should shut up but instead he barreled on. "What is it about the name that you hate? Or is it the family? My brother wasn't perfect, but it is a decent name and respected around these parts. It's a good name for Lily. Makes me wonder what my niece will think of her pa's side of the family when she's grown. She doesn't even know us."

"Garrett!" Her voice shook. "You're not being fair! You have no right to judge me for the past five years. You weren't there. You don't know what I went through. Besides, sometimes I get the feeling that it's you that has the secrets."

That stopped him cold. Had she learned about Sadie? About the fight? At Molly's front door he splayed his hand on the wood, barring her entry. "What have you heard?"

"Nothing."

"That's because there is nothing."

"Fine. Then let me go inside."

His face was inches from hers. So close he could feel her soft breath on his skin. So close he could... He shook his head to loosen the cord of tension that pulled him closer. He...had to...protect her, and this was not the way.

Her eyes were wide with confusion.

Abruptly, he spun around and strode away. It had been five years and nothing had changed. He'd told himself that this was all about Lily and about setting things right with his brother's memory. But it wasn't. He still cared too much, still wanted Kathleen for himself with a need so intense that it choked him.

But it could never be. Not when he'd made her a widow by his own hand.

Kathleen entered Molly's house and closed the door. She leaned against it, her heart racing.

What had just happened? They'd been arguing and then suddenly everything had changed. She'd thought…he might kiss her the way he'd been looking so steadily at her. But no. It had to have been her imagination. He'd never cared that way for her before. Josh had even said so. Garrett had never felt anything for her at all.

His accusations ricocheted through her head. He had a right to his anger. She had gone along with her parents' constant refusal to speak of anything pertaining to the Sheridans. She'd been weak. And they'd used that weakness. How many subtle jabs and stinging comments about Lily's heritage had she let slide by? They'd never wanted the marriage and did their best to drive out any goodness that came from it. It just happened that Lily was the best part. Lily—being a Sheridan—never measured up. Just as Kathleen had never measured up for marrying one.

Garrett would never understand. How could he? He was so strong. Even Josh had been unable to live in his shadow. But she had to explain things to him once they both calmed down. He'd been there for her, for Lily, these past weeks. Family meant something entirely different to Garrett than what it meant to her. She understood that now. Not all families were like hers.

But he was so angry. She'd never seen him lose his temper before. Josh had plenty of times, but never quiet, steady Garrett. It unnerved her. Would he ever give her the chance to explain?

Chapter Six

Four days later Kathleen stood, hands on hips, as she looked out the front window at Garrett reining in two horses harnessed to a flatbed wagon.

Molly pulled the rocking chair closer to the fireplace to make room for the pine that would soon go in the corner. "Lily deserves a Christmas tree and for that matter, so do I. I haven't had one since Beaudry's passing."

Kathleen sighed, wishing there was some other way. Garrett hadn't come around since their argument. This entire outing would be uncomfortable. Lily, however, seemed ecstatic about a chance to choose her own tree. She stood on tiptoe, watching Garrett stride up the path to the house.

Lily had peppered her with questions ever since Barbara Sheridan's visit. Kathleen had finally explained that side of her daughter's family. "Get your coat. Your Uncle Garrett is here."

Molly let him in. He dwarfed the entryway, standing there in his leather duster, a dark silhouette against the bright sunlight behind him. He tipped his hat. No smile. Just serious, as though he didn't want to be here, either. "I'll wait by the wagon."

Before he could turn to step outside, Lily dashed into the room and Kathleen helped her slip into her coat and mittens. She tugged on a red knit hat and tied it securely under her daughter's chin. Garrett watched her ministrations, but when she looked up, he quickly spun on his heel and left.

"Come on, Mama!" Lily skipped down the path after Garrett.

Kathleen had nothing to do but grab her cloak and hurry after them.

"Choose a good tree, now, Lily!" Molly called from the doorway.

Garrett stopped at the wagon and swung Lily up to deposit her on the seat in one smooth arc. Then, avoiding her gaze and as if she weighed no more than her daughter, followed through and did the same with Kathleen. She was left a little breathless.

He walked around to the other side of the wagon and climbed up. Reaching behind the seat, he dragged up a heavy blanket, spread half over Lily's lap and offered Kathleen the other corner. "The best trees are on the east edge of our property. Won't take long to find a good one, depending on how choosy Miss Lily here is."

Her daughter giggled. He'd already won her over and he hadn't said more than two sentences to her.

Well, she wasn't her daughter, nor was she so easy to win over. "Garrett…we should talk."

He indicated Lily with a tilt of his head. "It'll keep."

"But—"

"Relax, Kathleen. Let's enjoy the afternoon." He flicked the reins and the horses started off at a slow trot, the sleigh bells attached to their harnesses clanging merrily. "How are things at the bakery?"

She pressed her lips together, frustrated. Two could play at this game. "Busy. Too busy for Sue alone. And the ranch? How are things there?"

He kept his eyes on the road ahead, but a quick grin flashed across his face. It made her pause, that grin—the first she'd seen from him in years. Intriguing how it transformed him. He was handsome—no denying that. Odd that he hadn't married by now.

He talked of easy things—people they knew, the changes in the area. She almost felt as if their recent argument hadn't happened. It wasn't long before she started to relax just as he'd urged. The wagon jostled and creaked. The air was crisp and cold, and the sun's pale warmth seeped into her skin. The scent of pine enveloped her.

When they stopped in a grove of giant oak trees, Lily noticed some tracks in the snow and Garrett hunkered down beside her. He knew them all—coyote, blue jay, chipmunk, rabbit, even cougar. Seeing them together, shoulder to shoulder, Kathleen wondered if Josh would have been as patient explaining things. He'd been all about the quick and easiest way to get something done. Oh, he'd have brought Lily out to find a nice tree, but he'd never make the outing more than that. With that thought came a large dose of guilt. It wasn't right to be thinking of Josh that way…

comparing him to Garrett. He'd done the best he could considering he hadn't really loved her—or she him. Things had happened so fast—the courtship, the wedding, the funeral and Lily—that it had taken her a while to realize that. Looking back, they'd both tried to make it work for the short time they had.

"Did you and Josh pick out a tree each year?" she asked.

"We'd take turns, but Pa had the final say. One year I tagged the tree I wanted a few weeks early. Josh snuck out, cut it down and dragged it to that ravine. He gave some long-winded tale about seeing some townies with a tree earlier in the week."

"All that just so that you couldn't have the one you wanted?"

"Yep. Just to rile me."

"Did it work?"

Garrett chuckled. "Yeah. I was pretty sore. He didn't own up to it until much later."

"How old was he?"

"Josh was thirteen. Seemed like we were always competing about one thing or another. When we were little it was all about who could run faster. Then who could rope and tie the fastest—first with sheep, and then later with calves."

"You were so much older. How could he ever win?"

"He didn't very often. When we were little, he'd get so frustrated that sometimes I'd lose on purpose. If he found out he wouldn't speak to me for weeks. As we got older, I spent more time on the ranch and he spent more and more time in town. Made it easier, but didn't change things much. We both still vied for the better horse, the better rifle…the better girl. Guess it made it all the sweeter for him when he did best me."

She smiled up at him, but he didn't return it. He studied her face instead, his brow furrowed. His gaze carried a distant look as though he wasn't really seeing her but looking back and remembering.

She tugged his coat sleeve, wanting to draw him from his pensive mood. "Time to find that tree."

The first one that Lily picked out was twenty feet high. Eventually, Kathleen talked her down to one that would fit inside Molly's house. The branches were lopsided and slightly bare on one side, but Lily was proud of it.

Garrett retrieved the ax from the wagon bed and chopped down the tree. By the time he was finished, a light sheen of sweat coated his face and neck. She helped him load it onto the wagon and secure it with ropes. Glancing over the tethered branches, she caught him watching her.

A slow, warm smile—just for her—spread across his face. Quiet, competent, steady. What would it have been like if she'd married him instead of his brother? If he had returned her affection after that first kiss? Instinctively she knew that he wouldn't have left her, pregnant and unsure, to go off with friends to the saloon. It was silly to wonder…it was all in the past now and nothing could change it. Besides, Josh was the one who had come courting and had left the book of sonnets.

"Ready?" He'd walked around the wagon during her musings and now stood close, prepared to help her onto the high seat. She could see the scar on his chin through the stubble of new whiskers. So close she could see the softness of his lips.

"Garrett? About the other day. I need to explain—"

"You don't." He seemed to consider his words before going on. "I shouldn't have said anything. You don't owe me an explanation or an apology. There are things…" His voice trailed off as his gaze slid to her mouth.

"What things?" she prompted. Something thrummed between them. Something warm and sweet and fresh.

"Mama?"

She blinked. Lily. She pulled from his grasp, gathered her skirt and was halfway up to the wagon seat when she felt his hands on her waist, helping the rest of the way.

Back at Molly's, he set up the tree and then took the ax and tools back to the shed. Leaving Lily with Molly and a cup of hot cocoa, Kathleen followed him.

"Get back inside, Kathleen. You don't have your cloak on." He stood at the door to the shed, looping the rope they'd used around his hand and elbow.

"Will you stay and help decorate?"

He shook his head. "I've got chores at the ranch."

She tried not to let her disappointment show. "It's been a good day. A perfect day…for Lily. Thank you for that."

He acknowledged her words with a quick nod and then hung the coil of rope over a long peg.

Was it her imagination or was he distancing himself somehow? She took a deep breath, unsure how much to say without sounding ungrateful toward her family. "Lily hasn't had many of those. I haven't, either."

He searched her face. "Explain that."

"After…moving to the city, things changed between me and my parents. Seemed I could never do enough to please them. It was like walking on wet sand, the surface shifting beneath my feet. I never could find my balance. I had been a disappointment beyond anything they could forgive. And by extension, so had Lily. To even mention the name Sheridan would set them off."

"You never should have left here."

"They weren't like that at first. Only later." When Lily had made her presence known in Kathleen's burgeoning shape and her situation could no longer be hidden. "I needed help."

"I would—" He stopped and amended his words. "We would have helped you."

"I didn't believe that then and…I was afraid." She stood on her tiptoes and brushed a kiss on his cheek. "I believe it now."

With those four simple words, she realized that she'd crossed a chasm. She trusted him—and the thought overwhelmed her. It wasn't with just her physical safety, it was with her daughter… and quite possibly her heart.

She turned and walked across the yard and into the house.

Chapter Seven

The morning of the Community Christmas Dance, Lucy cornered Kathleen in the bakery and again urged her to go, promising to help watch Lily. Molly had said as much—several times. Women were in short supply in the small gold-mining town and a nice turnout of the feminine gender would make for a lively dance. Sue closed the bakery early in the afternoon so that they could get ready.

When Kathleen burst through the front door of Molly's, she found Lily twirling around the parlor, her new white Christmas dress flying out around her legs. "Mama! Mama! Look! Look at me!"

Kathleen smiled in spite of her harried thoughts. And then she went stock-still. In her daughter's hair was pinned a baby-blue ribbon with slightly frayed ends. The same ribbon that had been tied around the old book of sonnets.

"Where did you get that?"

At her tone, the shining excitement disappeared from Lily's face. "I found it in the trunk. Look! It matches my dress."

So it did. Kathleen hated to have been the one to dampen her daughter's day. "I'm sorry I snapped at you," she said. "It startled me—seeing that ribbon after so long."

Lily tugged at the bow. "I'll take it out, Mama. I don't want you sad."

Kathleen stilled her daughter's hand. "No. Leave it." She patted her hair back into place and smiled into her daughter's eyes. "You look lovely."

She looked up and found Molly watching the exchange. "Well. It appears you are both ready and I am the one who is late. Just give me two shakes of a lamb's tail and I'll be ready."

"It's okay, Mama," Lily said, her sunny nature returning. "Aunt Molly says it is better to be a little late."

"Oh? Why is that?"

"Well…so everyone can see me when I walk in, of course!"

Kathleen laughed as her daughter twirled around once more and skipped from the room.

Later, when she stepped outside with Lily, the fine mist floating in the stillness lent a magical quality to the evening. Molly had left earlier to help set out the food at the social, leaving Kathleen and Lily to walk to the dance on their own. Kathleen couldn't help it—she was nervous about this first foray back into the social life of the community. It had been years since she had done anything lighthearted or fun. Events like dancing hadn't existed for her after having Lily. And yet excitement raced just beneath the surface of her thoughts. She'd see Garrett tonight! And maybe instead of seeing her as a sister-in-law or Lily's mother, he would look at her as a woman. She drew in a shaky breath. And what would she do if he did?

Lily's small hand slipped into hers. The look in her eyes mirrored Kathleen's feelings. She squeezed her daughter's hand. "Your first party! Excited?"

Lily nodded.

"Me, too." She let her daughter lead her on to the town hall, where music spilled out onto the street.

She had come.

Garrett stopped in the doorway and watched Kathleen dance with Eduardo. The dark green dress she wore hugged her small waist and would have shown a lot more creamy skin but for the wine-colored shawl she had pinned loosely around her shoulders. As it was, he—as well as every other buck in the room—got a small teasing glimpse of lace at her neckline. She'd pulled the blond hair that framed her face back into a loose, curly tail, held there by a matching red bow, and let the rest of her hair hang free.

"Hello, Garrett. Garrett?"

He pulled his gaze away from Kathleen and found Lucy Mae at his side. He tipped his hat, and then remembering where he was, took it off.

Lucy smirked. "It's no secret who you want to dance with, but it looks like you'll have to stand in line. While you're waiting, could you help Alan bring in a few more tables from the restaurant? There's a bigger crowd than last year."

"Sure thing, Lucy."

"Good. And save me a dance? You owe me after bowing out last year."

He stifled a smile. "Glad you don't hold long grudges. Anything else?"

"No. That will do."

"At your service." He handed his hat and leather duster to her to hang up. She rolled her eyes in friendly exasperation. After all, he was helping with the tables. An even exchange.

Kathleen kept dancing, kept laughing. When she stopped, old school friends gathered around and she introduced them to her daughter. Seemed she was having a good time. He wanted to catch her for a dance, but was nervous just the same. What exactly did that peck she'd given him on the cheek mean? Thanks? Or something more? He'd tried to focus on that and not put anything more into the act as he helped set up the tables and a few more chairs.

When he finally stopped to rest, Paul approached.

"You're lookin' a mite tied and dragged. Figured you could use some liquid courage," Paul said with a smirk, and handed him a mug of spiced cider. "To hear the women talk, you're a regular saint with all the help you're giving old Widow Birdwell."

"Not if you could read my thoughts."

"Not so noble? Fancy that."

"Shut up, Paul. Go dance or something. Mabel has been eyeing you all night."

"Well, the company would be an improvement."

Garrett fell silent again as his gaze found Kathleen. She was with Lucy in the midst of a cluster of women. Talking. Always talking. What the heck did females find so interesting to say?

Slowly he became aware of a small dark-haired figure at his hip. Lily.

"How do, Miss Lily. You havin' a good time?"

A small sniffle escaped.

Uh-oh. He crouched down to her level. "What's wrong?"

She took two shaky breaths, her lower lip trembling. "Tommy

Mulligan spilled punch all over my new dress!" She held up the offending material. A smear of pink stained the hemline.

He glanced up at Paul. How did one handle a situation like this? Paul looked just as perplexed as he was. Garrett swallowed.

"Well, now. Boys can be clumsy at times. Comes with growing too fast."

Her china-doll eyes widened. "Tommy can't help growing."

"No. That he can't. And I'll tell you another thing about boys. They 'bout never say they're sorry."

"Why?"

"Comes real hard to them. Harder than just about anything else. Just ask my friend here, Mr. Ham."

She looked up at Paul and then seemed to ponder Garrett's words. "Di…did you spill punch?"

Mesmerized by her large brown eyes, so like Josh's, he vaguely realized his leg had started to cramp in his crouched position. He rose to his full height. "Happened a time or two."

Lily heaved a big sigh…and her small hand slipped into his.

He stood stock-still. He'd been content that she was finally talking to him, but this! It was more than he'd hoped for. Warmth spread though him. It humbled him—this acceptance, this trust from Josh's daughter.

Kathleen could only half listen to the man she'd just danced with, her attention pulled to the unfolding drama at the edge of the room. What was her daughter saying to Garrett? It looked as if she was bombarding him with questions. She wished she were closer so that she could hear! All evening she'd danced with other men when all she really wanted was to find out what it would be like to be in Garrett's arms.

"Should I be jealous? Or just offended?" The twinkle in Eduardo's eyes said he was neither.

"I'm so sorry!"

A black brow shot up. "Not the answer I wanted."

It had been a long time since anyone flirted with her. "Then—neither. I was curious what my daughter was doing."

"Lily? She's with Señor Garrett."

It was a bit disconcerting to realize this stranger knew who her daughter was. "You know the Sheridans?"

He grinned. "I've worked their ranch for two years now."

"Oh."

"Another dance? If I plan just right, I could maybe stop right under that." He pointed to a cluster of green dangling from the wagon-wheel chandelier. Mistletoe.

"Try that move, Eduardo, and I may have to banish you to the north forty for a week."

She recognized the deep voice behind her. Eduardo tipped his hat to her, winked and walked away. She turned to face Garrett. "About time you made your way over, Mr. Sheridan."

"Took a while to bolster my courage. You've been in demand all evening." He handed her a glass of cider. "Figured you could use that."

He waited for her to finish her glass, and then took it from her and set it aside. "You ready?" His invitation to dance might lack finesse, but his gaze was warm as he held out his left hand—warm and hopeful and slightly unsure. Her fingers touched his and shivers raced up her arm. If he noticed, he didn't say anything. She stepped into his arms for a slow waltz.

He didn't talk as he danced, but then she hadn't expected that of him. She let the music take her, trusting him to maneuver them both around the dance floor. He took her in circles, making her feel deliciously dizzy. Once, when she misstepped, he gripped her tighter and they both laughed.

"I haven't heard that enough," Garrett said. "Your laugh."

"I'm just finding it again," she admitted. "And it's your fault."

A slow smile—full of comprehension—spread across his face. Heat rose in her cheeks. "I mean…what I—"

But his smile only widened…and then he pulled her closer. Her heart did a somersault inside her. There was something special going on here. Was it just friendship? Or more?

All too soon, the music ended.

"Thank you for the dance."

He bowed slightly. "The pleasure was all mine, ma'am. However, looks like Lucy is glaring at me. Guess that means I'm up for a dance with her."

She sighed inwardly, wishing he'd stay by her side. "You do owe her."

"I was trying to forget. Excuse me." He walked toward Lucy as a lively square dance started up. Before long Kathleen realized she was tapping her toe to the music. She was having fun for the first time in years. She sighed happily.

"Kathleen."

She froze, recognizing the voice. Franklin—her brother-in-law. Her spirits plummeted.

"Did you think I wouldn't find you?"

Slowly she turned. "I wasn't hiding."

He stood there in his overcoat and bowler. Snowflakes dotted his shoulders. "You left without telling anyone."

"I left a note."

He snorted. "And now you've had your little holiday."

"What do you mean?"

"I've come to take you back."

Chapter Eight

❧⦿❧

Garrett finished the dance with Lucy, fetched her a glass of cider and then turned to head back to Kathleen. He stopped when he saw that she stood with a newcomer. The man wore clothes a cut above the rest of the townsfolk—a black silk vest with a gold watch fob dangling from the pocket, boots that looked to be made from alligator rather than the traditional leather of the area. A man of means.

"You gonna stand back and let that stranger move in?" Paul said in a low voice, coming to stand beside him.

"It's her choice who she wants to talk to." Even Garrett could hear the underlying tension in his voice.

"And you can see that if you don't step in, she doesn't have a choice."

Garrett pressed his lips together. Sometimes Paul was just too blunt, but he guessed that was why he got along with him. He knew where the man stood. Unfortunately, he didn't care for his opinion now—probably because it was true.

"Anyone with eyes in their head can tell you care for her."

"It's complicated, so you just might want to talk on something else since it's none of your business." He was pretty sure that wouldn't stop Paul one bit.

"You've been mooning over her since I first met you. Time you own up to it."

"Like I said—it's not that simple. Go find Lucy and ask her for a dance yourself."

"Good idea. I can talk to you any ol' day." He cuffed Garrett on the shoulder.

Once his friend had ambled away, Garrett looked back at Kathleen. What was going on?

Mr. Gator Boots leaned closer to her. Criminy, but she was pretty tonight with her skin flushed from dancing. She blended right in with all the holiday decorations. But this guy—all silk vest and slicked-back hair—jarred the whole picture. Garrett had a bad feeling about the man.

He felt a tug at his sleeve. Lily was back. "Tell him to leave my mama alone!"

At the moment, he could think of nothing he wanted more. He didn't like the way the man's body shut out the rest of the room to her. Yet, the way she stood there and answered right back—hands on her hips—seemed she knew him.

Garrett crouched down again. "Your mother's a big girl. I expect she can handle herself if she wants him to go away."

A scowl marred Lily's sweet face and made him chuckle. "Tell you what. Let's head over to Miss Molly and have a piece of her pumpkin pie."

Lily's eyes lit up. "Pumpkin's my favorite!"

"Fancy that!" he teased. "Mine, too."

They made their way through the men, women and children standing around the three tables of food. Apple, mincemeat and pumpkin pie appeared to be the staple fare. The air was thick with their warm aroma. On the far table were cutting boards with rounds of cheese and beside them, jugs of cider.

"You havin' a good time?" Molly asked Lily from her place behind the tables. She suddenly whisked out a rolled newspaper and shooed away a fly that had the audacity to test the food before everyone else. "Wish I'd brought my swatter," she mumbled. "I'd shorten a life, and that's the truth. That fly don't know it's winter. Must have been hiding out for a month just a-waiting for this party."

Lily giggled.

Garrett raised his brows. "Had no idea you were so violent, Miss Molly."

"Only when it comes to my pies."

Garrett picked up a dessert plate and cut a wedge of pumpkin pie. He looked up to see if Kathleen was coming over when he saw the man grab her arm and move her toward the doorway. He set down the pie. With a glance at Molly, he made it clear she was to watch Lily, and then strode over to Kathleen.

"Everything all right?"

Was it his imagination, or did her shoulders relax?

He nodded to the stranger. "Garrett Sheridan. And around here we don't manhandle the ladies."

The stranger let go of Kathleen's arm and looked him over. "So you're a Sheridan. I've heard a lot about your family."

"Sure it's all good."

Instead of commenting, the man turned back to Kathleen. "Where are you staying?"

"I'm not going back, Franklin."

"Of course you are. Julia is having heart palpitations and your mother is sick with worry."

"And Father? Why didn't he come?"

"It's a busy time of year for him."

"So he sent you."

"I volunteered." A smile played about the corners of his mouth. His black eyes, however, were cold.

Kathleen pressed her lips together. "I have a job here and Lily is adjusting to her new surroundings. I'm not going anywhere."

"A job?" Franklin echoed, his voice coated with sarcasm. "You have a job back home."

"I'm fully capable of deciding where I want to live." Was it Garrett's imagination or did he detect slight desperation in her tone?

Franklin snorted. "You've proved you can manage on your own. I take it that was the point in all this."

Garrett had heard enough. Seemed the man wasn't used to taking the word *no* for an answer. He held out his hand to Kathleen. "I hate to break up this reunion, but you promised me one more dance. I'll collect on that now."

Before Franklin could object, Garrett pulled Kathleen into his arms. The fiddler struck up another tune—a slow box step. Good. Anything faster and they wouldn't be able to talk. Tension radiated off her. What she needed was quiet—and maybe a little holding— in which he'd be glad to oblige, but he needed answers first. "How do you know that man?"

"My sister's husband, Franklin Farthington." She hesitated slightly in her dance step and pulled back to look up at him, her expression puzzled. "I didn't promise you anything about a dance."

He grinned. "Seemed the easiest way to frustrate good ol' Frank."

A hint of a smile lifted the corners of her mouth. "He's not one to trifle with. He's a powerful man. And can be persuasive."

"But he's not your husband. Which means he has no right to force you to go anywhere."

She was quiet at that.

"Do you want to go back?" He had to be sure. It had to bother her, having her mother and sister worrying. "What's really going on here, Kathleen?"

From her expression she seemed to be thinking mighty hard. After the music's second refrain, she met his gaze. "I don't want to leave, Garrett. This is my home now."

Garrett stopped dancing. "Clear enough." He started toward the man.

Kathleen grabbed his sleeve. "Please don't make a scene."

He patted her hand and then extricated himself. "You stay here."

He strode up to Franklin. "This is a community dance and last I knew you were not a part of this community. I'll ask you to leave."

Franklin smirked. "I'm not going without Kathleen. She needs to come with me. Her daughter, too."

Garrett took hold of his arm. The bulge beneath the man's shoulder warned of a weapon. Garrett whipped him around and forced him through the doorway. Behind him, a few ladies gasped at the sudden commotion.

Franklin fumbled for the gun—which now resided in Garrett's grip.

"I'm not so slow as to let you get the upper hand, mister." Garrett pushed him forward toward a fancy carriage. "I figure this one is yours."

"Don't you think I see what's going on?" Franklin snarled, but he climbed onto the seat. "If Kathleen doesn't come with me now, she'll never be welcome back in her own home. Her father barely will take her back as it is."

Garrett emptied the bullets from the derringer into the dirt and then held up the gun. When Franklin leaned down for it, Garrett grasped his collar, pulling him close. "Don't you ever call her character into question again. She's a Sheridan, and as such, you'll give her the respect she's entitled to. Now get!" He shoved Franklin away. Grabbing the bridle on the lead horse, he pulled the conveyance around to face the road to San Diego. He let out a loud whistle and slapped the animal's rump with the flat of his hand.

Startled, the horse took off at a gallop.

Garrett turned. Paul, Eduardo and Lucy stood at the door flanking Kathleen, their faces set in determined anticipation should he have need of their help. That extended to Kathleen now, he realized, and was thankful for it. He strode over to her. "I'll get your cloak."

"I'd like that," she said, her voice shaking.

Outside, a fairy ring haloed the full Christmas moon. He carried Lily and hadn't taken more than five steps when she laid her head on his shoulder. They crossed the main road before Kathleen spoke.

"Thank you, Garrett. Thank you for everything."

"Should I expect a bullet in my back?" He wasn't afraid, just trying to jostle her out of her worried mood. It worked.

She smiled. "Franklin is not a violent sort, but you may notice a few restaurants in the city that won't buy your beef in the future. He'll go back to my family, they'll throw up their hands that I'm beyond redemption now and perhaps will leave me be until spring."

"That include your father?"

She shook her head. "My father is done with me. That's why Franklin came. Not him."

They passed the large wooden doors of the livery and turned the corner, and then walked by the Krueger and the Vancini homes—still dark since both families were at the dance. When they reached Molly's, he stopped on the porch. A small animal scuffled over his boot and rounded the corner of the house.

Kathleen stood on tiptoes to see her daughter's face. "Lily is half-asleep. She looks so content I hate to move her, but I'll take her now."

He wrestled Lily around and into Kathleen's arms, all the while wishing he could just take the sleepy child to the back room and tuck her in. But he understood. Kathleen had to be careful of "talk," and that meant staying outside in full view—even if the only ones getting a good view were the moon and the hoot owl in the old pine.

"Will you wait?"

He nodded, wondering what more she had on her mind. She disappeared into the shadows of the house.

Five minutes later, she stepped outside.

"All snuggled in," she said, speaking of her daughter. Quietly, she closed the door. The light from the moon changed her hair to silvery white and lent her face a translucent quality. She looked like he supposed angels must.

"For weeks you have been underfoot—making sure Molly had firewood, making sure the roof was sturdy for the winter snow, walking me home."

"Guess I feel a certain responsibility to you and Lily."

"Is that what it is, Garrett?"

He swallowed. *That and more.* "Yes."

Kathleen looked away. "I thought…" She sighed.

"What?"

"Do you remember that time in Satterly's barn?"

His breath hitched and he glanced at her lips. "That was a long time ago."

"But you remember."

"Yes." That kiss had seared him with her sweetness. Fumbling, tentative, he'd known it was her first. It had all but carved her initials on his heart.

He studied her, the upturn of her nose, the way she'd twined the red ribbon in her hair. Small touches…feminine touches. He could smell the soap she'd used in her hair mixed in with the scent given off by the pines surrounding them. Awareness of her raced through him and set his skin to tingling.

"People make assumptions about widows. Other men would have expected…something…in return for all the hard work they did around here, but you haven't asked for anything from me."

"I asked to see Lily."

"That's not what I mean."

"I know." He stared at her, wanting her more in that moment than he could admit. Brother-in-law or not, she was a beautiful woman inside and out. He tried to remember why he'd stayed away. For his own sanity, right? It became harder and harder to think straight with her so close. "I'm no saint, Kathleen. Don't make me out to be."

"I don't think I am." She stepped toward him.

Something inside slid into place, as if it had been off-kilter for half of his life. She tilted her head back to look up at him with her eyes half-closed. She looked for all the world like a woman who wanted a kiss...*his* kiss.

Refusing her never entered his thoughts. Slowly, mindful that his heartbeat pounded loud in his ears, he removed his hat and lowered his mouth to hers.

His lips, warm and tender, molded to hers, and she felt as though, at long last, this was where she was supposed to be. In his arms. Safe. Protected. The utter gentleness of his touch, his soft nibble at her lower lip made her tremble. For the first time in her life, she felt cherished.

Currents of pleasure pulsed through her. This kiss was all Garrett. Gentle but firm. Strong and sure. And she wanted it to last. The wanting, the need, became an ache low inside her. He wasn't one to give his affection lightly. On that realization, she pulled back. What was she doing? How could she hope to measure up?

His face came into view. He looked as stunned as she felt. For a heartbeat, neither spoke.

"What's going on here, Kathleen? What is it you want?"

She touched her finger to his lips. Shook her head. Her feelings, her thoughts were all jumbled inside. "I don't know."

A muscle ticked in his cheek.

"I'm..."

"Confused?"

She nodded. "I feel as though I'm being disloyal to Josh."

"That was a long time ago...but...I know how you feel. I feel it, too." He let out a long breath and rubbed the back of his neck. "We'll take this slow. Figure it out as we go. You can pull the reins anytime. That suit you?"

Relief flooded through her.

"I'll stop by tomorrow. After chores." He didn't move to leave.

She should go inside, she knew that. But…one more light kiss… just one… She stood on her tiptoes and started to press a kiss to his cheek when he turned his face and captured her lips once more. This time any pretense of sweetness was gone. A rawness she'd suspected but never seen in him had him pulling her hard against him and pressing his warm mouth to hers, destroying any illusion that all he wanted was platonic.

Inside, an answering desire gripped her, overwhelming and turbulent. She pushed against his chest.

He pulled back immediately, raked his fingers through his hair, slowed his breathing.

"I should go inside."

He slipped on his hat. "Tomorrow?" And he waited as if he half expected her to reject him.

She nodded. "Tomorrow. Good night, Garrett."

She entered the house and shut the door. Placing her forehead against the cool wood, she listened to the sound of his footsteps fading away. Then she sat down in the rocking chair. Her body still thrummed from his kiss.

She loved him—had loved him for weeks now and possibly since way back, before Josh, when she'd first thought to kiss him in the barn. She hadn't recognized it at first. This love was so different from the rush of emotions she'd felt for Josh. This was deeper, stronger, steadier, and she knew in her heart it would burn longer. And that scared her.

Seeing Franklin had cleared things up. She hadn't measured up before. Not in her parents' eyes. Not in Josh's eyes. As hard as she'd tried, they'd never been satisfied. Dare she open herself to that hurt again?

She couldn't stand to let Garrett down. To see in his eyes the disappointment she'd seen in Josh's. And if he tired of her like Josh had—what then?

Now all she had was Lily and herself. Maybe it would be best to keep it that way. She'd be free to raise Lily as she wanted. Free to live her own life. She could almost picture it. Alone. Independent. No one would expect any more of her.

Only she would.

Deep down she knew. She expected more. She *wanted* more. For herself. For Lily. A real family.

She closed her eyes and rocked. Remembering Garrett's first kiss...and then remembering the second.

She wanted more. She wanted...Garrett.

Surely with Garrett it could be different.

Chapter Nine

Snow fell that night and into the next day. A good amount. Enough that the road from the ranch to town was impassable.

Garrett couldn't stand it.

He wanted to see Kathleen. To talk to her. Be with her.

Instead, once the snow finished pelting down that afternoon, he loaded the wagon with hay and hitched up the oxen, then drove them out to the meadow. Standing atop the flatbed, he scattered the hay over the ground. The cattle pushed close, fighting to get the choicest stalks, bellowing until they were satisfied.

He straightened, stretched his back and looked out over the rolling hills, now covered in white. He knew every rock, every oak tree that dotted the meadow. The snow had started just after the dance. By the time he and his folks had made it back to the house, a good three inches had fallen—one for each mile from town. And then it had continued on through the night.

He loved this ranch. Had always planned to start a family here. Maybe build a house near his folks. He was the one who would stay. Josh had always talked of leaving. Always wanted to see far-off places. Josh craved constant change…adventure. He never did get his wish.

And now Garrett could think of nothing but his brother's wife. Something about that didn't set right with him. Maybe in Bible times men married their brother's wives to keep them safe and to keep the children protected. People didn't do that anymore. Not that he cared what people would think…but Kathleen might. Especially if it affected Lily.

He stopped of a sudden. Marriage? He was thinkin' marriage after one…no two…kisses?

But a woman like Kathleen didn't just give out kisses. The way she'd responded—there *was* something between them. Something strong. He'd felt it long ago, but then Josh had intervened and pushed his way into Kathleen's life.

He'd hated his brother for that. That hate had eaten at him for a long time. It took a while for him to realize Josh was grasping for Ma and Pa—even himself—to notice him. That was why he joked all the time. Quiet praise or admonition fell on deaf ears. His brother had been bigger than life and needed bigger-than-life attention and excitement. If it hadn't come to him, then Josh had gone after it or created it. The day-to-day life on a ranch had stifled him. Still, it didn't excuse him from stealing the one girl Garrett had ever cared about. Josh, who all the girls liked, who could get any girl he wanted. Why'd he have to go after Kathleen?

He finished distributing the hay and reined the oxen back toward the barn. Maybe it was a good thing the snow had made travel impossible. He needed the time to figure a few things out. By the time he got back to the ranch and had unsaddled Blue, he had a grip on what he wanted to do.

"I'm going to marry her. My mind's made up," he said, striding into the parlor. "I want to bring Kathleen here until I can build a house."

Ma stoked the fire in the grate and then straightened, turning to him. "Then you know what you have to do. Marriage is too important to go into it with secrets."

Which meant he had to tell her his part in Josh's death.

Emotions stirred inside. His chest tightened. The things he'd said to Josh. The fight they'd had…over Kathleen. He'd hated the way Josh treated her. How he'd stepped out on her, not thinking about her feelings or caring who knew. Garrett could still hear his brother's cynical laugh when he'd told him to go home and take care of his wife. Josh had dug his heels in even further, like any Sheridan would have done, and drank till daylight crept into the saloon.

"It wasn't your fault."

When had Pa come into the room? He didn't want anybody, especially his own kin, letting him off easy. "I could have done things differently."

"Josh was hell-bent on kickin' up his own trouble. Remember that. He was grown with a baby on the way. It was his decision to act like he did. He's the one who made the wrong choice. You've got to let go of the notion you helped his death along."

Garrett blew out a long, slow breath. As much as he didn't want absolution for his part in Josh's death, he still needed to hear that his folks understood, that they'd support him if he needed them.

Unshed tears glistened in his mother's eyes. "Like I always said…we're family. Through whatever may come."

"I want Kathleen to have that, too."

"She does, son," Pa said. "But she has to be the one to accept it."

He closed his eyes. "All right," he heard himself say. "All right."

Kathleen stared out the frosty window, wondering for the thousandth time what Garrett was doing right at that moment. Eight inches of snow covered the ground, with more falling. Two days of it! Hers had been the only footsteps disturbing the carpet of white when she'd traipsed the half mile to the bakery that morning to fire up the ovens. The warmth in the shop was a welcome relief compared to outside. Even the few brave souls that had ventured out for bread and baked sweets had tarried a while inside to warm themselves. She thanked Garrett silently for the fifth time that morning that he'd had the foresight to store up a veritable fortress of chopped wood for Molly.

But truth be told, she wasn't thinking about wood that much. No…what she couldn't get out of her mind was Garrett's kiss. Soft, warm and gentle at first, and then changing. With the thought of how insistent it'd become, how it had stirred things to a frenzy deep in her belly, she felt her cheeks warm. She wanted that kiss again with a desire so strong it took her breath away.

Sue glanced up from rolling pie dough. "You were having a good time Saturday night."

Kathleen's cheeks warmed even more.

Sue laughed. "No need to be shy about it. You had one of the most eligible bachelors watching over you all night."

"What will people think? Him being Josh's brother?"

"I think it shouldn't matter. But to let you know, most the folks around here are happy you're back. And they're glad Garrett is looking out for you. You're the one making it complicated."

"I've got my daughter to think about."

"You've got your own happiness, too. Don't forget that. Lily will know if her mother's unhappy."

"My happiness doesn't depend on Garrett. It's just…he's been around so much lately and now he's not here. I miss him."

"The snow might have something to do with that." Sue pinched the edges of the dough, shaping it into a pretty pattern before pouring in the berry filling.

With the clear skies, by afternoon Kathleen had glanced out the front window half a dozen times hoping to see Garrett. Every time a man's heavy footstep landed on the boardwalk in front of the door or a shadow passed by she looked out. Finally, her constant vigil was rewarded. He caught her closing up the shop and stepped inside with her.

"I didn't think I'd see you," she said. "It's so late."

"Things kept coming up at the ranch, but I'm here now. Sue gone already?" he asked, scanning the dim interior of the bakery.

At her nod, he moved toward her. She thought he would kiss her, but instead he took her cloak from its peg and settled it over her shoulders, drawing it close at her throat. His gaze never left hers, however, and she *felt* kissed.

They stepped outside. She jiggled the door slightly while turning the key in the lock.

"Got that figured out now," he said, smiling slightly.

Lanterns blinked on in the hotel down the road as they crossed. When they rounded the corner and the shadows grew longer and darker, he moved closer. She slipped her hand through the crook of his arm. His nearness sent a thrum of excitement through her. Everything seemed so right. "Will you stay for supper?"

"Are you inviting me?" he whispered low, his breath warm against her ear. All teasing was gone from his voice and the question hung in the cold air between them.

She remembered another time when he'd been asked to stay for supper by Molly…and his response. The thought quickened her pulse as he followed her onto the front porch. "Yes. I'd like you to stay."

He pulled her close, wrapping his arms around her, his face hovering over hers. "Kathleen, there's something I need to tell you." His gaze fell to her mouth and then he looked back at her face. "Later." He touched his lips lightly to hers. She didn't resist—couldn't resist if she'd wanted to. She'd thought of nothing but this since the dance. Her entire body tingled with anticipation as she pressed her mouth gently to his and returned the kiss.

Slowly he took her lower lip gently, sucking, encouraging her to open her mouth, let him inside. And she did. Fire raced through her like liquid gold—and in its wake—desire. He moved, his mouth sliding from her lips down her throat to the base of her neck, near the bit of lace at her collar. Then, pulling away slightly, he looked down into her eyes. With his hands on her shoulders, he set her away from him, a determined look on his face.

"Seems like you and me have been dancing close without touching ever since your family moved to the area. Something always came between us. First your age—you must have been all of nine the first time I laid eyes on you, though I didn't notice you much until you were about fourteen. Then you living in town with me always out at the ranch. Then Josh."

"Josh? What are you saying, Garrett?"

"That I've given this a lot of thought—years of thought—and I can't let you slip away for a second time." His voice was raw with emotion. "I'm in love with you, Kathleen. I've loved you ever since that kiss in Satterly's barn. I want to marry you."

Chapter Ten

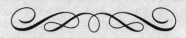

Slowly, as if pulling away from a fog, her eyes focused on him. "Marry? Garrett…I…"

Had he spoken too soon? She wasn't ready…might never be ready now. He backed away from her, lowered his hands.

She looked confused. This wasn't the way it was supposed to happen.

Her brow wrinkled. "What do you mean? You've loved me since that kiss?"

"Yes."

"Why didn't you say anything?"

"Like I said—you were too young at first, and later…you were with Josh."

She blinked, then clutched at her scarf. "Josh knew how you felt?"

He nodded. "He knew, all right."

She moved down to the path. Looked up into the inky night. "All that time? He never said a word to me."

"There was nothing to say. You loved him. You married him."

"Is that why you didn't come to the wedding?"

"Yes." Tears glistened in her blue eyes. He'd do anything not to have put them there. This wasn't at all how he'd imagined his proposal going.

"I don't see how I can marry you, Garrett."

The words cut into him. "Why not?"

"Don't you see? I couldn't make Josh happy. He never said so, but I could tell he didn't like marriage. He felt trapped, frustrated. He wanted so much more. And I had tied him down. He took that job in the mine to make a better life for me and for Lily. He wouldn't have done that if it wasn't for us. It's my fault he was there the day of the explosion."

How could she blame herself? He wanted to shake her…or

hold her. "It was never your fault! Josh didn't like doing anything for very long. He was always moving on to the next new thing."

He knew what he had to do—tell her the truth. Walking away now wasn't an option. Thing was, he knew with each word he uttered, it would ruin any chance he had with her.

"Do you remember the night before Josh died? I came up to the house? Just before he rode off, I heard Josh hollerin'…at you."

She looked startled. Then she covered her face with her hand. "I didn't think anyone knew."

It hurt him to open old wounds, but he had to see it through. "I'd heard him a time or two before," he admitted. "That night my folks were out visiting friends, and since I had moved to the bunkhouse, Josh felt free to be loud. You were sitting all alone in the parlor—sewing or mending—and crying. I could tell by the wet splotches on the shirt in your lap—and by your face.

"Something inside snapped. Nothing you could have done was so bad that you deserved that. He left you alone a lot. It wasn't right. I rode into town looking for him. I aimed to bring him back to the ranch house, make him apologize."

He swallowed. It was hard to continue. He hated this. Hated admitting he'd been wrong…done wrong.

"I found him getting liquored up in the saloon. We argued. I said some things I'm not proud of. He told me to stay out of his business. It turned to fists. I…broke his nose before Russell and Paul separated us."

"You broke his nose!"

"He grabbed his hat and left with…a friend." He wouldn't tell her the other part—that Josh had slept till morning in the willing arms of Sadie Darnell. "That's the last I saw of him alive, but I heard that he drank more—drank into the morning. And then he went to his job at the mine."

"A job that entailed handling dynamite," she said quietly.

Garrett took a deep breath. "So you see, it's my fault he died. Not yours. It's on my head." There. He'd said it. She knew.

"He'd been late before…but he'd never stayed away all night. Until then."

"I only made it worse…interfering like that."

"But family looks out for family, don't they?"

The way she said it, it wasn't a good thing. She sounded lost. Hurt. And was striking out like a wounded animal. He swallowed. Nodded.

She took a step back, her expression closing, shutting him out. "Please—you better go. I need time to sort through this."

He couldn't leave—not like this. Not without a grain of hope. "I want you and Lily in my life." He clenched his teeth to keep from saying more. Anything more would be like heaping coals on his words. He slipped on his hat. "Good night, Kathleen." He looked once more at the one woman he had always loved and then stepped off the porch and walked away.

His tall figure disappeared into the night. He'd been around so much, done so much for her, for Lily, for Molly—all because he felt guilty! He felt guilty about his brother's death and needed atonement…or redemption. But to marry her! What was he thinking?

It hurt worse because he'd made her believe—as much as she'd tried to deny it—that maybe it wasn't her fault Josh had been unhappy, that maybe it was something inside him—not her. Garrett had made her hope—and made her feel beautiful. She'd wanted to say yes, right then and there, despite what had happened with Josh. She'd wanted to try again. Wanted to know what love from a man, given freely, would be like. With Garrett she'd thought she knew. He'd made her feel special.

She entered Molly's house.

"Mama?" Lily called from her room. "Come tell me a story."

Her pasted-on smile wobbled precariously. "In a minute, sweetie." In the kitchen she filled the enamel basin with water from the pitcher and splashed it on her face. If she were lucky the coldness would numb her feelings as well as her skin.

It was no use at all. Hot tears squeezed through her closed lids. She pressed a towel to her face, and then heard Molly in the hall.

"Is that cowboy stayin' this time?" Molly asked, coming into the kitchen. She stopped short when she got a look at Kathleen's face. "Oh, my. What happened?"

She swiped once more with the towel before draping it over

the back of the chair. She couldn't answer, just shook her head, her thoughts and emotions a chaotic jumble inside.

Molly pulled out the chair. "Sit on down and I'll get supper going. You can peel." And with that she handed Kathleen a paring knife and set a ceramic bowl filled with potatoes in front of her.

The mundane task calmed her some. Lily came back in and set the table, her gaze frequently shifting to her mother.

"Can we decorate the tree tonight?"

Molly glanced at Kathleen. "I don't think so. It's late. We'll have an earlier supper tomorrow and get it done. There are still a few days before Christmas."

"Can we at least make the popcorn?"

Kathleen put down the knife and gathered Lily close. She kissed her on the forehead. "Of course we can. And string it, too. That way it will be all ready for the tree."

"Maybe Uncle Garrett can come tomorrow."

"I think he's busy," she hedged.

"But you'll ask him?"

Kathleen didn't know what to say. She didn't want to lie to Lily.

Molly bustled over and took the bowl of potatoes. "I'll just set these to boiling. Lily, why don't you go play for a while. I'll call you when the food is ready."

With Lily out of the room, Molly turned to Kathleen. "Now, I don't know what happened, and it's fine if you don't want to talk about it, but it seems strange to me and probably even stranger to Lily that you are so close to tears. You're probably scaring her."

"I know. It's just…" She let out a sigh.

Molly crossed her arms over her ample chest. "You got a good half hour before we're ready to eat."

"Garrett said something…about the night before Josh died."

"Umm. I was busy tending to Beaudry then, but I recollect some of the things happening in town."

"Josh was upset. I don't remember what it was about, but he shouted at me and Garrett overheard. After Josh left, Garrett stopped in to make sure I was all right."

Molly raised a brow. Waited.

"Josh didn't strike me, if that's what you are thinking. He wasn't like that."

"A body can strike with things other than their fist. Words hurt, too. It was good of Garrett to check on you."

Kathleen nodded slightly. "After that, Garrett followed Josh into town. He found him in the saloon, drinking. They...got into a fight. A bad one, because Josh didn't come home. It was his last night and he didn't come home." Her voice trembled. "I thought it was me—my fault, all these years, but it was..."

Molly sat down in the chair opposite her. "Did he tell you what the fight was about?"

"He didn't like the way Josh had been treating me."

"Garrett holds things in...sometimes for a long time before he acts. Something must have been building inside him for quite a while to let it out in a public place like the saloon."

"Josh probably had a gigantic headache that next morning. Even though he knew how to handle dynamite, he shouldn't have been anywhere near it."

Molly sat back in her chair. "Garrett sure has been feeling a lot of guilt all these years. I had no idea."

Kathleen stood suddenly, unable to be still, unable to make her thoughts even the slightest bit coherent. "Don't you see? He's been doing all this—the outhouse, the wood, all the visits to make sure we were okay, even the tree—out of guilt!"

"Now you're supposing a lot."

"It's true! Otherwise, why would he take it further? Why would he ask me to marry him?"

Molly raised her brows. "Well, now. It could be that he loves you."

"But how can I believe it?" She squeezed shut her eyes. "I want to. I...I love him...but if that fight hadn't happened, Josh might still be alive. How can I marry the man who sent Josh to his grave? How can I?"

"Now, you know that's not so. It's no more Garrett's fault than it is yours."

"Somewhere inside I understand that, I just don't see how we can ever be together. There's too much between us for it to ever be right."

Molly stood, walked over to her and pulled Kathleen into her arms. "You sure have had your share of heartbreak in your young life. Can't you just take some happiness? If he loves you and you love him…"

She took a deep breath and swiped the tears from her eyes. As much as she wanted to give in and tell Garrett yes, she had Lily to think about. None of this would be good for her daughter. Lily might come to hate her should she learn her mother married the man who beat up her father—and ultimately had a hand in his death. "I…can't."

"You sure about this?" Paul asked, his voice hesitant.

Garrett stuffed the last wrapped parcel of smoked beef into the large sack, cinched it and threw it over his shoulder. "I'm not staying here. Might as well be useful."

Paul followed him. "I really appreciate it, Garrett. Just wasn't up to the traveling this year."

"Works for me, too." Taking the smoked beef down to the orphanage was an annual pilgrimage for Paul. Garrett had joined him once, a few years back. He remembered the route.

"You're coming back?"

Garrett hesitated. Pressed his lips together. Nodded.

"Good." Paul helped hoist the pack over the mule's back and center it. "She'll come around."

Garrett didn't hold out any hope. "It'd take a miracle."

Together they secured the sack on the mule. Garrett mounted Blue.

"See you at church services Christmas Eve." Paul shook his hand and then handed the mule's lead to him. "Keep your rifle close."

Garrett reined Blue toward the main road.

The journey would take four days—two down at a slow pace, one there and one back up. He welcomed the chance to be by himself. The only thing he'd have to watch out for would be mountain lions tempted by the scent of the meat. Paul had wrapped it well enough, but he'd still have to take care.

However, mountain lions were the least of his worries right now. Before heading out of town, he'd have to pass the bakery.

So many things about the other night troubled him, but deep in his soul, he knew he'd done the right thing. It wouldn't have been right to lead Kathleen into a union without knowing his part in Josh's death. He loved her too much to take advantage of her like that. She thought he felt guilty—and she was right up to a point. But Josh had made his own choices—to drink too much, to dally with Sadie, to go to work the next morning still half-drunk and angry. He'd been angry at himself more than anything. Garrett understood that now.

It would take all his willpower not to stop, not to look in the window. He kept his gaze straight ahead, kept his mount at a steady pace and headed out of town.

Chapter Eleven

Christmas Eve service was a gathering of most of the townsfolk and many outlying families. The wooden building was decorated with fragrant pine boughs, mistletoe and red bows. Kathleen watched Lily's face light up in wonder as she passed into the large room lined with pews, and was handed her own small candle. For a moment Kathleen felt a wave of guilt that she hadn't brought her daughter here sooner, but she hadn't been ready when she first moved to town. She'd needed time.

She preferred to take a seat in the rear of the room, however, Molly, on seeing a friend and empty seats halfway to the front, took Lily's hand and led her that way. Once they were settled and the opening hymn sung, Kathleen dared a look at those seated around her.

No Garrett.

It seemed the ranch had swallowed him up. She set her jaw. Well…good. At first she had been so upset and confused that she didn't know what she would have done if he'd stopped by the bakery. Probably given him the cold shoulder. Probably refused to wait on him. But then he didn't come in, didn't even come to town as far as she knew. It had weighed on her. And she went from being angry to worrying. Maybe they should talk, now that the shock of what he'd said had worn off. Although it wouldn't change her mind. She'd finally asked Lucy, who knew just about everything about anything happening in town, and learned he'd left the area. He was doing just what she'd asked—giving her time.

She settled back into the pew, feeling a strange sense of loss that he wasn't here.

She turned her attention to the service.

Lily sang the carols in her sweet, high voice. Her eyes became as round as saucers when two boys walked down the aisle with candles and everyone took their turn lighting their own. It was then Kathleen noticed Brent and Barbara Sheridan across the aisle a few pews back. Barbara nodded to her—and smiled. A surprise.

When the singing was done and the service over, people milled about outside, wishing happy Christmas to each other, exchanging hugs and well wishes. Lucy made her way over to Kathleen.

"Garrett must not be back. He usually hands out the gifts to the youngsters."

Kathleen glanced over to see Brent opening his carriage boot and pulling out a small box. He called a name and a young boy ran up to accept the present. More names and presents followed. "There were…words between us. I wasn't…kind."

Lucy frowned, then led Kathleen away from those milling in front of the church and over to the freestanding bell tower. Kathleen checked for Lily and found Barbara Sheridan crouched down, talking to her with Molly standing close by.

"What happened?" Lucy asked in a hushed voice.

"He asked me to marry him."

Lucy's shoulders sank. "Guess I saw that coming. He's loved you since forever."

Startled that Lucy would know, Kathleen asked, "He told you?"

"Course not. You know how Garrett is—tight-lipped as a nutshell. It's plain in how he treats you, how he lights up when you walk into a room. I'd hoped last Christmas that he was over you. That's why I twisted his arm about going to the dance. But then you came back."

"It doesn't matter. There's too much between us to ever marry. Just too much heartbreak."

"He must have told you about that night. About the fight." Lucy shrugged. "So he stood up for you."

"I guess you could say that, but he took it too far. Josh didn't come home that night."

"He would have if Sadie hadn't stepped in."

The name was unfamiliar to Kathleen. "Sadie?"

"Yes. Sadie and Josh."

A knife wedged in Kathleen's chest. "Don't…" she whispered.

"Garrett left that part out, didn't he?"

"Josh…was with another woman?" She'd known he'd been

drinking more, spending more evenings away. But she hadn't known he was seeing someone.

"When Garrett broke Josh's nose, the fight ended and Josh was ready to go home. Garrett walked over to the bartender to get a cloth for the blood, and in that moment Sadie Darnell sidled up to Josh. Your husband grabbed a bottle of whiskey and left—leaning on Sadie."

"I didn't know…."

"Course not. Garrett knew it would hurt you."

Kathleen straightened. "It doesn't change anything. Garrett's been looking out for Lily and me out of guilt. He would marry me…out of guilt over what he's done. Marriage is hard enough without doing it for the wrong reasons. It's better I don't see him again. There's too much that's happened. Too much to ever put things back together again."

"Not if you love him."

She looked up to heaven. Stars blurred in the cold night sky. "I don't even know what love is between a man and a woman! It sure wasn't the way Josh treated me! All I have is Lily. And I'm trying to do the best by her." She was shaking, and not from the cold. Where had that outburst come from? She'd never told anyone about the way Josh treated her, never said anything bad about him. She was falling apart here. Coming back to Clear Springs had been a terrible choice.

Lucy pressed her lips together and then stepped forward and hugged Kathleen. "Don't be too hasty in making this decision. You won't get another chance—not from Garrett. Besides, it's Christmas. A time to remember, but also a time to forgive. Soon it will be a new year." She turned and headed back to the small knot of people left in front of the church.

Kathleen swiped the tears from her eyes and stood there, piecing together all that Lucy had said.

"Mama! Mama!" Lily ran up to her and tugged on her hand, leading her back toward the Sheridans. They were the last people Kathleen wanted to see just now.

"Honey. We need to head back to Molly's. It's getting late."

"Grandmother told me to get you. She wants to give you something."

She let Lily drag her toward Barbara, girding herself for the moment. Like Lucy had said, it was Christmas and should be a happy time—at least for children. She'd take Lily back to the house and make some hot cocoa. It would be okay. She'd make it be okay for Lily.

When she neared, Barbara smiled hesitantly. "Merry Christmas. I…I want to invite you and Lily and Molly out to the ranch tomorrow to spend the day with us."

It was a lovely invitation, and Kathleen wondered whether or not Barbara and Brent knew what had transpired between her and Garrett.

"Thank you, but Lily and I have other plans." She saw Molly's surprised expression from the corner of her eye.

Barbara's shoulders slumped. "Oh. I see."

Did the woman really want to spend the day with her?

"Well, then, since we won't be seeing you, I have a gift for each of you in the carriage. Brent?"

Her husband stepped to the boot and withdrew four packages.

Why? Why were they being kind to her after so long? Had she been mistaken five years ago? Had she only seen what she wanted to? Had her own shortcomings with Josh distorted what had really happened back then?

Each present was wrapped in white paper and tied with a red ribbon—all save one. Barbara handed them out, giving two to Lily. "Please, if anything changes your mind…you are welcome tomorrow. I'll hold on to the hope that you'll come."

Kathleen shook her head. She couldn't even speak. Confusion roiled like yesterday's breakfast in her stomach.

Brent helped his wife into the carriage and then climbed in after her. He glanced at each one of them in turn, and in his quiet gaze, Kathleen could see Garrett's patient look. There wasn't a bit of condemnation in it. Just…caring.

"Merry Christmas," Barbara said, and squeezed her husband's shoulder. Brent took the hint, flicked the reins and set off toward the ranch.

Kathleen couldn't sleep. Molly and Lily had been asleep for an hour when she tucked the covers around her daughter and left the bedroom. The parlor fireplace glowed with the last of the embers. Blue moonlight filtered through the crack in the window curtains. She pushed the heavy fabric aside and looked out to the road. A new dusting of snow had fallen since they'd returned from church, but now the clouds had passed over and the sky was clearing. The world seemed changed somehow, in these hours between dusk and dawn. An illusion. Only an illusion.

How could she stay in Clear Springs with how things were? She couldn't bear to see Garrett at odd times in the bakery or in town and not speak to him. Couldn't bear to know he was as close as the ranch. Was it really as simple as Lucy said?

Restless, she stirred the embers and added a few small sticks from the wood box. She tiptoed quietly back to the bedroom and to the foot of her bed. Lily's soft breathing broke the silence pressing down all around. Kathleen opened the large trunk and wedged the dowel to hold the lid. Digging down in the far right corner, she searched until her fingers brushed against the ear of the stuffed bunny she'd made for her daughter. She pulled it out, straightened the silk vest and fluffed its tail. Her gift to Molly came next. Warm slippers she'd knitted whenever Molly had been gone to her quilting group.

She placed the bunny and the slippers under the tree with the gifts from Barbara and Brent. The lone one from Garrett pulled her gaze. What was he giving Lily? She could open it and then rewrap it. Molly might know, but Lily wouldn't know any better. Still, that seemed dishonest. It *was* dishonest.

She settled into the rocking chair and picked up her needlepoint. She rocked back and forth. Back and forth. All the while, staring at that present.

"Enough!" she muttered under her breath. She grabbed the package and untied the string before her good sense could stop her. A book. A simple book! She sat down and stared at it. No title, nothing on the outside to suggest what it was about. On the inside cover Garrett had written the words, "For my niece, Lily Sheridan, on her first Christmas in Clear Springs."

She read the first few lines. It was about Josh—his life as a boy growing up on the ranch—his favorite pastimes, colors, horses, pets. She flipped through a few pages. There Garrett had written about a Fourth of July parade that Josh had been in when he was twelve. She remembered that parade! A coyote had spooked the horses and they'd run every which way that year, causing pandemonium. The entire book was a story for Lily about her father that she could treasure the rest of her life. Kathleen's throat thickened with emotion.

But how did Garrett end it?

She turned to the back.

> Josh Sheridan was one of the friendliest, fun kids in school, and that never changed as he got older. Your ma was the prettiest gal in Clear Springs. When your Ma caught Josh's eye and he caught hers, they fell hard and fast into love. When he found out a baby was coming—you!—he was the happiest man on this mountain and couldn't wait to see you.

> But accidents happen. And it did to Josh. We all miss him. But I know he's watching from heaven and so proud of his little girl. And real happy that she's moved back to the mountain he loved so much and called home.

She closed the book—and realized her face was wet with tears. A gulpy sob escaped. This gift was so precious. Not just to Lily, but to her, as well. There were parts of Josh's life she'd never known. And the ending, well…it was true. Josh *had* been happy about Lily. He'd been ecstatic. It was only later when the doubts had crept in about supporting a family that the tension started.

How had things reached this…this mess? Josh hadn't been perfect. Far from it, apparently, with Lucy's recent revelation about Sadie. But didn't she have to stay true to Josh and his memory? For Lily?

What about what she wanted?

She began to rewrap the book, but paused once more to look at the writing. It looked so familiar. Where had she seen it before?

An eerie feeling washed through her. Slowly, she rose and walked back to the room she shared with Lily. She opened the trunk and searched through the layers of garments until her fingers touched the leather book of sonnets. Unable to discern its color or shape in the dark, she was yet vividly aware of them anyway.

Back in the parlor, she took a deep breath. At least she was smarter now…wiser. She flipped through the pages to the beginning.

For Kathleen McCrory
With affection
JGS

She stared at the writing as if she'd never seen it before. Trouble was…she had. She closed her eyes, unwilling to give room to the suspicion that tried to crowd her thoughts. It was just a coincidence. They were brothers. Of course their handwriting would be similar. It happened like that in families, didn't it? Josh Grover Sheridan. Or could it be Garrett Joseph Sheridan? The *J* and *G* were hopelessly intertwined. She blinked and a tear dropped onto the page, smudging the indigo ink.

What had happened that night? She closed her eyes, trying to see it all again in her memory. Josh shouting at her, then leaving in a fit of anger. Garrett racing into the room to check that she was all right and then following Josh. What had Josh said? What piece of the puzzle was missing?

She'd known Josh was restless. Something had been bothering him for a while, but he'd not confided in her. Ever since the wedding he'd grown more distant. More unhappy. It had scared her. With Lily growing inside her, she had become bigger and more awkward. She'd needed his reassurance that everything was all right, because it didn't feel all right to her. She'd thought he married her out of love, but toward the end she'd felt like a burden.

That night she hadn't wanted to be alone—not in his parents' house. He'd left her alone so much. Maybe he would stay if she could get him talking. That was when she'd asked him to read to her. The book of sonnets was beside her and so she'd suggested it. And then everything got worse.

She forced herself to remember, aching inside again just as she had that night. Josh had mumbled about being the wrong one. It had been in such a low voice that she'd asked him to repeat it. He'd looked directly at her, and the stark frustration in his eyes had taken her aback. His jaw had tensed and finally he had said, "I can't do this." Then he'd stormed out.

And she'd thought it was her fault. That she couldn't hold on to him. He was slipping away. She was too young, too inexperienced, to hold on to her man. The shame had overwhelmed her.

Until now.

She stared at the writing…Garrett's words. Garrett had given her the book and Josh had taken the credit. And she'd believed him. After all, Josh was closer to her age. He had flattered her with his sudden, all-consuming interest and swept her off her feet.

Like a challenge—a competition.

Why had Josh done it? What kind of man would do that to his own brother? And why hadn't Garrett spoken up? Her entire marriage had been based on a lie! Could it be true, then, what Garrett had said? He really had loved her all this time?

Her hands shook as she turned the book over in them, smoothing her palm over the page. Calming a bit, Lucy's words came back to her. *He's loved you since forever.*

Well, she saw it now. He loved her. And he'd risked that love not once but twice. First, by stepping back when she'd fallen for his brother and again when he'd been honest with her and revealed the truth about the last night of Josh's life.

She closed her eyes and leaned back against the chair, her heart, her very soul aching as she realized the truth. Garrett had been more interested in Josh's happiness, and in her happiness, than his own. A selfless love. Just like the sonnets proclaimed.

And she'd thrown it away….

Chapter Twelve

"Everything is ready," Ma called out from the kitchen window.

Garrett held up his hand to acknowledge her. He'd returned late yesterday from his trip, so this year Pa had been the one to shoot a pheasant for the table. His stomach rumbled just thinking of the special Christmas dressing and gravy. He'd caught a whiff of it earlier. He pounded his ax through the thin layer of ice on the water in the horse trough and immediately Blue pushed up to his side to drink. Garrett slipped from the corral and latched the gate.

The whinny of a horse pulled his attention to the lane. A buggy approached—one from the livery. Molly held the reins, with Kathleen and Lily sitting on the front seat beside her.

He stopped in his tracks. She was the last person he had expected to see. Four days away had done nothing to ease the ache inside, and he'd finally admitted to himself that it never would go completely away. He'd have to live with it. He took a steadying breath.

Pa stepped out onto the porch, followed by Ma. They each exchanged glances, then looked at him as if he knew what was happening. He walked over to join them.

Molly pulled the rig up before the house and tied off the reins to the brake. "Well, don't just stand there. Help a body down," she said good-naturedly. "I got fixin's in the back to haul in."

He helped her down and then he turned back to Lily. "Miss Lily. Welcome and happy Christmas." He grabbed her under the arms and swung her in a wide arc to the ground, enjoying the sound of her giggles.

She crooked her finger at him. "Can I see Dixie?"

"The colt? Sure. After dinner I'll take you to the stable."

He turned back to Kathleen and his throat constricted. She looked more beautiful than ever in her dark blue cloak and what looked to be a new, cream-colored scarf. Strands of her blond hair had escaped from her bun and her cheeks were pink from the brisk winter air. He helped her down from the high step, wanting more than anything to keep hold of her.

"Thank you, Garrett." There was a new shyness to her voice as she avoided his gaze and smoothed her cloak.

Something was different. Something he couldn't quite place. He braced himself. Having her here today would be difficult after all that had gone on between them, yet he wouldn't want her anywhere else.

Ma wiped her hands on her apron. "I'm so glad you had a change of heart. Come right in. Brent? Help with those things in the buggy."

Kathleen wasn't paying attention. She was looking directly at him. "Your mother invited us at the church service last night."

He'd heard. "You declined."

"I thought…I wanted…" She clenched her hands, took a step toward him.

Ma and Molly turned briefly on the porch and then moved inside with Lily.

Kathleen watched them go and then drew in her breath. "I changed my mind, Garrett."

"I can see that." He shrugged as if it was nothing to him one way or the other.

"I…changed my mind about a lot of things."

He let out a slow breath. A lot of things?

"That book Josh gave me? There's this poem in it…about gold. It says there's the kind that glitters in the river—sitting right there just waiting to be picked up."

He rubbed his neck. "You're talking in riddles, Kathleen. What are you getting at?"

She swallowed. "Josh was that kind of gold. On the surface, easy to see, fun, exciting. I'll always love him for giving me Lily."

So that was it. She still loved Josh. He didn't figure into her life—other than as an uncle to Lily. "All right. I understand."

"The other gold," she continued, "is more difficult because it is hidden deep in the earth. But it's pure and even more of a treasure for all the work it takes to find. A person has to chip away at the surrounding rock to get to it."

He stopped. Turned. Was she still talking about gold?

"Josh didn't give me that book. You did."

His heart thudded in his chest. "Finally figured that out."

"Garrett, I couldn't recognize your love. It was buried deep. Hidden."

"You sure about it now?"

She nodded. "When I look back, you've always been there watching out for me, strong…protective…caring—ever since that day when you helped me from the creek. I don't want you to stop."

"Couldn't stop if I wanted to," he admitted.

"Good." Tears pooled in her blue eyes.

Did this mean…? After all this time he was afraid to hope.

"Because I love you, Mr. Sheridan."

He drank in the sound of her words, committing the moment to memory. Somewhere along the way, she'd forgiven him! The huge weight he'd carried ever since Josh died dropped from him. It was a miracle, pure and simple. A Christmas miracle. He swallowed. "Then you'll stay awhile—after dinner?"

"Yes."

He had to know. Had to be sure. "Longer?"

"If you'll have me." She looked back at the ranch house. "And Lily."

He could almost see his future stretching out ahead of him, and Kathleen was part of it. He took a deep breath. "Forever?"

"I like the sound of that." Her eyes shone with happiness and love. "Forever."

"Nothin' short of that will do." He pulled her into his arms and kissed her soundly on the lips, sealing their future together.

* * * * *

CHRISTMAS
IN SMOKE RIVER

LYNNA BANNING

Dear Reader,

Christmas in the Old West was like all of life in the Old West, especially on ranches and farms and in small towns—"homegrown." Nobody had much money, so Christmas was a time when mothers and daughters baked cookies, fathers and grandfathers built doll cradles and hobby horses, and grandmothers knit sweaters and scarves for gifts.

A tree would be dragged in from the woods and decorated with paper chains and popcorn balls and strings of cranberries. People gathered to sing songs and play games, to eat and laugh together. Schoolchildren in town went caroling up and down the streets and pored over store window displays of dolls and toy trains; in the country, older kids went on sleigh rides and collected in kitchens to make divinity and fudge.

My grandfather was raised on a ranch in Oregon. He told me that one Christmas when he was a boy, he felt truly blessed when he received a single fragrant ripe orange in his Christmas stocking.

I wish all of you the rich blessings of the holiday season that people enjoyed in the Old West.

Lynna Banning

DEDICATION

In memory of my grandfather, Claude Earl Banning, and with grateful thanks to Suzanne Barrett and Ignacio Avalos.

Chapter One

Lilah

The house came as a shock. It was much larger than I had expected, much too big for just myself and Miss Mollie, the kitten I had brought with me on the train from Philadelphia. And no garden! Instead there was an expanse of dry, dusty ground punctuated with a single overgrown maple tree in the far corner and surrounded by a scruffy picket fence that in some earlier life must have been white but now looked mottled and in some places was peeling down to the bare wood.

Aunt Carrie, you lied. Well, of course she had. That had been my aunt's forte, had it not? Which was why it was I, and not she, who was now taking possession of this big old rundown place in this little scrap of a town three thousand miles from Philadelphia and civilization.

Oh, mercy, this *is what I wanted?*

I unlocked the front door and inspected the interior, upstairs and down. Horrors! It looked as if no one had set foot in the place for at least twenty years. Cobwebs drooped from the ceiling beams, dust balls six inches in diameter lolled in the corners. The wallpaper was peeling and the dingy paint was cracked. My heart curled up under my starched white shirtwaist and quivered in despair.

Thoroughly discouraged, I settled Mollie in her basket, walked into town and engaged a room at the Smoke River Hotel. As soon as I registered, I stepped next door to the restaurant and ordered a large, comforting pot of tea. At least I had a house to live in, and a quiet place to pursue my calling, far from Mama and her disapproving sniffs. *Lilah, you simply must learn to fit into society.*

I gazed wistfully out the front window of the restaurant. I was now way out West in Oregon, far from anything civilized. Across the street were a barbershop, a mercantile, a dressmaker and a bakery. And that was it, except for the sheriff's office.

I scratched behind Mollie's ear and slipped a morsel of my buttered toast into the basket at my feet, then wished I hadn't. The waitress might hear the kitten's purring.

The house—*my* house—needed everything: a thorough cleaning top to bottom, fresh paint and new wallpaper in the three upstairs bedrooms, one of which I would use as my office when my typewriter and desk and filing cabinet arrived from home. The room was light and airy, with large many-paned windows and a high ceiling.

I sipped my tea and quivered at the prospect before me. Except for a huge nickel-trimmed stove in the kitchen and my two travel trunks, there was not a scrap of furniture in the entire house. No bed, no bookcases, no china cabinet, no…anything.

On the way back to my room at the hotel I stopped in at the mercantile. Aunt Carrie had left me pots of money in her will, so cost was no deterrent. As soon as I found a Montgomery Ward catalog, I would simply order what I needed.

At Ness's mercantile, the proprietor—surely not the owner, as she could not be more than fourteen years old—located a catalog and, with a stealthy glance at the curtain behind her, the girl let me take the catalog up to my hotel room. That evening I mulled for hours over beds and end tables and settees, and the next morning when I presented my filled-out order form, the girl's brown eyes popped.

"Ma'am, you sure you want to order all this?" she gasped.

"I am. And have you any flower seeds? What once might have been a garden at my new home is now bare dirt."

She nodded so enthusiastically her braids bounced. "Oh, I love gardens! And you'll need a shovel, and a hoe, and…"

I must have groaned, because she, her name is Edith Ness, laughed and asked me where I came from. When I told her, her eyes rounded. "You must have had servants," she said in a hushed tone. "And a gardener."

Servants, yes. But a gardener? It was Mama who had mulched and planted and pruned in our large expanse of land by the river, and there were always scads of blooms and bouquets in every room.

I told Edith that I planned to be my own gardener and that I wanted flowers, and lots of them, in the worst way. As soon as possible.

My furniture would be shipped by rail from Omaha within three weeks. While I waited, I worked on the house, scrubbing floors until my knees ached, combing spiders' webs off the walls, pulling the garish, faded wallpaper down and burning every last scrap in the stove.

I also made good use of the shovel, and while I had never had any instruction in spading up the earth, I managed to dig a wide bed all along my front fence and planted the seeds I had purchased. I watered them with used wash water and fussed over them for weeks while wagonloads of the furniture began to arrive from the station.

Finally, three weeks later, I was thrilled to see beautiful, brave green sprouts poking up from the earth.

Now each afternoon I sit in my new porch swing, which came unassembled and cost me three broken fingernails before I figured out how it all fit together, and envision how lovely my garden will look in another month when the nasturtiums and black-eyed Susans and baby's breath will be in bloom. Lately I even wrestle my typewriter out to the front porch, where I prop it up on an upended apple crate and clack away at my writing.

I cannot wait for my flowers to bloom!

Chapter Two

Gale

Dammit all to hell, running cattle through town to get to the railhead is the craziest idea since Whitey Poletti used his hair clippers to shear his daughter's pet lamb. I keep telling Charlie, my boss, that it's nuts to drive cows down main street, but can I tell the owner of the biggest ranch in Lane County what to do?

"You're just the foreman of the Rocking K, not the boss," he yells. "I'm making the decisions, not you."

Right. Old man's getting gray hairs in his brain. Anyway, yesterday me and Skip and Jase and two vaqueros rounded up a hundred head of prime beef and got as far as the outskirts of Smoke River when I realized it wasn't gonna work. The cows kept straying away from the herd, and just as we started through town, Skip and Ernesto lost control over them.

It was too late to backtrack. Nothing to do but drive 'em on through and pray. Jase rode on ahead to clear everybody out of the way, and we thundered on down the road, riding like crazed Indians. I brought up the rear. For a few minutes I couldn't see a damn thing for the dust, but when it lifted I wished it hadn't. I sure hated to watch what was happening.

The cows were spread out over the road, and Skip and Ernesto couldn't hold 'em. Goddamn, it was hard to watch.

The left flank barreled down that road like the Lord won't have it, and just at the edge of town where the road narrows there was no place to go, so they milled around and trampled some lady's front fence all to hell.

I caught a glimpse of her as I rode past, but I was so busy trying to control those darn cows I didn't pay her much mind. She was standin' on her front porch and her mouth was open as if she was screamin' at us, and I guess she was. Anyway, by the time we got the herd penned up for the night it was way past supper-time, so I stopped in at the saloon for a shot of red-eye and a bit of cool-off time.

After dark I rode out of town on my way back to the Rocking K, but I knew I'd have to stop where we'd taken the fence down and make amends. I hate this part of bein' the foreman, but I wouldn't feel right if I didn't.

Sure enough, the pickets were plumb ruined, split and shattered every which way. And some little nubby green shoots that had poked up were flattened. I tied my gelding to the only fence post left standing, swatted the dust off my Stetson and tramped up to the front door and knocked.

Nothing happened, so I knocked again, louder.

Still nothing. Hell's bells, maybe she'd gone for the sheriff.

Nah. I'd have run into the sheriff at the saloon.

I raised my fist and was just about to bash a good one on the door when it jerked open and the lady peered out at me. Right away I started to explain about the fence, but when I got a good look at her, my tongue went numb and I just stared. I'd never seen a female anything like her.

She had red hair, dark like good wine or that rambly rose that spangles over the bunkhouse door, and it was knotted up into a thick bun at the back of her neck. Little tendrils had escaped and curled around her face.

She stared back at me with dark blue eyes so big they looked like pansies. In the lamplight spilling from inside the house they seemed almost purple.

She didn't smile. I stood there for a full minute wondering why I couldn't talk and why she didn't smile or say anything, and then she opened her lips and spoke.

"Yes?"

"Ma'am, I—" I swallowed hard. "I came about your fence."

"Oh, I see." Her voice got real icy.

I swallowed again. "My boys kinda lost control over the cows this afternoon, and I sure am sorry about your fence."

"And my garden," she said. Her voice was awful quiet.

"Oh, yeah, I guess we tore up the ground a mite."

The way she kept looking at me with those eyes of hers kinda unnerved me, and I couldn't think what to say next.

God, I'd never seen a woman as beautiful as she was. I looked her over real quick like and that just made it worse. She had on a ruffly red-striped shirtwaist with the sleeves rolled up to her elbows, tucked real neat into a plain gray skirt. Looked like denim or twill, and it flared over her hips just right.

"My fence?" she reminded. Still icy.

I tried like hell to get my eyes past where her breasts pushed out those red stripes. "Uh, yeah, your fence. I'll send one of my hands out to repair it tomorrow, soon as we get the cattle loaded."

"And what about my garden?"

"Well, I s'pose he could fix that up, too. Sure am sorry."

"A garden cannot be 'fixed up.' It is destroyed beyond repair and must be replanted."

"Okay."

"I grew it from seed, you understand. That takes time. Eight weeks, to be exact."

She didn't sound so frosty now. She sounded as though she'd like to brain me with a two-by-four. She looked at me as if I was gonna fix it, but hell, I didn't want to take that on. Now I didn't know what to say.

"Eight weeks, huh?"

She nodded. "I was anxious to see the flowers bloom because… well, I was anxious."

"Sure sorry to have ruined it, ma'am. My name's Gale McBurney."

"Mr. McBurney."

"I'm the foreman at the Rocking K, and like I said, I'm real sorry."

"You will, of course, have everything repaired?"

"Yeah, well, hope I didn't interrupt your supper."

"Actually, I was hanging wallpaper in the upstairs bedroom."

Now, that caught my interest. This old place had been empty for years. Probably needed a bunch of work. How come her husband wasn't hanging the wallpaper? Or maybe she lived here alone?

"What is the Rocking K?" she asked all of a sudden.

"It's a ranch, ma'am. About six miles out of town."

"Oh. I arrived on the train from the East. To me, it all looks like one big ranch."

I caught myself watching her mouth as she talked. "The Rocking K is the biggest ranch in the county, Mrs....?"

"My name is Lilah Cornwell."

I nodded. "Missus Cornwell."

"It's *Miss* Cornwell."

Miss. As in not married. For some reason that made me real happy. Not that there was a shortage of single women in the county, and not that I hadn't had some dealings with one or two over the years, but...Well, it just made me feel good. She was sure something to look at.

I settled my hat on my head, then snatched it off again. "Like I said, Miss Cornwell, I'll have one of my hands fix your fence."

"And replant my garden," she reminded me.

All the way back to the ranch I thought about her voice, kinda low and throaty, like a nesting dove. Miss Lilah Cornwell, huh?

Chapter Three

Lilah

The man stood there on my front porch in an open-collared blue chambray shirt stuffed into tight, dusty Levi's, looking like a character in one of those dime novels. He was very tan, with eyes the color of green leaves. As he talked, an unruly shock of black hair kept flopping onto his forehead. I wondered if he was part Indian. Probably not, with a name like McBurney. Black Irish, perhaps.

But he was promising to fix my fence. And my garden. Studying his obvious chagrin over the destruction his cows had wrought on my property, I felt my fury ebb. So he would send one of 'his' hands tomorrow. That must be what a ranch foreman did all day, boss people around.

I decided that I disliked him.

Still, something about the man was arresting—perhaps the odd hunger in his eyes. I found it disturbing. For that alone I should dislike him even more.

But I did not.

The next morning, after my breakfast of tea and marmalade toast, I commenced hanging the yellow-flowered wallpaper in the second bedroom, which would serve as my office. I filled a bowl with the lumpy paste and lugged it and the roll of wallpaper upstairs. For hours I smeared the sticky stuff on the wrong side, slapped it on the wall, smoothed it out and trimmed the edges. I worked steadily until I was lightheaded with fatigue and famished to boot.

During my lunch of bread from the bakery and hard yellow cheese, I wondered why I didn't just hire a man from town to hang the wallpaper? But the answer was so obvious I had to laugh. After Aunt Carrie's cautionary tales, I wanted no man inside my private space, for any reason. So I would cope on my own.

After lunch I finished up the wallpapering and began to paint the downstairs, starting with the front parlor. The paint I'd selected from Ness's mercantile was a creamy yellow, which I liked because it reminded me of the daffodils that bloomed each spring in Mama's garden.

By midafternoon my shoulders ached, but I pressed onward, loaded up my paintbrush and carefully painted around the door molding and the window frames. The paint smell made me dizzy and a bit headachy, but I resolved I would finish at least one wall before I collapsed. I had just restirred the paint when I heard a rhythmic pounding coming from my front yard. I climbed down from the ladder and looked out the window.

A cowboy was bent over my decimated fence, hammering nails into the pickets. His back was toward me, but I guessed it was one of the ranch hands Mr. McBurney had promised to send. The afternoon sun was simply broiling, and a damp patch of perspiration showed on the back of the man's shirt.

I kept on painting, and he kept on hammering. By teatime my neck felt as if a carriage wheel had rolled over it, so I rescued the pitcher of lemonade from the cooler, poured a tall glass and gulped it down.

Never had anything tasted so good! I sank down at the kitchen table and laid my head on my folded arms. I had one more yellow wall to paint in the parlor, but I wasn't at all sure I could drag my aching body back to work.

Another glass of lemonade and an aspirin powder gave me courage. On my way back to the parlor, I passed by the front window and glanced out at the man still laboring over the fence pickets. By now the sweaty spot on the back of his shirt was platter-size.

Poor fellow, working away on orders from that slave-driving foreman, Mr. McBurney. I set my brush in the paint bucket, poured him a glass of lemonade and took it outside.

"Would you like a glass of—?"

"Sure would, whatever it is." He rose and turned to face me.

"Oh," I blurted out. "It's you!"

He pushed his hat back with his thumb. "Who'd you expect?"

"I expected your ranch hand. You said you would send one of your ranch hands to fix the fence."

"Sorry. All the hands are busy down at the rail yard." Without shifting his gaze from mine, he reached out and lifted the lemonade glass out of my hand.

"This for me?" The skin at the corners of his eyes crinkled. He brought the glass to his lips and gulped half of it down.

"I thought you would be too busy bossing around your ranch hands to bother with my fence."

"'Bossing around'?" He polished off the rest of the lemonade. "You think I work a crew of slaves, is that it?"

I could not think of one sensible thing to say, so I kept silent. When I didn't respond, he grinned and went on.

"I don't 'boss' them around with a bullwhip. Ranch hands get paid like everybody else."

"Oh. I see."

"No, you don't, ma'am. I can tell by that little frown between your eyes."

I hadn't realized I was frowning. Or that he was watching my face that closely. I found myself watching his face as well, especially his eyes. I was embarrassingly aware of his green eyes. I felt my cheeks grow hot.

"I did not mean to be insulting, Mr. McBurney."

He handed back the empty glass. "You hangin' more wallpaper?"

"What? Why would you think that?"

"Your hair." He brushed a finger over the tendrils of hair straggling onto my face. "Looks kinda spotted."

"I've been painting the walls of my parlor."

"Yellow, right? Nice color for a parlor. You like to paint?"

I had to laugh at that. "I have no choice, unless I want to live with dingy gray walls."

He looked at me for a long moment, and then he smiled. The man's mouth was beautiful, his lips well formed and…well, curved into a smile like that, they were most attractive.

Mercy! My belly flipped up into a slow somersault and my cheeks grew even warmer. Never in my entire life had I admired a man's mouth. I felt as if I were thirteen years old!

"What about the fence?" he asked.

"What about it?"

"You want it white? Yellow?"

I had to laugh. "I cannot imagine a picket fence painted yellow."

The shoulders under the blue work shirt lifted in a brief, eloquent shrug. "I can."

"The townspeople will think I'm crazy."

"You care what the townspeople think?"

"Well, no, I suppose not. But I am new in town. I don't want people to think I am eccentric."

"You mean like old-maid eccentric? I mean no disrespect, ma'am, but you've got a far piece to go on that score."

"What score?" I heard myself ask. "Old maid or eccentric?"

"Both." He handed me the lemonade glass. "Me, I like colors."

"Then you choose the color, Mr. McBurney."

He tried hard to curb his grin. He had beautiful teeth, too, straight and white against his tanned skin.

"Okay. S'long as you promise not to make me repaint it if you don't like it."

"Very well, I promise." I turned toward the porch.

"Hey, Miss Cornwell?"

I glanced back at him. "Yes?"

"Name's Gale. Gale McBurney."

Chapter Four

Gale

I had the new pickets nailed in place and the whole fence standing upright by suppertime. I even reinforced the wobbly fence post. Tomorrow I'd slap on a coat of paint. I knew I could send out Skip or Jase, but I wanted to do it myself, partly because I looked forward to picking out the color. And partly, I guess, because I wanted to spend more time in the vicinity of Miss Cornwell.

Lilah, she said her name was. Damn pretty name.

Damn pretty woman.

Before I rode back to the ranch, I stopped in at Ness's mercantile to pick out some paint. Carl didn't much like my choice, but little Edith did. I could tell by the enthusiastic bobbing of her head. That kid had good color sense.

I dropped off the two-gallon cans of paint just inside Miss Cornwell's repaired gate and whistled all the way home. Missed supper at the ranch house again, but I had some bacon and leftover corn bread at my cabin.

I couldn't sleep for the second night in a row, so I rolled off my cot, chunked up the fire and started a new drawing. Couldn't quite get her chin right, but tomorrow I'd take a closer look.

Chapter Five

Lilah

Orange! He's painting my fence *orange?* I leaped out of the chair and upended my toast onto the kitchen floor, marmalade side down. While I scrubbed off the sticky jam I could hear him whistling out by the front fence. "The Blue Danube" waltz? Unusual choice for a cowboy/ranch foreman.

My first impulse was to storm outside, but then I reminded myself I had let him choose the color, so it served me right. Mama always said I was too impulsive.

By lunchtime I couldn't stand it any longer and stepped out onto the front porch.

"Good morning, Mr. McBurney."

"Gale," he reminded me without looking up. "Like the color?"

"It's, well, unusual," I allowed. "It's sort of a peachy-orange-sherbety shade."

He rocked back on his heels and sent me a look from under his battered wide-brimmed hat. It shaded his eyes, which looked even more green, exactly the color of a fresh Christmas wreath made of fir fronds.

He sent me a frown. "'Sherbety'? What's that?"

"You know, like ice cream, only made with ice."

"You mean that Persian stuff?"

"Yes. They call it sorbet."

He thumbed his hat back and sent me that smile again. "Sounds seductive."

I stopped breathing. *Seductive?* Did he really say that?

He did. I know he did because his eyes had that crinkly look in the corners, and he wouldn't meet my gaze. The man knew exactly what he'd said.

Chapter Six

Gale

That night at the supper table I got ribbed but good, not just by the vaqueros, Ernesto and Juan, but by Jase and Skip, and even Consuelo, the ranch cook.

"Where you been past two days, Señor Gale? Ees she pretty?"

"Yeah, Gale," said Skip. "Tell us all about it."

Jase poked the younger man's arm. "Ya mean 'her,' doncha, Skip?"

With a knowing grin Skip unfolded his long legs and slid his lanky body down in his chair. "Yeah. Tell us about 'her.'"

"Bueno," said Juan and Ernesto together. Juan reached out to pinch Consuelo's ample posterior, but she adroitly sidestepped his seeking fingers.

Only Charlie Kingman, owner of the Rocking K, kept his tongue from flapping, and maybe that was because of Consuelo's beef stew. He was shoveling it in as if there wasn't gonna be a tomorrow.

After the hoorah died down some and the boys were chin deep in Consuelo's brandy-apple pie, Charlie caught my eye and lifted one silvery eyebrow. I stared right back at him, but inside I was squirming.

Just because I'd started Skip and Jase on breaking the new mustangs Ernesto and his nephew had brought in, everybody thought I must have a girl in town who was more important than a few wild horses. Everybody except Mrs. Kingman. Alice said nothing, just studied the dabs of orange paint on the backs of my hands and sent me a slow smile.

"I visited the dressmaker in town this afternoon," she said casually to her husband. She sat up straighter so he could admire her new shirtwaist. "Do you like it?"

From the opposite end of the big walnut table Charlie gave her a slow once-over, and I could see he liked it because he grunted and his cheeks turned pink. Old codger was still male, wasn't he?

I knew then that Alice had figured out where I'd been all day. Nobody, not even an Irish cowboy, has orange freckles all over his arms. They wouldn't scrub off when I washed up at the pump, even when I used a fingernail brush.

Skip and Jase sure razzed me about breaking those mustangs. "Kinda a five-man job, if you get my drift," Skip drawled.

"Kinda hard with just us four."

Charlie leaned back in his chair and gestured to Consuelo for more coffee. "About that string of horses, Gale."

Jase snorted. "Horses! I'd wager the man's got his eye on a pretty little—"

"Have some more pie, Jason," Alice Kingman interrupted.

"Yeah," I said real low. "Fill your mouth with something other than idle talk."

Consuelo did her part, too. "More coffee?" She managed to accidentally touch the hot coffeepot to Jase's meaty hand, and when he jerked it away he knocked over his cup.

"Now look what you make me do!" the plump Mexican woman complained. "All today I spend ironing clean tablecloth, and now must wash all over again. Ay-yi-yi!" She rapped her knuckles on top of Jase's shaggy blond head. "You behave!"

When he wasn't looking, she sent me a wink.

"What about those mustangs?" I asked Charlie. "You want 'em green broke or saddle ready?"

"Saddle ready. They're goin' to the army at Fort Hall."

I nodded. That oughta keep me workin' hard all day and sore all night for weeks. No time to admire my orange fence.

Or anything else. Unless…

"I'm turnin' in, Charlie." At his nod, I stood up and tipped my head at his wife. "Mrs. Kingman."

I fully intended to head straight for the cabin I'd been given as part of my wages as foreman, but halfway across the meadow I changed my mind. The Lord loves a fool, I guess, because nobody saw me saddle up my gelding and leave the ranch.

Chapter Seven

Lilah

I yanked the paper out of the typewriter, crumpled it into a big, crunchy ball and added it to the pile in the wastebasket by my desk. I'd been writing steadily ever since my supper of scrambled eggs and biscuits, but my story just wasn't coming.

I lifted my head when an odd sound drifted through the open window, an irregular chuff-chuff, followed by a pause. What on earth? I raised the sash and peered out. There was just enough moonlight to see a dark shape hunched over close to the ground by my new front fence.

I slid the sash up, and the figure froze.

I kept a small Colt pistol in my top desk drawer, and now I grabbed it and started down the stairs with the gun in my right hand, clinging to the banister with my left. I eased the front door open, pulled back the hammer on the gun and stepped out onto the porch.

"Hold it right there, whoever you are!" I sounded braver than I felt. At least I hoped I did.

A voice cut through the darkness. "It's all right, Miss Cornwell. It's me, Gale McBurney."

The strength drained from my body. "Could you not have knocked on the door?" I snapped. I hated sounding so waspish, but now I was shaking, and that made me mad. I detest being frightened.

"What on earth are you doing out there?" I winced at my tone.

"Planting nasturtiums."

"Whaaat?" My knees were feeling quite wobbly.

"And black-eyed Susans. Edith Ness told me that's what you bought before, so I thought I'd…"

He stepped into the faint lamplight spilling out the front door.

In his hand was a trowel, *my* trowel, if I wasn't mistaken, and on his face was the ghost of one of those unsettling smiles. But now I was so angry I was immune.

"...replant your flower seeds," he finished.

"At this time of night? Mr. McBurney, it's past midnight."

"Yeah, I know. But it's the only time I have, so I figured I'd better get it done tonight."

Chapter Eight

Gale

I straightened up real quick when I saw that little pistol in her hand. She had it aimed straight at me. "That thing loaded?"

"Yes, it most certainly is."

"Mind pointing it somewhere else?"

She didn't answer for way too long, and I started to sweat. Then I noticed her bare toes peeking out from under her dark skirt. Part of me went cold and still as I studied them.

The rest of me went as hot as July at noon.

She still hadn't lowered the gun. "Miss Cornwell?"

She didn't answer.

"Uh, Miss Cornwell? Lilah?"

She jerked her gun hand down against her skirt and sent me a questioning look. "Did you plant any baby's breath?"

I was still staring at her bare toes, I guess, because she repeated the question.

"Baby's breath? What's that?"

"*Gypsophila.* It's a flower. I had planted baby's breath seeds."

So, I thought irrationally, there would be more planting to do on some other night. First chance I got between breaking a new bunch of wild mustangs and making another stop at the mercantile.

"Guess I missed that baby's whatever, Miss…Lilah." Damn, I loved the flavor of her name in my mouth. "But I got the other seeds planted just fine. Kinda spread them around some. Flowers in straight lines aren't too interesting."

"What would you know about flower gardens?" She worked her lower lip between her teeth, and right away things inside my gut moved from July straight into August.

"Look, Miss—Lilah. I'll make you a wager. If you don't like your garden when the flowers bloom, I'll dig it up and start over."

"No, you won't," she said. "It will be too late in the season to start over."

"Does that mean you'll leave it planted like it is? Or that you'll be replacing me?"

"I am quite sure you have your hands full with your ranch job."

"That's a fact, ma'am. Lilah. Right now we're breaking horses."

"Well, then?"

I couldn't answer a 'well, then' question, so I dropped the trowel I'd found in the shed off her back porch and moved up the walk toward her. When I reached the bottom porch step I stopped and looked up.

"I want to come back." I said it flat out. I watched her tongue slip out and wet her lower lip and it was all I could do to keep from groaning out loud.

"You have no reason to come back," she said.

"I know. I want to anyway."

"Why?"

"I'm not real sure, to be honest. Outside of the obvious."

Her eyebrows went up. Funny how dark they were, not red, like her hair. Dark like…hawk wings.

"The obvious? What, pray tell, is 'the obvious'?"

I couldn't answer that without saying too much and getting myself in a whole passel of trouble. So I just climbed the three steps to where she stood, lifted the Colt out of her hand and brushed my lips against her cheek.

I stood there for a full minute with my heart bulupping under my breastbone, waiting for I didn't know what. Then I went right for the passel of trouble—hooked one hand around the back of her neck and tipped her chin up with one finger.

"Lilah?"

She didn't make a sound, so I kissed her.

She still said nothing, so I backtracked off the porch and turned to go.

Then I made a mistake. I spun back around, and she was still standing there, not moving and not saying a word.

God, in for a penny, in for a…

I tramped back up the steps, pulled her close and let myself enjoy her mouth until my privates ached.

Big mistake. Big, damn mistake.

Oh, hell no, it wasn't. It was big, damn wonderful.

Chapter Nine

Lilah

Never in my life had I been kissed like that. It went on and on, his mouth questioning, questioning, while my body trembled. I never wanted it to end.

Eventually he did end it, though I could tell he didn't want to because his breathing was even more ragged than mine. That made me feel wonderful, knowing that being close to me, touching me with his mouth unsettled him as much as it did me.

I had a fleeting memory of Adrian Borrey back in Philadelphia, how dry and flat his lips had felt, and in a flash I saw both the deceit and the hilarity of writing my love stories when I knew next to nothing about the subject.

When I opened my eyes Mr. McBurney, Gale, was striding through the front gate, and while I watched he pulled himself up onto the horse he'd tethered to the fence post and rode off into the dark.

I must have stood there on my front porch a good ten minutes after the hoofbeats faded away, and all that time I kept asking myself what had just happened. Crickets scraped in the yard. The slight breeze was soft on my skin, and I could smell the heady sweet perfume of the damask rose on the trellis in the side yard. My breasts felt swollen and achy.

My mind felt addled and at the same time dazzlingly clear, as if I had just gulped down a mouthful of stars. I walked back into the house, climbed the stairs and lay down on my bed fully clothed and stared up at the ceiling.

An hour passed, then two. I could still feel the delicious pressure of Gale's mouth on mine, smell the sweat-spicy scent of his skin.

Dear God in heaven, I have missed so much of life.

Chapter Ten

Gale

I got back to my cabin around three in the morning, feeling like I'd had too many slugs of whiskey. At five o'clock I hauled myself out of bed, pulled on my jeans and stumbled down to the ranch house for breakfast. My head ached like it did that time I cracked it on a tree limb rescuing Mrs. Kingman's cat, but damned if I could stop grinning.

Jase and Skip were bleary-eyed, hunched over their coffee mugs with their gazes fixed on the basket of biscuits Consuelo set on the table in front of Charlie. Juan was hungover, maybe for the first time in his seventeen years, and he paid no attention to anyone. But Ernesto studied me with his sharp black eyes and pursed his lips.

Charlie reached for a biscuit. "Soon as you finish eatin', Gale, I've got twelve horses waitin' for you in the corral."

The boss was in a hurry to deliver the animals to the army post at Fort Hall, and he expected me to hustle because another twenty-five horses were waiting in the holding pen.

Jase and Skip groaned. Ernesto gave me a thumbs-up.

By noon I'd spent more time on the ground in the corral than in the saddle. I was covered with dust and my shoulder hurt where I'd smacked into the fence on one of my unplanned trips off the back of an ornery stallion. When the dinner gong clanged, I staggered over to the horse trough and dunked my head in.

Didn't help much. When I came up for air, Juan handed me a towel, but he looked at me funny. "You okay, *amigo?*"

"Mostly."

"Too much beer?"

Too much something for sure, but it wasn't beer. And it wasn't meant for Juan's ears.

The fried chicken and mashed potatoes Consuelo laid out on

the big dining table helped some, but back in the corral that afternoon things went from bad to very bad.

"¿Qué pasa?" Ernesto said after one really spectacular fall. "Not like you."

I shrugged off his concern and worked the last four mustangs as if there was no tomorrow. Except there *would* be tomorrow, and another one after that, and on and on until the job was done and all the horses were being trailed east to the army post. Skip and Juan usually drove the herd; that'd give me a breather.

But it didn't help that I couldn't sleep at night thinking about Lilah Cornwell's bare toes and the feel of her soft mouth under mine.

Chapter Eleven

Lilah

For the next two weeks I watched my seedbeds like a hawk eyeing a nest of baby chicks. It was now May, and day by day the air grew more balmy and springlike, but the ground remained just that: flat, dry ground. I could see nothing that hinted of a single leaf or a flower.

Where were my nasturtiums? My black-eyed Susans? All these years I had clamored to be on my own, free to pursue whatever path I wished, and now I was proving inept. Even a weed would be gratifying.

Every morning I dribbled the remains of my wash water onto the dirt under which I prayed a seed or two would be sprouting, and hoped no passerby would judge my mental faculties deficient for watering a sunbaked patch of bare earth.

Trips to the mercantile for soap or potatoes or thread were an agony. With each visit little Edith Ness looked at me expectantly, and I had to shake my head. No sprouts yet. No seedlings. No flowers.

I had not confessed to Edith that it was not I who had replanted the garden but Gale McBurney. Perhaps it didn't matter whether saint or sinner poked a shriveled seed into the dry ground. What mattered was that I was now the faithful custodian of God's promised bounty.

Eventually anyway.

One morning as I slopped my scant cupful of water onto the bare flower bed, a trim little horse and buggy pulled to a stop in front of the fence and a well-dressed woman in a bright calico skirt and matching shirtwaist leaned out.

"That fence of yours is a most unusual color."

"Yes," I said. "I know."

"Did you intend for it to be orange?"

"Um…well, no. It just happened." I couldn't admit that it was Gale McBurney who had painted it orange.

She bobbed her graying head. "My name is Alice Kingman. My husband, Charlie, owns the Rocking K ranch." She rested the buggy whip at her side.

Heavens! Mrs. Kingman was well-known in town. She would surely say something to the townspeople about my outlandish fence, and then the whole story about who had painted it and why would come tumbling out.

I managed to smile. "How do you do, Mrs. Kingman. I am Lilah Cornwell."

"New in town, aren't you? I haven't seen you around before."

"I traveled from Philadelphia a few months ago."

"I've often wondered about this old place," she said. "It must have needed some work."

"And some furniture," I added with a laugh. "My aunt left the house to me, but I don't think she ever lived here. It needed everything."

"Ah."

"For the first month I ate off tin plates and slept on the floor."

"Ah," she said again. She looked me over with intelligent gray-blue eyes. "You must come out to the ranch for Sunday dinner."

My heart almost stopped. "Oh, no, I couldn't. Thank you, but—"

"Why couldn't you?"

There were a thousand reasons why I couldn't. For one, Gale McBurney was foreman at the Kingman ranch, and he had kissed me so thoroughly I hadn't slept soundly for two weeks. I simply couldn't face him again. That memory took care of excuses two and three and four as to why I could not appear at the Kingman ranch.

"Oh, I—I wouldn't want to impose."

"Nonsense." She picked up her whip. "I'll send one of the ranch hands with the buggy to drive you out. Four o'clock Sunday. And mind you plan to stay over."

For the rest of the day I was in a nervous flutter. Did Alice Kingman know about Gale? What should I wear to dinner at a ranch? I had brought exactly three dresses suitable for church or a social, but I hadn't attended church since I was twelve, and the thought of a social of any kind made me physically ill. Perhaps that was why Aunt Carrie had willed me this house far off in the West; she had always known how shy I was.

I would much rather talk to flowers than people. And there were *people* at the Rocking K ranch. Especially Gale McBurney.

Chapter Twelve

Gale

It was a good two weeks before I got most of the wild mustangs saddle broke. By the last day, I ached all over and thought maybe I'd cracked a rib. As we washed up for supper, Jase started to tease me.

"You goin' into town tonight, Gale?"

"Nope. Don't want to even look at a saddle. Hurt too much."

"Hell, it's Saturday night! Oughta be dancin' at the Golden Partridge. I hear there's a new girl in town, Lilah something."

My fists clenched of their own accord. *Keep your damn hands off her.*

"I don't think she's the kind to be hangin' out at the Golden Partridge," I managed to say.

But I realized I really didn't know the first thing about Lilah Cornwell except that I'd swear she didn't wear a corset, and when I kissed her she tasted so sweet I got hard.

I knew she hung her own wallpaper and had painted her parlor by herself and that she liked flowers, but that was all. The thought of Skip or Jase or anybody else laying a hand on her made my gut knot up.

After supper I limped across the meadow to my cabin, heated water and scrubbed off three layers of dirt and sweat, then saddled my gelding and hauled my aching ass up onto his back. All the way into town I kept thinking what a fool a man could be.

An hour later I stumbled into the saloon and found Jase and Skip sprawled at a table, nursing what looked like one beer too many.

Skip lifted his glass in my direction. "Thought you weren't comin', Gale."

"I thought so, too."

"Beer?"

"Nah. My head already aches."

Jase squinted at me. "What didja come for, then?"

Hell if I knew.

Wrong. I did know. I had come to make sure no randy cowboy laid a finger on Lilah Cornwell.

I scanned the entire room, including every couple stomping around on the dance floor. Should have saved myself the trip; Lilah wasn't here.

Well, shoot's sake. I was too keyed up to stay at the saloon and too tired and sore to do anything else but ride back to the ranch and hit the sack.

On the way out of town, I passed Lilah's orange-sherbet picket fence, and I tried real hard not to look up at the house. There was a light on upstairs, and I tried not to look at that, either. I felt better knowing she wasn't at the dance, but I sure wanted to see her.

Hell's bells, I couldn't come calling in the middle of the night. I couldn't toss pebbles against her bedroom window like a love-sick kid, either. She'd think I was way out of line.

On the other hand, I'd already strayed so far out of line the night I kissed her I wondered if I'd ever be able to face her again.

I gigged my heels into the horse's flanks and moved on down the road.

Chapter Thirteen

Lilah

By Sunday afternoon I had worried myself into a kerfuffle that would have made Aunt Carrie laugh. *Just pretend you are someone else,* she would say when I confessed my uncertainties. *Lie a little.*

Oh, dear aunt, don't lecture me. Lying is what got you killed.

I decided on my yellow dimity with the tiny pearl buttons all the way to the hem. I'd given up trying to lace myself into the corsets I'd packed in my trunk, but I felt woefully unfashionable without one. I did wear my prettiest hat, a wide-brimmed straw with a yellow ribbon, and by the time I had secured my flyaway tendrils into a neat bun at my neck, I heard a horse and buggy roll to a stop in front of the house.

A handsome older man, dark skinned with gray streaks in his longish black hair, sat in the shiny vehicle.

"Buenas tardes, señorita." He climbed down and tipped his hat, then walked through the gate and lifted my portmanteau out of my hand.

"Good afternoon," I managed as he nestled my tapestry bag on the buggy floor.

"I am Ernesto Tapia," he explained. He gave me a wide grin. "And you are Señorita Cornwell. Boss lady send me to bring. I am honored."

As I moved down the walkway, I came to a dead stop and stared at my feet. A pale green fuzz covered the ground. My seedlings were sprouting! It was all I could do not to drop to my knees and kiss each one of them.

Reluctantly I stepped out through the gate, and with a twinkly-eyed look in his dark eyes, Ernesto handed me into the buggy and we were off.

The countryside beyond my little house grew greener and more lush with each passing mile. I couldn't take my eyes off the grace-ful trees that towered beside the road, or the broad swaths of open fields dotted with red-and-yellow wildflowers. Ernesto drove in silence, but each time I exclaimed over some patch of red daisy-like blooms or a bush covered with tiny white flowers, he chuck-led and explained what they were. Mayweed and yarrow.

Finally the wide gate to the ranch loomed. Ernesto climbed down to unlatch it and drive the buggy on through, and I gazed about in awe.

The house was huge, painted a blinding white that glowed in the late-afternoon sun, and its windows looked out from all three floors. A scarlet rose twined around the front-porch posts and drooped over the lattice. Beside the house, green fields stretched away to a rusty red barn and a series of sturdy-looking pole fences. Corrals, I guessed. Inside one enclosure milled the most beautiful horses I had ever seen, all colors and some even in two colors.

"Criollos," Ernesto said. "Wild."

I knew exactly how they must feel.

Mrs. Kingman appeared on the front porch, dressed in a simple skirt of dark blue denim and a white very plain shirtwaist with a cameo at her throat.

"Welcome!" she called.

Ernesto handed me out of the buggy, and Mrs. Kingman came down the broad wooden steps, her hands outstretched.

"Heavens, my dear, you look wide-eyed. Have you seen a wolf? Or a bear?"

"This is a very beautiful country, Mrs. Kingman," I managed. "I expect I am, well, bowled over. Everything is so *big!*"

She laughed. "Do call me Alice, remember?" She motioned for Ernesto to set my portmanteau on the porch. Just as the Mexi-can drove away toward the barn, the front door opened and a tall, rangy man with silver hair that brushed his shirt collar stepped out. He had very blue eyes, and when they lit on me they widened.

"This is my husband, Charlie," Alice said. "Meet Miss Lilah Cornwell, from Philadelphia."

Mr. Kingman engulfed my hand in both of his and tipped his

head toward his wife. "Gonna be interesting, Allie. Real interesting."

Interesting? Whatever did he mean? Inside, my stomach knotted.

Alice showed me to a lovely bedroom on the second floor where I laid my hat on the quilted bedcover, unpacked my few things and washed my hands and face. A gong clanged long and loud, and I surmised that was the call to dinner.

I gulped a deep breath of air and steeled myself to go downstairs and make conversation.

Chapter Fourteen

Gale

Along about dinnertime Charlie strode out to the pump, where the hands were lined up to wash and took me aside. "Got a surprise for you, Gale."

"Yeah? Couldn't be another herd of mustangs, could it?"

"Nope."

That was a relief. My shoulder was still so sore it ached when I put on my shirt in the morning, and my cracked rib hurt if I forgot and leaned up against a fence.

The boss looked kinda funny, the way he gets right around Alice's birthday. Probably a present for her, maybe a new horse he'd want me to gentle.

"Come on," he said. "It's inside."

"Consuelo's fried chicken?" I guessed. "Chocolate cake?"

Charlie just grinned.

I was the last person to enter the dining room, and right away I noticed an extra chair had been set directly across from me. Everybody else noticed it, too. Ernesto was the only hand not whispering about it.

Oh, no. It had to be Alice's spinster aunt. Charlie knew I hated the old woman, and Charlie always liked playing jokes.

Damn the man.

I heard the rustle of petticoats coming down the staircase and I gritted my teeth and swore under my breath.

But it couldn't have been Alice's maiden aunt, because one by one Jase and then Skip and then Juan and Ernesto jolted to their feet. Suspicious, I dragged myself upright, too. Ernesto pulled out the empty chair, and then the wearer of the petticoats appeared.

Lilah Cornwell slid into place and I about swallowed my tongue. *Double damn the man.*

The ranch hands just stood there, mouths gaping open, until Alice murmured, "At ease, gentlemen," and they dropped into their chairs.

Lilah didn't look up right away, and that gave me a split second to compose myself. My God, she was beautiful. In that yellow dress she looked like a ruffled lemon drop. Some of her dark red hair had pulled out of the bun at her neck and curled across her temples and her cheeks in little swirls that made my mouth water.

I sure hoped my mouth wasn't hanging open like Skip's and Jase's. Oh, what in hell was she doing here?

Alice explained it, along with the introductions. "This is Miss Cornwell," she announced. "I have invited her to dinner."

Alice went around the table introducing everyone, and by the time she got to me I thought I'd pretty much recovered.

Lilah smiled and nodded at all the boys, and when Alice mentioned me, Lilah glanced up and blushed. I couldn't have said a word anyway, so I just nodded.

I was saved when Consuelo entered with a huge platter of fried chicken, and everything got back to normal.

Except for me. My tongue stayed glued to the roof of my mouth through creamed corn and biscuits and mashed potatoes and gravy while Jase and Skip tried to outdo each other with tales of dangerous cowboy exploits, and Alice and Charlie looked at each other and smiled.

Jase was seated next to Lilah, and I noticed he kept hitching his chair closer and closer until Consuelo barged in between them with a basket of fresh biscuits and elbowed him away.

That brought a big har-har from Skip, and even quiet, self-contained Juan forgot his mama's instructions in table manners and snickered.

By the time Consuelo's double-layer chocolate cake was served, I was drawn up tighter than an overpulled cinch. Whenever I got the chance I watched Lilah out of the corner of my eye, and it seemed to me she was aware of my discomfort. She never looked directly at me, but she said little things I knew were meant just for my ears.

"Today I saw the new seedlings in my garden," she said at one point. A while later she coughed and said, "I like bright colors, purple and red. And orange."

I couldn't say a damn word. She liked orange? Glory be!

After dinner we all strayed out to the veranda, where Charlie and Alice sat on the lawn swing holding hands. Juan got out his guitar and sang some songs in Spanish that made my throat tight. Lilah sat in the high-backed wicker rocking chair with Jase and Skip sprawled at her feet.

I sat on the top porch step with my back to her, working my thumbnail into my palm. Consuelo brought coffee.

Then Alice blew whatever peace of mind I had managed to work up all to hell. "Miss Cornwell will be spending the night."

That did it. I decided not to stay and duke it out verbally with Skip or Jase but to cut and run. Bad enough that Lilah was here for dinner, but it was hard not to think about her sleeping just across the meadow from my cabin.

I couldn't take it any longer. I jerked to my feet and stomped off into the dark. Consuelo's voice followed me. "You want no coffee, Señor Gale?"

"No, thanks, Consuelo. Gotta get up early tomorrow and break some more horses. Night, Miss Cornwell."

"Good night, Gale."

What hearing my name on her lips did to my body was downright embarrassing.

Chapter Fifteen

Lilah

The following morning I entered the dining room to find Alice sitting alone at the huge table, a blue ceramic mug of coffee cradled between her hands. I took the chair to her left, relieved that conversing with any of the ranch hands, especially Gale, or Mr. Kingman, would not be necessary.

But I was shortly to learn something about the life of a cowboy on a ranch like this one. Apparently they got up before dawn and worked at their assigned chores until the sun was a big gold ball in the sky and Consuelo rang the gong announcing breakfast at seven o'clock.

The men tramped in, their hair slicked down, their Levi's dusty, followed by Mr. Kingman in a blue work shirt and a worn leather vest. Consuelo brought in platters of fried eggs, pancakes the size of dinner plates, thick slices of bacon, fried potatoes, plus a big ceramic bowl of hot biscuits. She circled the table pouring mugs of coffee and slapping away any fingers that crept to touch her ample posterior as she passed.

The woman was well past forty but very handsome, with black hair in a single thick braid that hung down her back and sharp brown eyes that missed nothing. She never seemed to hurry, never seemed ruffled by the little flirty gestures and remarks the ranch hands indulged in, and I had to laugh inside. It was Consuelo who ruled this roost, not Charlie Kingman.

I wondered where Gale was. The men passed the platters of food in silence and fell to cleaning their loaded plates and gulping down Consuelo's coffee while I picked away at my small pile of fried potatoes and buttered a biscuit. When talk resumed, not one mention was made of Gale.

"Gotta fix that back pasture fence, Skip," Mr. Kingman said.

"Yeah. Find that roll of barbwire yet?"

"Let's finish working those horses in the corral first."

"Too many to do in one day, boss. Too green yet."

I sat quietly sipping my coffee until Mr. Kingman startled me with a question.

"Do you ride, Miss Cornwell?"

I gulped. "Why, no, I do not. To be honest, I am afraid of horses."

The man's bushy salt-and-pepper eyebrows shot up. "Afraid of horses? We can fix that, can't we, boys?"

The chorus of yesses made me nervous. Then Alice turned to me. "Do you have a split skirt?" she asked.

"A what?" I had never heard of a split skirt. It sounded most unladylike.

"Or a pair of britches?" Mr. Kingman added. "I'd bet the mercantile in town would have a pair of boy-size jeans that'd fit you just fine."

Jeans! I was horrified at such an outlandish suggestion. Besides, I didn't want to learn to ride a horse. I wanted to go back to my house in town and watch my seedlings grow.

Alice caught my eye and smiled. "Maybe next time you visit. In the meantime, ask the dressmaker in town, Verena Forester, about making you a split skirt. Denim should work nicely."

Gale still had not shown up, and I began to wonder why. Was he too busy with some task outside to stop for breakfast? Or perhaps he did not wish to see me. Last night he had sat on the porch with his back to me while everyone told stories and joked and laughed, but Gale had spoken scarcely two words to me.

It was clear he'd been surprised to see me at dinner yesterday, but he'd spared me not one single glance. A dreadful suspicion entered my mind. Had he been disappointed in that kiss? Perhaps I had done it wrong somehow. I could barely swallow at that thought, and I roused myself just in time to catch the tail end of Alice's comment.

"…go riding next time."

"Y-yes, I will," I said. I didn't say another word until breakfast was over.

"Charlie," Alice said when Consuelo began to clear the table.

"Someone will have to drive Miss Cornwell back to town this morning."

All four of the ranch hands suddenly sat up straight and looked at Charlie expectantly.

"Can't spare you, Skip. Jase, you and Gale have to work those two stallions we talked about. How about you, Ernesto?"

"Bueno," the stocky Mexican said. "I like drive Señorita Cornwell. She no talk much."

Everyone laughed, but relief surged through me like a tornado. *I have found a friend.*

So later that morning I found myself once more ensconced in the trim little buggy with the kindly man with the understanding eyes and no interest in making conversation.

Despite Gale's puzzling absence from the breakfast table, I smiled all the way home.

"Split skirt!" The dressmaker, Verena Forester, rolled her eyes. "What d'you want with a split skirt, I might ask?"

"For riding," I replied calmly. *As if it is any of your business.*

"Riding? Huh!" Verena's voice rose in accusation. "You got a horse, have ya?"

"I will use a horse, yes. How else does one go riding?"

She huffed and bustled away to her pattern books like a fluffed-up hen. "A skirt like this?" She spread a page out on the counter.

"Yes." I jabbed my forefinger on the drawing of a young woman standing splay-legged in an odd-looking garment split up the middle. It looked for all the world like a severed turkey carcass.

"Yes, just like that," I said. "What sort of fabric would you recommend?"

The dressmaker narrowed her eyes. "What I'd recommend, young woman, is to give up the whole idea. It's indecent."

I just shrugged.

"Who're you going riding *with,* if I may ask?"

"Alice Kingman. Do you know her?"

The transformation in Verena was instantaneous. She leaned forward across the counter and lowered her voice. "You mean Charlie Kingman's wife?"

"Why, yes." I understood immediately that I had touched a

nerve of some sort, and with the dressmaker's next question I knew what it was.

"You've met Charlie, I assume? Did he look...well, happy?"

Aha! Verena had a *tendre* for the owner of the Rocking K. Possibly she was carrying a torch for him. I managed to smile. "Mr. and Mrs. Kingman both look extremely happy."

"Denim!" she snapped. "That's what you want for your split skirt. All I have is blue."

"Blue will be fine."

"Stand over here so I can take your measurements."

I stood and turned and lifted my arms on command while Verena circled her tape measure around various parts of my anatomy.

"Be ready on Friday," she said at last. "You want to open an account? I figure if you're friends with Alice Kingman, you'll be going to plenty of ranch shindigs."

At the word *shindigs* I must have blanched, because Verena sent me a strange look. I certainly did not want to attend any "shindigs" where I would be expected to make polite conversation. They would be just like Mama's afternoon teas, which I had always loathed.

I wasn't sure I wanted to learn to ride a horse, either. In fact, the more I thought about it, the more sure I was this was the *last* thing I wanted to do. I wanted to write my stories.

And water my flowers.

Nevertheless, I opened an account with the dressmaker, and on her advice went across the street to the mercantile where Edith helped me find a pair of calf-high leather boots and what she termed a "cowboy" hat. It was light tan suede with a wide brim, which Edith showed me how to "train up" into a curl.

My goodness, people out here in the West certainly dressed oddly. With any luck I would never have to wear either the split skirt or the hat or the heavy leather boots; I could just keep making excuses until Alice Kingman gave up.

I took my package under my arm and left the mercantile with Edith gazing after me with a bemused expression. She was an intelligent young girl; perhaps she had guessed my disinclination to ever wear a cowboy hat or a pair of boots.

Chapter Sixteen

Gale

"Aw, hell, Gale, it's Saturday night!"

I turned my back on Jase. "So?"

"So..." Across the dining table, Skip managed to look exasperated and curious at the same time. "Ya gotta cut loose and have some fun now that we've got most of those horses broke. Even the boss says you need lightenin' up."

That made me laugh. Charlie Kingman worked me hard and I'd never once heard him use the phrase *lighten up*. Alice, maybe, but not Charlie.

"You're a lying son of a... All you and Jase want is a poker game. Ask Juan to go into town with you."

"Juan plays poker like a fish learnin' to square dance."

"Ask Ernesto, then."

"Huh!" Skip worked the crease of his hat between his thumb and forefinger. "Ernesto plays poker as if he invented the game, and I ain't got that much money. That man always wins. Always."

"Gonna be dancin' at the Golden Partridge," Jase said, dropping his voice to a wheedle.

"Sorry, boys. Don't have time."

Skip raised his sandy eyebrows. "Gonna be some of Selma's girls there, too, if you've got the inclination."

"Don't have the inclination."

Both men looked at each other, then back at me. "You funnin', Gale?" Skip said. "'Cause you always had time for—"

"No, I'm not funnin'. Go on, get out of here before I think up something for you to do."

Within two minutes I was left in peace, and Consuelo approached with what I'd asked her for earlier. With a puzzled look in her dark eyes she plopped it into my hand; it was satisfyingly heavy and wrapped in a clean huck towel.

I trailed Skip and Jase into town, and every mile I wondered what the hell I thought I was doing. But the minute I spied that orange picket fence, I knew exactly what it was.

A light burned upstairs. She was home. Was she hanging more wallpaper? Painting her dining room? I tied Randy to a maple tree around back and stomped up onto the front porch, purposely making a bunch of noise so she'd know someone was there.

I knocked. Knocked again. A plaintive little cry came from a wicker basket at my feet, and I scooped up a tiny orange cat and snuggled it against my chest. Right away it started to purr, and at that instant the front door swung open.

"Oh," she said. She didn't look paint speckled, which was a good sign. Her gaze left my face and traveled to the cat at my chest.

"Whatever are you doing here?"

"Hello, Miss Cornwell. Lilah."

"With my cat," she added.

"Well, it mewed, and I—"

"I see."

She didn't sound mad, so I went on, "Have you had supper yet?"

She frowned. "No, not yet. I was working and quite forgot about eating supper."

"In that case, Miss Cornwell, Lilah, would you consider having supper with me?"

Chapter Seventeen

Lilah

He just stood there waiting, with Mollie cuddled against his crisp blue shirt. "I often eat only cheese and a few crackers for supper," I said. I reached out to take the cat and he trapped my hand in his.

"Lilah. I brought supper fixings. I was hoping maybe you would—"

I cut him off. "I don't cook."

"But I do." He said it with such assurance I almost laughed. I extricated my hand, and Mollie, from his grasp and stood wondering what I should do about Mr. Gale McBurney standing here on my front porch. He answered the question with his next words.

"I brought two prime-beef steaks."

My mouth watered.

"And two potatoes."

"Potatoes?"

"For baking. You've got an oven, haven't you?"

Yes, I had an oven, and an appetite, so I invited him in. Before he stepped through the door I slipped Mollie back into her basket and picked it up by the handle. As I led the way to the kitchen I could still hear her purring.

Gale set something wrapped up in a towel on my polished wood kitchen counter and folded back the top. A potato rolled out. He caught it in one hand and tipped his head toward my shiny nickel-plated stove.

"Pretty fancy," he said. "Got a wood box?"

I pointed. He opened the firebox, stirred up the coals left from my afternoon tea and chunked in three pieces of wood one of the neighbor boys, Billy Rowell, had split for me.

"Got a broiler?"

I must have looked blank because he began checking the contents of the warming oven. "Ah," he said, extricating a round mesh-looking thing I'd never seen before. "Your broiler."

He laid it on the stove, then unloaded the contents of his towel-swathed bundle. Another potato, a small ceramic crock of butter and two of the thickest steaks I had ever seen.

"Those will never cook through," I warned.

"Don't want 'em to." He stabbed both potatoes with a fork, popped them into the oven and turned to me. "A steak's no good if it's cooked till it's as tough as leather. My daddy used to say a good steak should be served bleedin' and bawlin'."

"Ugh." I couldn't help the shudder that ran through me.

"My daddy," he explained, "was from Texas. Now, what're we gonna do for an hour while those potatoes bake?"

Chapter Eighteen

"We could…talk," Lilah suggested. "In the parlor."

"What else?"

"We could…play chess?"

"I used to play chess with my dad," I said. "But that's so long ago I probably couldn't give you a good match. What else?"

She thought for a moment, then hitched herself up onto a tall kitchen stool. Oh, Lord, her feet were bare. And her toes…well, they peeked out from under her petticoat, and it plumb took my mind off the conversation.

"We could read aloud to each other," she suggested. "Dickens? Sir Walter Scott?"

"Got any poetry?"

I could see that surprised her because her eyebrows went up. "Poetry?" she echoed. She didn't for one minute believe I liked poetry.

"Yeah. You know, Tennyson? Byron?"

She stared at me as if I had green onions growing out of my ears.

"Or," she said after a long minute, "we could play, well, poker." She sounded pretty doubtful, but I kept quiet.

She bit her lower lip and I had to look away. "That's what people out here in the West play, isn't it? I bet I could learn quite rapidly."

All kinds of things started going through my mind. Playing for…kisses, maybe?

"Sure you wouldn't rather read some poetry?"

She shook her head. The bun at her neck shook loose, and a couple of long shiny curls slipped free. Goddamn, her hair was beautiful, like polished mahogany. Between her hair and her bare toes, I was having a tough time hiding my arousal.

"Uh, since I'm cooking supper tonight, would you have an apron I could wear?"

That made her laugh. It sounded soft and kinda drowsy, and I gritted my teeth against the picture that climbed into my brain. Wish I hadn't hung my hat on the peg near the door, but I'd better hurry up with the apron.

Without a word she lifted a ruffly pink gingham apron off a hook and handed it over. She watched me tie it around my waist and I prayed she wouldn't notice the bulge in the front.

"Would you like to see the new wallpaper I finished upstairs?"

That came out of nowhere, and it was a few seconds before I could talk. "Sure."

She led the way. All I could think about was that no man wearing a pink apron could seduce a woman, no matter how bare her toes were or how her hips swayed in front of him while she climbed up a staircase.

The first door we came to was closed. Must be her bedroom. I wanted to know what it looked like in the worst way. Were the walls yellow? Blue? What color was the quilt on the bed? How *big* was the bed? And on and on until I thought I'd choke.

"This," she said, pausing in the second doorway, "is my office. It's where I work." She gestured at a huge walnut desk facing the windows. A black typing machine sat on top and notebooks were scattered around like lily pads on a pond. A vase of pencils perched next to the typewriter. The wastebasket beside the desk overflowed with crumpled-up balls of paper.

"You work? What do you work at?"

She hesitated half a second, and I figured she'd had some hassle over what she worked at.

"I…um…I am a writer."

That knocked my socks clean off. I'm sure my jaw dropped because she gave me an odd, shy little glance and blushed a pretty rose color.

She caught me looking at her, and she said, "Close your mouth, Gale."

"A writer?"

"Does that shock you?"

"Yes. No! Hell, I don't know. I never met a lady writer before. What do you write?"

This time she waited so long to answer I felt my equilibrium begin to tilt.

"I write…stories," she said.

"For a newspaper back East?" I guessed.

She shook her head. "For myself."

I was beginning to understand. In fact, I understood much, much more than she could ever know. I wasn't about to ask what kind of stories.

She led the way back downstairs in silence so thick you could have heard an ant cross the floor. In the kitchen she picked up a silver-plated clock. "We have forty minutes before supper. I want you to teach me how to play poker."

Chapter Nineteen

Lilah

I discovered that I loved playing poker! It was a challenge to bluff when I had nothing but a pair of fours. Perhaps my flair for duplicity came from Aunt Carrie, but I surely hoped I would meet a better end than she had.

We played for what Gale called "truths." The winner could ask a question which the loser had to answer truthfully. Unlike Aunt Carrie, I answered all my forfeited truths honestly. Fortunately, I won the first hand I was dealt.

"What is Texas like?" was my first question.

"Big. Raw. Surprising," he answered.

He won the next hand, and I had to confess why I had never learned to ride.

"Don't they have horses in Philadelphia?"

"Oh, yes. And riding clubs and hunts and equestrienne balls and…" And so much more I did not wish to remember.

The man did not give up easily. "How come?" he pursued. "What's wrong with clubs and hunts and balls?"

With the loss of my next hand I knew I was trapped. I looked everywhere but at Gale, sitting across the kitchen table from me in that ridiculous pink apron, but he stared at me and waited as if he had nothing better to do than pry painful answers out of me.

I could hear Aunt Carrie's voice. *Lie.*

"Lilah?" His green eyes held mine, and I knew I could not lie. There was something open and unstudied about Gale McBurney that made it impossible for me to deceive him.

"I…I find it difficult to…talk to people. I am quite shy."

"You're talkin' to me," he pointed out.

"Yes, I am. Reluctantly."

He didn't say a word, just smiled and shuffled the cards and dealt out another hand.

Thank the Lord I won with two queens to his pair of eights. "My turn," I gloated. "Tell me about your father."

"Big," he said. Then he added, "Raw. Surprising."

"But that is exactly what you said about Texas," I protested.

"Yeah. They're the same."

It was my turn to stare at him. "Your father is…surprising?"

"Yeah. That's why I left Texas."

A thousand more questions popped into my head, but Gale glanced away to the clock, folded his cards back into the deck and stood up. "Potatoes are about done."

I laughed. "I don't believe that for one minute. You just don't want to talk about your father."

"Damn right. You don't get another question until you win another hand." He snaked a potato out of the oven, squeezed it experimentally and slid it back onto the rack. Then he removed the iron rounds over the firebox and settled that broiler thing right over the coals.

I watched him. Maybe cooking wasn't so difficult. It had annoyed me that Mama's cook had always shooed me out of the kitchen. I wanted to know how to *do* things. Even at eleven years old, I had wanted to be independent.

Gale's question startled me. "Got a couple of sharp knives?"

"In the drawer. I'll get them."

"Put the plates on, too," he ordered. "And that little crock of butter."

Within five minutes the meat was sputtering as the grease dripped onto the hot coals, and the kitchen began to smell heavenly. Gale forked over the steaks and gestured for me to sit down at the table. He split the potatoes in two, slathered the halves with butter and slid them onto the plates, followed by the sizzling steaks.

Then he untied the pink apron and sat down across from me. I was almost sorry about the apron. He looked so out of place in ruffled gingham it was somehow endearing.

But he certainly wasn't out of place in a kitchen. I had never eaten such a perfectly grilled piece of beef, not even at the fancy restaurant Mama favored in downtown Philadelphia.

"Got any wine?" Gale asked after his first bite.

I retrieved the bottle I'd purchased at the mercantile and kept in the bottom cabinet and set out two water glasses.

"Kinda big, aren't they?" he said with a grin. "Never figured you for a drinkin' woman."

"I drink wine only when I have a cough. I mix it with honey."

"Must be pretty healthy, then. This bottle's never been opened." He twisted the cork out and sloshed some into my glass. And his.

"What'll we drink to?" The corners of his eyes crinkled.

I had not the foggiest notion. I couldn't propose a toast to my not having to visit the Rocking K again, could I? I lifted my glass.

"To not having to learn to ride."

Gale choked on his wine. When he stopped coughing and caught his breath, he gave me a long, puzzled look.

Chapter Twenty

Gale

"How come you don't want to ride? Is it the horse? Being out at the ranch? *Me?*"

"Of course it's not you." She said that right away, so I felt better. A lot better. Matter of fact I felt so good I gulped down the rest of my glass without thinking. Then her tongue came out and licked a drop of wine off her upper lip.

I forgot the other two reasons why she might not want to ride a horse. I thought about snagging that frilly apron and dropping it across my lap, but then I realized Lilah couldn't see what was happening to me underneath the table.

"It is difficult for me, being at the ranch," she said at last. "Having to talk to people."

"You seemed to do okay when you came to dinner that time. With Alice and all."

"With Alice, yes. The 'and all' I could not really manage. Perhaps you didn't notice how quiet I was."

"Yeah, I noticed. I thought it was me. You know, seeing me again after…"

Hell, I couldn't say that. The word *kiss* would flood the air between us with too much unspoken feeling. I wanted to eat supper with her, not send her off upstairs in a huff.

She studied the butter crock. "Well, I admit it was awkward. After a while I began to wonder if—"

I stopped her just in time. "Don't go there, Lilah. Just let it be."

She licked her lips again and I thought I was gonna explode. "Gale, there is one thing I do want to say."

"Okay. I'm listenin'."

"If I do want to learn to ride, could it be just you who would teach me?"

"Well, it could be, sure. But why?" I held my breath.

"Because I would have to talk with Jason or Skip, or even Mr. Kingman. With you, I don't have to."

I just looked at her sitting there across from me with her cheeks flushed from the wine and her lips like ripe raspberries. *She doesn't have to talk to me? Hell yes, she has to talk to me!*

I didn't want to startle her, or scare her, but I sure wanted her to know that. It wasn't just the taste of her mouth under mine, or the ache in my groin when I admired her backside or spied her bare toes. It was more than that.

As a matter of honest fact, it was so much more than that it kinda set me back on my heels. She didn't know anything about me, really. What the hell would she do when she found out?

Chapter Twenty-One

Lilah

Something was closing down inside Gale. I could see it as clearly as if he'd written it out on one of my parlor walls. But I had no idea what it was.

He would not have invited himself to supper if he did not like me, would he? Or if my kiss had been so inept that he would never want another?

Of course, there were things I was hiding, too. And all at once it struck me funny, the two of us dancing around each other like youngsters at our first ball, studiously trying not to look at each other. Trying hard not to like each other.

I deduced that liking me was some sort of a threat to him. But why? Aunt Carrie would know. Aunt Carrie had understood men because she knew them so well, had dealt with them under difficult circumstances where they had to rely on each other. Trust each other.

But, Lilah Marie Cornwell, you are not Aunt Carrie.

I supposed when it came to men I would have to live and learn, as Mama always said. I only hoped I would survive. Aunt Carrie had not.

I heated water to wash the plates and silverware while Gale cut up tiny morsels of leftover steak for Mollie and took them in his cupped palm out to the front porch, where I'd set her basket before supper. He did not come back.

I washed the plates and dried them and put them away in the walnut hutch, then set the coffeepot on the stove. Even if Gale had slipped away, I wanted to sit in the lawn swing with Mollie on my lap and admire my garden in the moonlight.

My flower bed was turning into a most intriguing mélange of colors and patterns; the beds were not separated, as Mama's gardens always were, but mixed together all which-a-way, like one of those Impressionistic paintings Mama had brought back from Paris where the paint all washed together in a riot of hues. If my orange fence was causing talk around town, my haphazard swirly carpet of flowers would bring the gossip to a crescendo.

Just imagine, being the subject of gossip not because of a relationship with the opposite sex, but because of the indiscriminate mating of red nasturtiums and golden-yellow black-eyed Susans!

Chapter Twenty-Two

Gale

I could see she had something on her mind when she pushed open the screen door and came out on the porch. I could see it in the way she held her shoulders. She settled at the far end of the lawn swing, reached over and lifted her orange cat out of my lap and sat petting it without saying a word. Real quick it got hard to watch her hands like that, stroking that ball of fur slow and gentle-like, back and forth, back and forth, and not in any kind of hurry.

She had a kind of faraway look on her face, and she kept staring over at the flowers I'd planted for her. They looked real pretty, all mixed up like that, like a Persian carpet I'd seen once in my daddy's front parlor.

I sure wanted to ask what she was thinking, but I figured if it was any of my business she'd tell me. And if it wasn't, maybe she'd tell me anyway. Don't know why I thought that; guess I wanted it to be true.

My stomach was getting all knotted up just being close to her, smelling her hair and the scent of her skin. She didn't have to say a single word to keep me interested. To be honest, I was more than interested. And when I realized that, my heart kicked like an unbroke stallion.

Must be it was time for me to go. But just when I made that decision she said something that took all the vinegar out of me.

"I write love stories."

"Huh?"

"You know, stories about handsome heroes and beautiful girls."

I swallowed twice. "You get any of these stories published?"

"No, not yet. I send them out, but I don't receive much encouragement."

"How come? Aren't they any good?"

"No, not very." She looked at me kinda funny.

"Why not? What's wrong with them?"

She was quiet for so long I thought maybe she'd decided not to answer. Then she opened her mouth and blew me out of the corral again.

"The truth is that I don't know much about it. What makes a love story, I mean."

Whoa. It was my turn to be quiet. Couldn't think for a minute, I guess. Everyone on God's earth knows about love, don't they?

"Lilah, are you saying you haven't had much, uh, experience?"

She nodded, but she kept her head down, staring at her cat, and I couldn't see her eyes.

"I'm gonna tell you a secret," I said. "You know all those dime novels about cowboys and bank robbers and sheriffs? They're mostly made up. Anybody that knows diddly about life out here in the West knows what's printed in those books isn't real."

"It doesn't matter, Gale. Those stories *feel* true. The reader is convinced because of the setting and the details. Gunfights and train wrecks are easier to imagine."

"So maybe…" Aw, hell, for sure that wasn't an invitation to take her upstairs and do some research. That'd be the dumbest thing since ginger beer. Instead I sucked in my breath and asked, "Why are you telling me this?"

"I wanted you to know what I wrote about."

"Why? You think it matters to me what you write? You think I'm gonna look at you any different because you write love stories?"

"I thought you would think it was frivolous. My mother thinks it is."

"Well, I sure ain't your mother."

"No. And I thank the Lord for that."

I had to laugh at her words, and then she laughed, and before I knew what I was doing I leaned over and kissed her. Damn near squashed her cat, but it was worth it.

She tasted like wine, and I couldn't get enough of her. Couldn't get close enough to her either, with that cat between us. Maybe that was a good thing. I was starting to ache so bad I wasn't sure how I was gonna mount my horse and ride the six miles back to the ranch.

I shouldn't have worried. She didn't move an inch to make it easier for me to get any closer, so I figured she'd had enough of a randy cowboy with a lot of giddy-yap and no manners. I got to my feet and walked to the edge of the porch.

"I'd best say good-night, Lilah. Thanks for havin' supper with me."

Chapter Twenty-Three

Lilah

He hesitated at the top step, his broad shoulders hunched over a bit, both his hands jammed in his back pockets.

"Gale?"

He half turned toward me, but he kept his hands where they were. "Yeah?"

"I liked the steaks. I liked playing poker with you."

I brushed Mollie off my lap, stood up and took three steps to where he stood. "But most of all, I like that you listened to me."

I stretched up on tiptoe and kissed his cheek. He didn't move, didn't say a word, just stood there looking at me. I stepped back, but he caught me, bent his head and covered my mouth with his.

His kiss was long and deep and very thorough, so thorough that my knees turned to jelly as his lips moved on mine. A hot, delicious light bloomed inside my body. Never, never had I felt anything so exquisite.

After a long time he lifted his head. "Gotta stop this," he murmured.

"No, don't." My automatic protest shocked me.

"Yes, dammit." He curved his fingers around my shoulders and moved me away from him. His hands were shaking.

My heart was fluttering like a hummingbird's wings. I watched him snag his wide-brimmed gray hat off the porch railing and tramp off behind the house where he had tied up his horse. I waited, scarcely able to draw breath.

Finally he appeared, the reins held loosely in his hand and his hat tipped low.

"I'm not gonna apologize," he said from the shadows. His voice was low and careful. "Won't happen again."

I felt like weeping. I *wanted* it to happen again. And I wanted to tell him that.

But of course I couldn't. No lady told a man what she really wanted.

Chapter Twenty-Four

Gale

I talked Charlie into letting me ride out to round up another herd of mustangs for delivery to Fort Hall. I took Ernesto with me. The Mexican was good at finding wild horses and rounding them up, and even better, he didn't flap his tongue like Jase or Skip. Didn't think I could stand any more words in my head than the ones already rattling around in there.

We rode hard and worked ourselves to exhaustion, and that suited me just fine. At the end of long, dusty days in the saddle I hunkered down by the campfire, nursing a full cup of Ernesto's double-boiled coffee and my empty helping of good sense when it came to Lilah Cornwell. It was getting cold now as fall got closer, but even sleeping right next to the campfire, I was hot all night.

Two weeks later, when we drove seventeen new mustangs through the Rocking K corral gate, I'd pretty well sorted things out. Lilah wasn't the kind of woman a man played fast and loose with. More than that, I wasn't a man who could risk getting beat all to hell again. I figured I could learn to live with the situation.

I figured that until the first night back at the ranch when Alice Kingman blindsided me at supper.

"Lilah Cornwell is coming to dinner again on Sunday. I think she's ready to learn to ride."

I managed to finish my beef stew and corn bread, but as soon as I could escape I headed across the meadow to my cabin and some 90-percent-proof comfort and some more clear-headed thinking.

Chapter Twenty-Five

Lilah

The prospect of Sunday dinner at the Kingman ranch had me so nervous I couldn't eat or sleep for three days. My blue denim split riding skirt had been ready for weeks; my nerves were not.

It wasn't the prospect of mounting the horse Alice said she had picked out for me or having to make conversation at the dinner table. Plain and simple, I was nervous about seeing Gale again.

Alice had mentioned that he'd been gone these past few weeks on ranch business. I was surprised how unsettled I was by his absence, but I knew I would be even more unsettled at his presence. By the time Sunday afternoon came and Ernesto rolled the buggy to a stop at my front gate, I felt as giddy as a schoolgirl.

"Señorita Cornwell." The old Mexican man tipped his hat.

"Hello, Ernesto. I hoped it would be you."

A flush darkened his wrinkled cheeks, and he helped me onto the hard leather seat beside him without a word. The horse trotted along the road past fields of wildflowers and tall gray-green grass and maple trees shimmering in the sunlight. The countryside always took my breath away, but it was almost fall, and today everything seemed especially lovely with the soft glow of the afternoon sun.

"Oh, Ernesto, just look! What are those brilliant yellow flowers?"

"Gold weed." He halted the buggy, climbed down and waded into the sea of blooms. He returned with a single flower held gently in his fingers, and as soon as he settled himself beside me he took my hand and shook the bloom over my cupped palm. Tiny black seeds sifted down.

"Grow in hot sun," he said. He closed my fingers over the seeds. "You plant in garden."

Too soon we left the road through the wildflower fields and turned in at the Rocking K gate. More nervous than I ever remembered being at one of Mama's soirees, I smoothed the skirt of my rose-pink lawn dress and tucked the loose tendrils of hair back into my bun. Mama always said a redhead should never wear pink, but I didn't care. Pink was my favorite color.

Ernesto drove the buggy off to the barn just as Consuelo came sailing out onto the porch to bang her metal spoon against the triangle of steel that served as the dinner gong. Alice came out to welcome me, and the ranch hands gathered in silence as I climbed up the porch steps.

"Haven't heard them this quiet since they all had the grippe last spring," Alice whispered. "They don't know what to say to you."

"As little as possible, I hope. I find conversing with strangers difficult."

She sent me a twinkly look. "Then you must come out to the ranch more often."

I tried not to look for Gale.

In the dining room, Charlie Kingman rose and took my hand in both of his and the cowhands tumbled in and jostled each other for the empty chairs. A few minutes later Ernesto entered with a quiet smile.

"How come *he* gets to drive the buggy?" sandy-haired Skip blurted out.

"Because he's an old man," the young blond one, Jason, offered.

"Because I am *muy amable*," Ernesto said, his grin widening. "Polite."

That brought silence until a familiar voice spoke from the hallway. "Because he's trustworthy with horses and other living things."

Gale stepped into the room and my pulse skipped. He nodded at Alice. "Mrs. Kingman." Then at Charlie, who grunted something unintelligible in return but lifted a hand in greeting.

Finally he looked at me. "Miss Cornwell."

Miss Cornwell? This from the man who had kissed me until I was dizzy?

"Gale," I responded. I watched his eyes grow even greener.

"Lilah," he said at last.

Mr. Kingman cleared his throat. "Gale's been rounding up some more wild horses for me."

"I see."

"You might like to watch him work with them tomorrow morning."

"Yes, thank you, I—"

"No, she wouldn't," Gale interrupted.

Every head swiveled toward him as he seated himself across from me. Even Consuelo, who had just entered with a platter piled high with fried chicken, stopped short and stared at him.

An imp took over my good sense. "I wouldn't?"

He caught my gaze and held it. "It's too early in the morning," he said.

I lifted an eyebrow in his direction. "How early is too early?"

"Yeah, Gale, what d'*you* know?"

"Shut up, Jase."

At that, Consuelo plunked the chicken platter down on the table and stalked toward the kitchen. *"Ay de mi,"* I heard her mutter.

Ernesto calmly picked up his knife and rapped it across Gale's knuckles. *"No más, mi amigo."*

"Gentlemen," Alice Kingman announced, "let us say grace."

All heads bowed but mine. I had not said grace since I was a girl and Aunt Carrie went off to the War. Across from me, Gale met my eyes with steady purpose, and while Alice spoke the words of grace, he gave me an almost imperceptible shake of his head.

I knew what he meant. For some reason he didn't want me to watch him work the horses in the corral.

The next morning I was up and dressed long before the breakfast gong sounded. Gale and the other hands stood up when I entered the dining room, but he glared at me until I was seated and Consuelo began pouring the coffee. I was *not* going to allow myself to be intimidated by his disapproval. My imp was even more obstreperous this morning, so I sent him a smile I hoped would melt his disdain into a puddle of chagrin.

After breakfast was over, the ranch hands excused themselves and disappeared. Mr. Kingman escorted me out the front door, down the porch steps and over to the fenced-in corral where a handful of restless horses were penned. I leaned against the split-pole barrier and adjusted my felt hat to keep the sun out of my eyes. I didn't want to miss one minute of whatever activity it was Gale did not want me to watch.

Alice joined me at the fence. "Watching Gale break a horse always brings tears to my eyes," she confessed.

"It must be terrible for the horse," I answered.

She looked over at me as if I had just recited the multiplication tables in Greek. "I don't mean tears over the horse, Lilah. Over Gale."

"What? What about Gale makes you cry?"

"Just watch," she replied with a slow smile. "You'll see." So I propped my elbows on the top rail and settled in to watch.

Ernesto and his nephew, Juan, shooed all the animals but one into a holding pen, and then Ernesto dropped a rope around the neck of a shiny chocolate-brown horse with a black mane and tail. While he held the rope taut, Juan slapped a saddle onto the fence, then laid a plaid blanket and something that looked like a leather cat's cradle on top. A noose of some sort, I gathered. I decided *I* would cry over the horse, not Gale.

Then Gale climbed through the fence and lifted the rope out of Ernesto's gloved hand. He wore boots and tight jeans like the other cowhands, but his head was bare and he wore no gloves.

One by one, Jase and Skip and Juan joined the Kingmans and me at the fence. Apparently watching Gale was a source of entertainment for the entire ranch.

Ernesto came to stand next to me, saying nothing in his usual fashion, but giving my split skirt a nod of approval.

The horse stood snorting and pawing the ground, watching Gale with one rolling black eye as he wound the rope around one bent arm and moved steadily closer. The animal whinnied and tossed its head, but Gale kept on walking.

Suddenly the horse reared. Gale waited, keeping the rope snugged about his elbow and when the animal stood still, Gale stepped forward and leaned in.

"Bueno," Ernesto muttered.

Then Gale moved in close and dropped the rope. I stiffened, expecting the horse to rear or kick him, but I heard Gale's voice

speaking soft and low, words I couldn't hear. But the horse seemed
to. It sent shivers up my spine.

He began touching the animal, running his hands over its muzzle, down its legs, all the time crooning whatever he was saying over and over in gentle tones. He kept touching and talking for a good quarter of an hour, never in a hurry and never letting his hands break contact with the horse's twitching hide.

"You see?" Alice whispered.

I did see. Watching Gale, I understood things about him I might never have known. He was gentle. Patient. And completely in command. My throat tightened into an ache.

Chapter Twenty-Six

Lilah

Gale stepped to one side of the horse. The animal followed him and then curved its neck toward him. He returned to stand directly in front of the animal, smoothed his palms over its muzzle, talking softly, then stepped away again. The horse shifted to follow him.

Gale walked farther away and the horse followed at his shoulder. He reversed direction and the animal followed; he even walked the perimeter of the corral and the horse stayed with him. It was almost as if he had hypnotized the beast.

They began a sort of game where Gale would run to one side and then quickly reverse direction. The horse stayed with him. Finally, he stopped, smoothed the animal's withers and spoke in its twitching ear.

"Now it comes," Ernesto murmured.

Gale moved to the corral fence and lifted the saddle blanket and the leather halter off the top rail. With slow, deliberate motions he spread the blanket on the animal's back, talking all the time, then slipped the harness over its head. The horse stood perfectly still.

Beside me, Alice clasped her hands together. "Now watch."

Gale moved to the fence. The horse followed. He hoisted the saddle off the rail and settled it atop the blanket and rocked it into place. Then he leaned against the animal and kept leaning. Finally he reached underneath and buckled the strap, the cinch, Ernesto called it, and pulled it tight.

Again he pressed his body flat against the animal's shoulder, still talking, rubbing himself against the withers, and finally he placed one boot in the stirrup and grabbed the dangling reins.

Ernesto pursed his lips and nodded. *"Sí, sí,"* he said, and Gale swung himself up into the saddle. The horse stood motionless for a long moment, then suddenly arched its back and twisted, kicking out its hind legs. Gale's arm went up for balance, but he kept his seat and held on to the reins.

The animal kicked and bucked for another few minutes while Gale stuck on its back as if he were glued there. Suddenly the horse stopped and stood still, snorting loudly. Gale leaned forward and patted its neck, spoke to it, patted it some more and finally touched his boot heels gently against its ribs, and the animal stepped forward. He reined it to one side and it turned. He walked it twice around the corral.

Alice swiped tears off her cheeks. Ernesto again murmured, *"Bueno,"* and I felt my own eyes sting. Alice was right; what I had witnessed was beautiful.

"Well," she said, her voice watery, "are you ready to learn to ride?"

I must have looked horror-struck because she burst out laughing. "Oh, no, not that horse!" She tipped her head at the animal Gale was now unsaddling. "Ernesto, get Lady saddled for Miss Cornwell, would you?"

Without a word the Mexican swung away from the fence and strode off toward the barn.

All at once I was so terrified my entire body began to shake.

Chapter Twenty-Seven

Gale

I turned over the stallion I'd just broke to Juan and stowed the saddle and bridle in the barn just as Ernesto was rustling up some tack and one of Alice's old saddles. "For Señorita Cornwell," he explained. "She is *muy nerviosa*."

I bet she was, having just seen me get bucked all to hell and gone. That was why I didn't want her watching me work with the mustang. Lilah sure could be stubborn, though.

So I wiped the sweat off my face, grabbed my hat and went to teach the lady how to ride.

Jase swaggered over. "Whyn't you let *me* teach her, huh, Gale? You already had a workout."

"I'm not tired," I retorted.

Skip sauntered up, too. "Prob'ly smell pretty sweaty, too. Me, I'm fresh as a—"

"Shut up. Go find a fence to mend."

I led Lady out to the corral, took one look at Lilah and decided this was a very bad idea. Her eyes were as big as one of Consuelo's cupcakes.

"You ready?" I said. Half of me hoped she'd back out. The other half couldn't wait to get close to her.

She nodded, and I turned to clear everyone away from the fence. As scared as she was, she sure didn't need an audience. I caught Alice's eye.

"Jason," she called. "I need some help with a barrel of apples on the back porch. You, too, Skip."

Both the boys groaned, but orders from the boss's wife took precedence over watching a pretty girl. When they'd shuffled off, I signaled for Lilah to crawl through the fence and stand next to the sweet old gray mare Alice's kids had learned to ride on.

She did crawl through, but she was moving real, real slow.

"You can back out of this venture," I said.

She straightened her spine. "I wouldn't think of it."

I just looked at her. "You sure?"

"I—I'm s-sure."

That got a claw into my heart. I laid my hand on the horse's nose. "This here's a real gentle mare. Name's Lady." I picked up Lilah's hand and laid it next to mine.

"Let her smell you," I said. "And talk to her some."

Lady blew out a gusty breath and Lilah backed away.

"That's her way of sayin' hello," I said. "Just stand quiet. Keep your hand where it was."

I could feel her tremble, and I wasn't even touching her. The ruffle down the front of her striped shirtwaist was shuddering.

"What should I say to it?"

"Anything that comes to mind. Doesn't have to make sense."

She gave a little pat on the horse's nose. "H-hello, Lady. I hope you won't mind if I t-try to ride you today."

"Keep talkin'," I said. "She knows you want to be friends. Horses are real smart."

Lilah bent toward Lady's ear. "I bet you can tell I'm a little frightened, can't you?"

"Okay, now come on over here." I guided Lilah over to the mounting block Juan had dragged over. "I want you to step up on this thing. When you're ready, lift your left foot into the stirrup, and I'll boost you up into the saddle."

She nodded, but she didn't move.

"Ready?"

She bit her lip and nodded again.

"I'm gonna have to touch your backside, so don't scream. Thought I'd warn you."

She got her toe into the stirrup just fine, and I laid my hand on her bottom. Goddamn, she was soft. And so warm my palm felt as if I'd picked up a hot coal.

"Stand up in the stirrup." I gave her behind a shove upward and gritted my teeth. "Swing your right leg over the saddle and settle onto the seat. Now reach your other toe into the stirrup on the other side."

When she was seated, I grabbed the reins and swung up behind her.

"Oh! I didn't expect you—"

I had to chuckle. "To climb up behind you," I finished.

"Well, no, I thought…"

"I can get off if you'd prefer."

She kind of leaned back against my chest. "No. Don't get off. Stay here with me."

For a minute I couldn't remember what the hell I was doin' up on a horse with my arms around her. So I gigged the mare and started walking her slowly around the corral.

Before we'd gone three steps, Lilah peered down. "It—it's quite far to the ground," she said in a small voice.

"If you're scared, hold on to the saddle horn." I grabbed her hand and positioned it, then walked the mare around twice more. Most of the time I had my eyes closed, just breathing in the scent of her hair. Roses, maybe.

She kept a stranglehold on the saddle horn, but after a while I felt her body relax.

"You doin' okay?"

"Yes."

The next time we came around I spoke to Juan. "Open the gate, *por favor*."

We moved out into the meadow. I didn't want to stop riding behind her, but this wasn't teaching her how to manage the horse on her own. I reined up after a few yards and dismounted.

"Gale? Where are you going?"

"Gonna get my horse." I laid the reins in her hand. "Just sit there and stay still. Horse won't move unless you do."

I walked off toward the barn to saddle Randy. When I got back she was still there, her back stiff, her hands white-knuckled around the reins.

"Now," I said. "Touch your heels to her sides, real light. When she steps forward, follow me."

I headed off toward the river, keeping my eye on Lady behind me until Lilah spoke.

"What is that building over there?"

"That's my cabin. I live there."

"Can I go see it?"

"Nope." Didn't mean to sound so sharp, but in all the years I'd been foreman at the Rocking K, I'd never invited anyone to my cabin.

"Why not?"

"Don't ask why, Lilah."

She was quiet all the way to the riverbank. I showed her how to dismount, and then I boosted her back up into the saddle again and we headed back to the corral. She didn't want to stop, but I knew she'd be plenty sore after her first time on horseback.

And anyway, I was having a real hard time keeping my hands off her. Figured I could only take so much.

Chapter Twenty-Eight

Lilah

I did not like riding a horse nearly as much as I liked playing poker with Gale, but after watching him tame that wild horse with such gentleness and skill, I knew I was in good hands.

And I was. I made "horse friends" with the mare Lady and I enjoyed the experience more than I thought I would. Possibly that was because of Gale. I appreciated that he did not allow the ranch hands to observe my fumbling first attempt and…well, just because it was Gale.

I like the man. I like him more than I thought I could *ever* like a man. I blush to admit it, but I especially like it when he kisses me. Mama would have an attack of the vapors at such an admission, but I think Aunt Carrie would cheer. Aunt Carrie lived life to its fullest, even though it cost her dearly in the end.

That afternoon Ernesto drove me back to town in the buggy, and I will never forget the gallant and thoughtful thing he did. When he pulled the horse to a stop in front of my house, he dipped his hand into the pocket of his worn leather vest and pulled out what looked like a man's sock. The top was knotted and something was tied up inside it.

He pressed it into my hand and gave me a shy smile. "For you, *señorita*."

Inside were thousands of tiny black seeds. "Flowers," he explained in his softly accented voice. "From the land."

"Wildflowers! Oh, Ernesto, thank you!"

He studied my garden, where drifts of daisies and baby's breath mingled in riot of color, like a painting. "*Muy bonita.* You grow more."

I was so touched I leaned over and kissed his wrinkled cheek, which embarrassed him. A flush colored his skin until he bid me goodbye and drove off down the road.

I was so excited I stripped off my riding skirt and donned the jeans I wore to work in the garden, dragged out the shovel from the shed off the back porch and started that very afternoon to spade up more ground.

The next morning I was so stiff and sore I could scarcely hobble downstairs for my marmalade toast and coffee. All the spading, no doubt. Or two hours on horseback. Gale had warned me to soak in a hot tub before bed, but in my excitement over Ernesto's wildflower seeds I forgot to follow his advice.

The next three days I spent sowing my new seeds and wondering when I would see Gale again. But when he did finally appear on my porch, it was unexpected. And terrible.

It was late afternoon on a beautiful fall day. I had just finished up a new story and addressed it to the publisher of a lady's magazine when I heard someone calling my name through the front screen door.

Gale. His voice sounded harsh. I clattered downstairs with a sudden knot of apprehension in my stomach.

"Gale! Come in." I pushed open the screen.

"I'd rather you came outside," he said. His face looked odd and tight. He sat me down in the swing and began pacing back and forth from one end of the porch to the other, his hands jammed in the back pockets of his dusty jeans.

"Lilah…" His voice caught. Something was very wrong.

"What is it? Tell me."

"Don't really know how." He turned toward me, snatched off his hat, and crowded close to me on the swing.

"Ernesto…" He stopped and swallowed, then started again. "Ernesto was moving some of those mustangs from the holding pen into the corral when one of 'em went kinda crazy. Kicked Ernesto in the head pretty bad."

He jerked to his feet and walked to the front steps, stood for a moment staring down at my newly spaded-up garden, then came back and sat down again.

"Doc came out. Said it was a concussion. Bad one." He drew in a rough breath. "Ernesto's dead, Lilah. He never woke up."

For a moment I felt nothing. This was not real, not happening. But when Gale reached his arms around me I knew it was true.

I cried and cried. Gale finally went into the kitchen and brought me a cup of wine. "Whiskey'd be better," he said. "Couldn't find any."

"I-in the hutch," I said, sobbing.

He brought that, too, and I drank all that he poured into my glass. After a while he poured himself half a glass and tossed it down.

"Funeral's tomorrow. I'll come get you with the buggy."

I could only nod and mop at my eyes with my skirt hem. Gale reached over and squeezed my shoulder, then untied his horse and mounted. He forgot his hat, but my throat ached so much I couldn't tell him.

We didn't talk much on the way out to the ranch. Every time my gaze lit on the clumps of goldenweed and wild sunflowers Ernesto had pointed out to me, my tears started in again. Both my handkerchiefs were sodden before we had gone three miles. Gale pulled his out of his shirt pocket and handed it to me; when I noticed that it, too, was tear damp, I started in again.

Alice met me on the porch. "We have an hour before the boys load the..." She stopped short. "Would you like something to drink? Lemonade?"

I wanted some whiskey, but I wouldn't dare ask. Consuelo brought out two glasses, and we sat in silence except for Alice's occasional shuddery breath.

The burial plot was a small square on top of a gentle hill, fenced in black wrought iron. There were two graves beside the deep hole that awaited Ernesto's remains. One headstone read Timothy Kearns Kingman, aged eleven. The other was for Charles Randolph Kingman, aged twenty. Alice studied each grave for a long moment before turning her attention to the coffin the men carried up.

Charlie read some verses from the Bible, but I could not listen. Consuelo blotted away at her streaming eyes with the sleeves of her black silk dress. Juan stood beside her, thin lipped but dry-eyed.

I felt sick and strange, as if I were wrapped in thick cotton. Skip and Jason and Alice bowed their heads for the Lord's Prayer, but I could not, and Gale did not. His face looked ravaged.

When it was over, the dirt shoveled over the coffin and the grave filled in, I stepped forward and laid the bunch of golden-weed daisies Gale had let me pick on the drive in from town on top of the mound of fresh dirt and numbly turned away.

Alice and Charlie walked back to the ranch house holding hands. The buggy stood at the porch. "Consuelo has made a light supper," Alice began. "If you would stay?"

I could not answer. I shook my head and pressed her hand. Then Charlie spoke. "Thank you for coming. Ernesto thought you were really something." He bent and kissed my cheek. "Gale will drive you home."

Oh, thank God. I could not stand being with anyone but Gale. I climbed up into the buggy, clenched my hands in my lap and waited.

Chapter Twenty-Nine

Gale

The minute we left ranch property I reined up the horse, stopped the buggy and pulled Lilah into my arms. She wasn't crying, exactly, but she wasn't acting normal, either.

"You all right?"

"No," she whispered. "Take me home."

I whipped the horse into a trot. I never whip a horse, but I could see something wasn't right with her. I pulled the buggy around in back of her house. Didn't know why, really, just thought I might be there for a while and I didn't want to start any talk.

She didn't seem to notice. Seemed kind of as if she was sleep-walking. I felt pretty low myself. Inside the house she went straight to the hutch for the whiskey, snagged two glasses from the top shelf and uncorked the bottle. She started to pour it out, then stopped and looked over at me.

"Do you want some of this?"

I lifted the whiskey out of her hand. "Nope. Do you?"

"No."

I stuffed the cork back in and we just stood there looking at each other. Her face was bone-white, and her eyelids were red and swollen. Her mouth...oh, God, her mouth was all twisted.

I reached for her. "Lilah."

"Kiss me, Gale." Her voice was so soft I wasn't sure I heard right.

"What?"

"Kiss me." She wound both arms around my neck and held on tight. "I need you to kiss me."

I needed her, too, but maybe this wasn't the right time. I knew if I kissed her I wouldn't be able to stop.

And I guess she didn't want me to. I kissed her until I couldn't breathe, and her mouth told me things I wasn't sure I could believe. I held her until her knees gave way, and then I gathered her up and climbed the stairs with her in my arms, pushed through her bedroom door and laid her down on the bed.

She moaned and pulled me down beside her. "Don't leave," she whispered.

I walked over to the china basin on her chest of drawers, poured in water from the pitcher and wet a square of linen and wrung it out. When I returned to the bed, she rolled toward me. I sponged off her face and neck and pressed my lips against her reddened eyelids.

"More," she murmured.

I unbuttoned the top seven buttons of her shirtwaist and ran the cloth over her upper chest. I was right—no corset. Might explain why my hand started to shake.

"Gale?"

"Yeah?"

"Would you stay with me?"

I sure couldn't answer right away. When I trusted my voice, I tried to say something sensible. "You don't know what you're sayin', really."

"I know exactly what I am saying."

"Lilah…"

"Don't stop me, Gale. I want you to stay."

"That's grief talking, right?"

"Yes. And more."

Oh, lordy. I undid all the rest of the buttons and undressed her slowly, all the way down to her camisole and lacy drawers, thinking she'd stop me any minute. But she didn't.

So I stretched out beside her and stared up at the blue-painted ceiling. I wanted her like I'd never wanted another woman, and I wrestled with it a long time. Finally she rose up on one elbow and began unbuttoning my shirt. When she reached for the belt buckle at my waist, I caught her wrist.

"Don't, unless you're real sure about this."

"I am sure." She smiled for the first time that day.

I rolled off the bed and stripped while she watched. Standing in front of her stark naked made the state of my need more than obvious.

"Gale, you are a handsome man."

"That's not what's important, is it?"

"Of course not."

I lay down beside her and tugged the ribbon on her camisole free, wishing like hell my fingers weren't shaking. She laid her hands against my bare chest.

"This is the most wonderful thing I have ever known," she said.

"What is?"

"Spending time with you."

"You know something, Lilah? Everywhere I go, everything I do, I think about you."

"I know," she murmured.

"You do?"

"Yes, I do."

"What else do you know?"

"I know that I like to be where I can talk to you."

"And kiss me?"

She didn't answer. She didn't need to. She shrugged off her camisole and I leaned over her. Her lips were warm and salty.

And when I touched her breasts I heard her breath hitch in.

Chapter Thirty

Lilah

Gale's touch was soothing at first, and I sorely needed soothing. I was heartsick over Ernesto's death, almost disoriented with grief. His hands were warm and slow as they moved over my body. Such a simple thing, really, to touch and comfort. He kissed my neck, the sensitive place behind my ear, my breasts. Heavens, what a wondrous thing it was, being with another human being. I felt him breathing with me while I struggled to put my sadness in perspective.

And then his touching turned into something else. Something inside me flickered to life—a sweet, sweet hunger. I moved my body to face his and looked into his eyes. What I saw there was humbling.

This man desired me. And he cared how I felt about what was happening. He put his mouth on me, on places that made me gasp and soar inside and beg for more. I gave myself up to the pleasure of it.

When I cried out for more, he kissed me deeply and rose up over me, hesitated and then thrust deep inside me. I felt a momentary stab of pain, and then he began to move.

I will never forget how it was between us. I have never known anything more glorious than the wave after wave of pleasure that swept me along. Gale called my name over and over, and at the end, when his body stilled and then convulsed, his face was wet with tears.

This meant something to him, and I knew it was more than just pleasure. When our breathing returned to normal, I laid my head in the curve of his shoulder and slept.

When I opened my eyes Gale's arms were wrapped around me. We didn't speak. After a while he began to remove the tortoiseshell hairpins that held my bun in place. He drew them out slowly, and one by one tossed them on the floor. He laced his fingers through my hair and brought his lips to my forehead.

"Being with you is better than anything I've ever known."

His words startled me. Suddenly I wanted to know more about this man—not his physical self, but his inside self.

"Gale, why did you never go back to Texas?"

He thought a long time before he answered, "There was someone else before you. Someone that mattered to me."

I touched his hand. "Tell me."

"It's not pretty, Lilah. Maybe you don't want to know."

"I do want to know. Tell me."

Again he waited before he spoke again. "She was pretty. Real pretty. Too pretty. She was older than me. Almost twenty-six. I was just eighteen. I wanted her real bad, but I should have known."

"Known what? What happened?"

"My father…" His voice turned hoarse. "My father got her pregnant. She married him instead of me."

"What did you do?"

"Joined the Confederate Army. Fought at Antietam and Chancellorsville. Would have done more, but I took a minié ball in my chest and damn near died. There were days I wished I had. When I got out of the hospital, I was mustered out. That's when I came north."

Chapter Thirty-One

Gale

Hell and damn. I'd never told a living soul about it, but all these years it's been eating my insides like acid. For the first time I wanted to spill it all out, get rid of it. Maybe it would heal some of the broken places inside me.

She traced the scar above my left nipple with her soft fingers. "Have you replaced her?"

"No. I'm afraid of it. Not of you, Lilah. *It*."

God, I wanted Lilah like a thirsty man craves water. That wasn't what scared me; what scared me was loving her.

She sighed and curled up against me.

"Lilah, I can't stay. Have to be at the ranch before sunup."

"It isn't sunup yet." Her voice was getting drowsy.

"Takes an hour to get there. And Jase and Skip will sure as hell want to know where I've been all night."

"Tell them a lie. My aunt Carrie taught me that lies can be... lifesaving."

"But you don't lie."

"Not to you, no."

I thought for a minute. "What happened to your Aunt Carrie?"

She lifted her head and looked into my face. "Aunt Carrie was a spy for the Union Army. She was caught and hanged at Richmond."

"My God. *My God*."

She snuggled back down and draped her arm over my chest. "I was twelve. She was my favorite aunt."

"Makes me sad to think of that."

"It makes me sad to think of your father and what he did."

"Funny thing, Lilah. Right now, I feel worse about your aunt Carrie than I do about my father."

"Gale?"

"Yeah?"

"Don't leave. I don't care about the ranch hands."

I edged away from her, stood up and walked across the room to dunk that linen washcloth in the basin. Then I sat down on the bed beside her and washed her gently.

"You sore?"

"No."

"Good."

"Why?"

I leaned over and kissed her. "'Cause I'm stayin'. And before sunup, there's gonna be more."

By the time I left Lilah that night, I knew I was running scared. Everyone at the ranch, except for Alice and Consuelo, was too hungover after the funeral to notice when I returned, even Juan, who never drank much because he couldn't hold his liquor. Consuelo made a halfhearted attempt at bacon and eggs, and I noticed Charlie was sitting at the other end of the table, close to Alice, talking in low tones when I came in.

Skip and Jase never even looked up. They all ate as if everything tasted like dust and I had to work to keep my appetite from showing. I'd honored Ernesto's memory in a way he would have approved of, and I was grateful for the silence around the breakfast table. Gave me time to pull my head out of the clouds and get my bearings.

Charlie tossed me a lifeline. "Gale, how'd you like to trail six of those mustangs to a rancher I know in Idaho and bring back a stud horse I'm looking to buy?"

I tried not to look too eager. Couldn't have come at a better time; I needed some space to breathe. Even so, Alice gave me a sharp look.

"Yeah, be glad to."

"Could you leave in the morning?" Charlie added.

"Yeah. You sendin' anybody with me?"

"No. We're shorthanded with Ernesto gone. You're on your own."

I spent the rest of the day packing up my gear and picking out the six mustangs so Skip and Jase could get them shod. Driving them from Oregon all the way to Idaho would take me the best part of two weeks. When I got back, it would be winter.

Consuelo packed me up a saddlebag full of biscuits and a slab of bacon. At the last minute I slipped in a bottle of whiskey. Figured I needed it.

When I rode out the Rocking K gate the next morning I had a strange feeling inside, part relief and part pain. Guess I pretty well knew that both had to do with Lilah Cornwell.

I had to stop thinking about it. Had to stop thinking about Lilah. She didn't know much about being with a man, but, God, when I showed her, she took my breath away.

The sun was just coming up, and when I looked back there was Alice, heading across the meadow to my cabin to do something I'd asked her to do. It was a long shot, but I figured I didn't have a choice. I had nothing to offer Lilah. Not a damn thing.

Chapter Thirty-Two

Lilah

I guessed that I would not see Gale much after the night we had spent together. Something about the way he'd looked when he had left that next morning...well, he'd looked almost scared. I kept busy writing a new story and sprinkling water on my new seedbed. They wouldn't sprout until next spring, but I wanted to give them a head start.

The front section of my garden was beginning to stop passersby. Crimson and orange nasturtiums trailed in profusion around swirls of yellow black-eyed Susans. What an eye for color Gale had! The way he'd arranged the blooms in drifts made me catch my breath every time I looked at them.

One morning I was out watering when Alice Kingman drove up in her buggy. "I'm on my way to the train station to mail something for Gale." She tipped her head at a large square package on the seat beside her. "Would you come for dinner at the ranch?"

I swallowed. "Thank you, but I'd rather not, Alice. I imagine you are all extrabusy with Ernesto gone."

"Gale is gone, too," she said. "Charlie sent him to Idaho to buy a stud horse."

Oh. That explained why I hadn't seen him for almost two weeks. "Alice, what is a stud horse?"

She had a fit of the giggles over my question. "My heavens, Lilah, you are a city girl through and through. A stud horse is a lusty male stallion. It mates with the mares."

I nodded, and Alice grinned at me. "And don't ask me to explain how a stallion mates with a mare."

My face burned. "I won't, I promise."

"Come out to the ranch next week, then, before Gale gets back. It will do you good."

I couldn't imagine what good it could do me, so the minute Alice drove off toward the train station, I forgot about it. But on her way back to the ranch she stopped again and made me promise to come out on Sunday. She insisted in a rather peculiar way, which struck me as odd for a woman as easygoing as a ranch owner's wife.

Lord knew I didn't want to go. Christmas was just weeks away, and I had a million things to do: letters to write, cookies to bake. I even planned to make paper chains and decorate a tree. Besides, with Gale gone I knew I would have to fend off the attentions of Jason and Skip; Juan was too well mannered to do much flirting, and Charlie simply didn't notice what went on under his nose.

I went back to my unfinished story. Lately I found myself saving more typewritten pages than I was crumpling up and tossing in the wastebasket, so I was writing in a fever. The words for my love stories were coming easier, and I blushed to think about why.

Sunday afternoon at the ranch proved to be even more uncomfortable than I had anticipated. I told myself it was not Gale's absence, but the truth was I suspected Gale's being gone had more to do with me than any stud horse Charlie wanted brought from Idaho. It made me feel all mixed-up inside.

I scarcely noticed the wild tales Jason and Skip bandied about; Juan was extratalkative, reminiscing about his uncle Ernesto and how they had come from Mexico together. After we had devoured one of Consuelo's double-layer chocolate cakes, I noticed Charlie and Alice sitting close together on the porch swing with his arm around her shoulders, and a pain laced through my chest. After a while Charlie ambled off to the corral, and the ranch hands followed.

"You look somber this afternoon, Lilah," Alice remarked when we were alone. "Are you thinking of Ernesto?"

"No. I've thought about him so often these past weeks I think my brain is tired."

"About Gale, then?" Alice's sharp eyes studied my face.

"N-no. Alice, the truth is it would do me no good at all to think about Gale."

She stopped the swing's motion. "Why is that?"

"Because I, well, I do not imagine he is thinking of me. I do not think Gale really cares very much about me."

Until I heard my voice say the words, I hadn't realized I felt that way, but it was true. I knew Gale had wanted me physically that night, but Gale was a man, a "stud," doing what a man will do. He hadn't even said goodbye before he'd left for Idaho.

All at once Alice again stopped the swing and stood up. "Come with me, Lilah. There is something I want you to see."

Uneasy, I followed her down the porch steps, along the gravel path in front of the house and out across the grassy meadow. We were heading toward the cabin I had noticed that day Gale had taken me riding. Gale's cabin.

"Gale told me no one ever comes to his cabin," I said.

"No one except me," Alice said with a smile. "Come on. I have his permission."

She climbed the three split-log steps, crossed the narrow plank porch and ran her fingers along the top of the door frame. With the key, she unlocked the solid wood door, pushed it open and stepped inside.

I followed her into a sunshine-filled room and caught my breath. The cabin was neat and well cared for, with shelves spanning the walls that were stuffed with a haphazard array of books. Pencil sketches were tacked all over one wall. A fieldstone fireplace faced a narrow bed and a plain wooden chest, and an array of iron skillets and pots hung over the spotless woodstove. Raw wood beams soared overhead.

I turned to Alice. "Who built this?"

"Gale built it. It took him six years."

One wall was completely covered with pictures. Paintings! Mountain scenes, rivers tumbling through rocky canyons; portraits, including a handsome one of Ernesto, one of Alice sitting in the porch swing, even one of Ernesto's nephew, Juan, squatting by a campfire. There were paintings of horses in a golden field, ranch hands branding cattle, Jason leaning against the corral fence, his face hidden by his wide-brimmed hat. There was even one of my flower bed!

Paintings covered every spare inch of wall space. In the center of the room stood a large easel bathed in light from one of the large windows. A canvas drape covered it.

"Did Gale paint all these?"

Alice nodded. "He did."

"You mean he is a…a painter?" I shook my head in disbelief. "But he's your foreman. When could he find time to paint all these?"

"During the day he works for Charlie. At night he works for himself. I often see a light burning."

"But…" I snapped my mouth shut. "This is what you wanted to show me?"

"No." She moved to the canvas-draped easel. "*This* is what I want you to see." She lifted the drape and I couldn't help but gasp.

My own face looked back at me. It was done in tones of peach and warm red-browns, and I couldn't stop staring at it.

"So you see?" Alice laid her hand on my arm. "Gale does think about you. He thinks about you all the time."

I was speechless.

She covered up my portrait with a quiet smile. "You must not tell him that I showed this to you, Lilah."

I was so overcome I could only nod. And then I burst into tears. I sniffled all the way back to the ranch house, where Consuelo gave me a worried look and brought me an extrabig cup of coffee.

I was still dazed the next morning when Alice drove me home in the buggy. At my gate, she made me promise, twice, that I would say nothing to Gale about seeing his paintings.

"Nothing," she repeated, looking into my face with serious, unblinking eyes. "Not one word."

Chapter Thirty-Three

Gale

I delivered the six mustangs to Fort Hall, picked up the stallion Charlie sent me to buy and headed home. Have to admit I diddle-daddled along the trail, in no hurry to get back to Oregon and the Rocking K. And Lilah.

Some nights I lay awake wondering what the hell I was doing. Other nights, sitting up late by a smoldering campfire, I thought maybe I knew. I'd fallen in love with Lilah Cornwell, and that was the last thing I'd wanted to do.

I twisted it every which way, but it still came out the same. I wanted to see her. Wanted to touch her and kiss her and watch her eyes after a shot of whiskey or in those quiet moments after I made love to her. But…

I had to face it. I had nothing to offer her. Making love to her was one thing. Letting myself really love her, care about her…that was something I couldn't risk.

It was a long, lonesome ride back to the Rocking K, and every single damn mile I was hungry for things I couldn't have.

After four hundred miles it got to the point where I saw her face everywhere I looked and heard her voice on every breeze.

When I got back to the ranch I just wanted to turn around and head back to Idaho. I unsaddled Randy and rubbed him down along with the new stallion, stalled them and dumped some oats in their feedbags. Then I tramped across the meadow to my cabin and drank whiskey until I couldn't see straight. I couldn't ever remember being this lonely.

I slept for two days. When I woke up and felt the sun warm on my face, I knew I had to see Lilah. I put it off for two days, and then Alice told me she was coming to dinner again on Sunday.

That made me sweat some.

"She may want to go riding again, Gale," Alice confided after supper. "You'll take her out? Consuelo could pack up a picnic lunch, and—"

"No." I snapped the word at her. "It's winter. Too cold to ride."

"Yes," she said quietly. I swore at her inside my head. That Alice was a woman full of yesses. Bet when she and Charlie were courting, she'd given him a run for his money. Maybe she still did.

When Juan drove up on Sunday on a crisp, windy day with Lilah sitting in the buggy in some sort of ruffly blue-striped dress I thought I'd died and gone to hell. Couldn't keep my eyes off her, but I had to wait until she wasn't looking to really gaze at her. Otherwise she'd see everything written all over my face.

Hell and damn, I couldn't string her along any further. Better make a clean break.

I decided I'd do it on our picnic. But first she wanted to see the stallion I'd brought from Idaho.

She stood for a long time peering into the stall, and when she turned away to mount on Lady, she had a funny look on her face. I climbed up on Randy and we rode out to the river. The day was cold, but she didn't seem to notice. Half a mile along the riverbank she reined in and sat waiting for me to catch up.

"I have something to tell you," she said.

"Yeah?"

"I've been waiting to tell you. It's a surprise."

"What is it?" My throat was so tight I could barely get the words out. "You're pregnant," I guessed.

Lilah laughed and all of a sudden I wanted to strangle her. "Oh, no," she said, those blue eyes dancing. "Although that would be nice, too."

"Well, what is it?" My voice came out as growly as a bad-tempered grizzly, and I opened my mouth to apologize, but she just smiled at me, and kept on smiling. Damn, under the brim of her felt hat her face was lit up like Christmas candles. Whatever it was, she was sure happy about it. I wondered if she'd feel that way if I *had* got her pregnant.

I reached over and tipped her chin up with my forefinger. "Tell me, dammit."

"I sold one of my stories. To a lady's magazine in New York."

I sure didn't know what to say about that except congratulations. So I said that.

"It's a love story," she said.

"Figured it was, since you told me that's what you write."

"It's a really *good* love story, Gale. One I am proud of."

She kicked Lady into a walk and kept talking. "It has lots of visual detail and suspense, just as you suggested, remember?"

Lord, yes, I remembered. I was afraid of what *she* might remember.

"You have a love scene in this story?"

"Oh, yes. An extremely romantic one."

I caught Lady's bridle and brought the mare to a halt. "You didn't…" I couldn't finish what I was thinking.

She tipped her face up to mine, and now her eyes looked troubled. "Oh, no, Gale. I could never, never write about that night with you. That is private. It always will be private."

I released the mare and we rode on side by side. "What happened that night was just between us."

"Just between us," she repeated. "I would never share it with anyone."

I waited for what I thought was coming next, a question about why I hadn't been to see her all these weeks. But she kept on riding.

And I kept on waiting.

The next thing out of her mouth was an even bigger surprise. "Could we go swimming in the river?"

"Swimming!" Was she nuts? I'd see her naked, or almost, and all my sensible hands-off talk would fly away on the wind.

"Don't think so," I managed.

"Why not?"

"Water's too cold."

"Isn't that why one goes swimming? To cool off?"

"Sometimes. Not today."

She paid no attention. "I think so, after we have our picnic. Over there, under those trees." She pointed to a stand of maples, rode over and waited for me to help her dismount.

I slid out of Randy's saddle and she held out her arms. Putting my hands around her waist cut my breath off. She came down way too close to me.

Her hair smelled good, like lemons. God, she had no idea what she was putting me through. I must have let out a groan because she got that little frown between her eyebrows I remembered from the first time I ever laid eyes on her.

She looked up. "Are you hungry?"

That made me laugh. "Hell, yes."

"Is this a good place for a picnic?" She waved one hand toward the slow-flowing river a few yards away.

"It'll do, I guess."

All at once she looked up at me. "You are not glad to see me, are you, Gale?"

Goodness, she could be direct. "Yes and no."

"Explain."

I swallowed hard. "Yes, because seeing you makes me damn happy. And no, because I'm trying like hell not to compromise you any more than I already have."

Without a word she turned away and moved to a grassy spot under a half-grown maple. I grabbed the blanket and the picnic basket tied behind my saddle and tramped after her. My jeans were starting to feel way too tight.

Chapter Thirty-Four

Lilah

I was so elated over the sale of my story I felt I could fly, but I sensed that Gale did not want to come on this picnic with me. Or even talk. We ate Consuelo's bacon sandwiches and hard-boiled eggs and chocolate cupcakes, but my mood drooped lower and lower as I realized that Gale was foreman out here on the Rocking K ranch and I was a writer who lived in town.

There was no future for us. Gale was strong enough to face it, and he was trying not to hurt me, but I could not accept it. Soon I would have to follow Aunt Carrie's example and lie to this man. I would have to tell him it did not matter.

But it did. No man had ever mattered to me the way Gale McBurney did. And I knew that no man ever would.

I swallowed the last crumb of my cupcake and stood up. Gale lounged on the picnic blanket, his hat pulled over his face. "Where are you going?"

"Swimming." I unbuttoned my blue chambray shirt and shed my boots and riding skirt.

"Don't." He spoke from under his hat.

"Don't what?"

"Don't take off any more."

"You're watching?"

"Damn right."

I turned my back, walked to the riverbank and dipped one toe in the water. It was freezing cold! I wanted the man to kiss me, but I couldn't ask him to. So I settled for a swim instead, no matter how cold it was.

"Watch out for rocks under the surface," he called. I shot a glance back at him, and he was still lying with his hat over his face.

I splashed into the deep pool closest to the bank and almost screamed as the icy water closed over me. *What was I thinking?* It was almost Christmas, too wintry for swimming in anything but a bathtub full of hot water. When I surfaced, Gale was stalking back and forth along the edge with a scowl on his face.

"C-come on in," I called, beginning to shiver. To keep warm I started to tread water.

"Not a chance in hell."

I splashed water at him, but he didn't even flinch, so I turned, gritted my teeth and swam to the deepest part of the pool. Gale did not move a single inch.

I gazed up at the specks of brilliant blue sky glimpsed through the tree branches and wondered what Aunt Carrie would do about a man like Gale.

Nothing. I could hear her voice as clearly as if she were floating beside me. *Do nothing. Pretend it does not matter. Go home and forget him.*

Chapter Thirty-Five

Gale

She came out of the river looking like a frozen water nymph, her hair straggling out of the bun at her neck and her wet skin glistening. I shut my eyes and turned away.

"I'm going to lie in the sun to dry my underclothes," she called.

"Yeah." I packed up the picnic basket, folded up the blanket and waited, grinding my jaw to keep from looking at her. How long did it take for a scrap of lacy drawers and a camisole to dry on a winter day? An hour? Two?

I knew I'd never make it.

All of a sudden I saw the humor in the situation. Didn't exactly make me laugh, but my tight jaw began to relax and my aroused body settled down a bit.

Or it would eventually. Before it did I worked up a pretty good ache in my groin, and Lilah sure wasn't helping matters. I couldn't let myself get close to her.

I couldn't live without her.

Dammit, I wish I'd stayed in Idaho.

While I paced up and down with my eyes focused anywhere but on her, she dried off and put her clothes back on, pulled on her boots and mounted her horse.

Hallelujah. Maybe I could heave my swollen privates into the saddle and make it back to the ranch before I hauled her off into the trees and did what I was aching to do.

I focused on the trail, the grass, the spindly little trilliums fighting for life in the shade, anything to keep from watching Lilah's body move with the motion of her horse. I kept thinking that underneath that riding skirt was just a single layer of white muslin. One single layer.

God help me. I tried not to think about it. Right before we

emerged from the trees I lost it, dragged her off the mare onto my lap and kissed her like tomorrow was a century away. She tasted of chocolate, and her skin smelled so sweet it made my mouth water.

"When we get back to the ranch," I said against her lips, "get Juan to drive you home. I don't trust myself."

She mmm-hmmed, but her voice was drowsy. I prayed to God she heard me. I set her back in Lady's saddle and we just looked at each other. What I saw in her eyes was understanding and quietness, and underneath that was banked passion. What she saw in mine, I don't know. Desperation, maybe. Raw hunger.

It turned out she wasn't going back to town. She was staying overnight at the ranch. I kept my jaw clenched all through supper and the front-porch antics of Jase and Skip after dessert, but finally I couldn't take anymore. I set off across the meadow for the safety of my cabin.

Fat lot of good that did me, with Lilah's portrait staring me in the face and no whiskey left in the bottle.

By midnight I'd had all I could stand.

Chapter Thirty-Six

Lilah

Gale was quiet all through supper, through Consuelo's cherry pie and coffee and then brandy on the porch while my body sang with wanting him. I knew I wouldn't sleep, so I stayed up as late as possible. Even after Gale went off to his cabin and Charlie and Alice went upstairs to their bedroom, I sat and rocked back and forth in the porch swing and tried and tried to stop thinking about him.

A fat silvery moon rose and set, and at last I climbed up to my third-floor guest room and crawled under the sheet.

My eyelids simply would not stay closed. After an hour I gave up and lay awake, staring up at the wallpapered ceiling in the darkness.

I must have drifted off to sleep, but I jolted awake when the door to my room silently opened and a shadow moved to the bed.

"Move over," Gale whispered. I heard his heavy leather belt drop to the rug, and then he slid his body next to mine and reached for me.

"Don't say anything," he murmured. "I make a hundred and thirty-five dollars a month as ranch foreman, and that's not enough to support a wife. Just let me love you."

We were quiet after that. He touched me all over and kissed me everywhere, even places I had only imagined in my dreams, and it went on and on until we were both breathing hard and nothing mattered any longer.

At the end he whispered in my ear. "I love you, Lilah. And I can't do a damn thing about it."

"It doesn't matter. This is all I want."

"It's not enough."

I had plenty of money, even more now that my stories were starting to sell. But I knew Gale would never, never accept help from me. I couldn't offer him a single penny because he would be too proud to take it. *Why are men so pigheaded?*

Toward morning he said something else. "The hardest thing I've ever done is to be in love with you and walk away." That just plain made me cry.

Juan drove me back to town before breakfast. Nothing was the same. Nothing would ever be the same.

To keep my mind off Gale I baked Christmas cookies, dozens of them—white-winged angels and fat Santas with a dot of red-current jelly for a nose. I baked and cried and baked some more, and in between batches I wrote.

I sold two more stories, and I stopped Charlie on his way into town one morning and sent word to Alice, hoping she would tell Gale about my success.

I thought a lot about Aunt Carrie. I couldn't bring myself to lie to Gale, so when my courses came I stopped Alice on her way out of town one day and sent a short note to him.

Mama wrote, asking me to come back to Philadelphia for Christmas. I wrote back and said no, and I lied about the reason. She would never understand wanting to live near a man who could not marry me.

Chapter Thirty-Seven

Gale

"Ya know what, Gale? Sure seems funny that Lilah's never visited all these weeks, don't it?"

We were mending the corral fence, and as usual Jase couldn't keep his mouth shut. "Maybe she's busy, Jase."

"Thought she liked us. You anyway."

I pounded in a nail. "Guess you thought wrong." I shut my mind down as best I could, and eventually Jase drifted back to the barn and let me finish the fence alone.

I'd just stretched the last section of barbwire when Alice drove up in the buggy.

"Gale, I want you to take something into town for me."

Chapter Thirty-Eight

Lilah

From my upstairs bedroom window I heard Gale's voice on the front porch, calling my name. "Lilah? Lilah, answer me!"

My heart all but stopped. I had never before heard him use that tone of voice. What was wrong? Was it Alice? Charlie?

"Gale? I'm coming." I rushed down the stairs in my dressing gown, still hearing his shouts.

"Hurry up!"

He stood there with a bushy, fragrant fir tree balanced on one shoulder. Snow dusted his hat and the collar of his sheepskin jacket.

"Christmas tree," he announced. "Where d'ya want it?"

"In the front parlor," I said, gasping. "Right in front of the window."

"Gonna decorate it?"

"Oh, I left all the tinsel and ornaments back in Philadelphia."

"Out here we use popcorn balls and strings of cranberries, stuff like that. Even paper cutouts to look like snowflakes."

He set the tree down where I pointed and snaked off his hat with a puff of snow dust. "I'll help with the popcorn balls. Alice has a good recipe."

Then he made a hasty retreat. I opened my mouth to ask about the popcorn balls, but he was already riding off.

I spent all the next day stringing cranberries and making lacy paper snowflakes. The whole house smelled like a Christmas tree, and I smiled and smiled when Gale came that evening to help me make popcorn balls.

Chapter Thirty-Nine

Gale

After we rolled the popcorn balls and hung them up on the branches, we walked out to the front porch to admire the decorated tree. "Look!" Lilah shouted. "It's snowing!"

The white flakes sifted down, frosting her hair. Before I could stop her she skedaddled off the porch and spun in a circle like a kid, opening her mouth wide to catch snowflakes on her tongue. I wanted to kiss her so bad I fought to keep my hands jammed in my pockets.

The whole world felt peaceful as everything turned white and silent. "You had snow in Philadelphia, didn't you?"

"Oh, yes, but it was nothing like this. The trees are so beautiful with their branches all white and sparkly, and look! The road looks like a wide path of soft white silk."

"And your flowers are getting covered up," I said. "All lumpy like little fat dolls dancing across your front yard."

All at once she froze. "Gale, listen!" She rushed to the front fence and cocked her head. "Carolers!"

Faint voices floated on the snowy air. "God rest ye merry gentlemen, let nothing you dismay…"

"Oh," she breathed. "How lovely."

"Yeah." But I was looking at her, not at the crowd of singers moving along the road.

She dashed into the kitchen, where I heard a clatter of dishes. When I got there she was loading up a platter with some of the Christmas cookies she'd baked.

"Schoolkids," I explained. "They do it every Christmas."

She turned toward me and I saw tears in her eyes. She gave me a shaky smile. "Christmas always makes me cry."

The singers drew closer. "O, come, all ye faithful…"

Lilah grabbed the platter of cookies and scooted out the front door. I heard oohs and aahs and a lot of laughter, and then the voices resumed singing and moved on down the road. "We three kings of Orient are…"

The music drifted off until there was nothing left but the sound of our breathing, and I knew I had to get out of there. I was coming undone. I left her without even kissing her, and I regretted it all the way back to the ranch.

Alice kept sending me into town on errands—pick up some needles from the mercantile and bring more raisins and another ten-pound bag of brown sugar. All the store windows had rows of little kids gazing at displays of toy trains and dolls and bows and arrows. I waded through them, made my purchases and carefully avoided slowing down when I came to Lilah's orange fence on my way out of town.

Consuelo outdid herself baking apple and mince pies, but I wasn't hungry. Skip and Jase and Juan ate like starving Indians, laughing and joking and telling tall tales like they always did. I didn't say much, just wasn't in the mood to celebrate.

By Christmas Eve I couldn't stand it any longer, and I left the dining table and headed across the frosty meadow to my cabin. Before I'd gone ten yards, Alice flagged me down.

Oh, no, not another damned errand in town.

"Gale, a letter came for you. I picked it up at the mercantile when I was in town."

"Not from Texas, I hope."

"No. From…" She peered at the envelope. "Chicago."

I studied the envelope. The return address read "Strellan Gallery, Chicago."

I ripped it open so fast it tore off one corner and unfolded the single sheet of heavy bond.

"Dear Mr. McBurney, we are pleased…"

A bank draft fluttered to the ground. I scooped it up and read the amount. Twelve thousand dollars? God, *twelve thousand dollars?*

I kissed Alice, raced for the barn where I threw a saddle up on Randy and headed straight for town.

Chapter Forty

Lilah

I was just admiring my beautiful popcorn-ball-and-cranberry-strung Christmas tree in the front parlor when I heard Gale's voice.

"Lilah! Lilah!"

His horse clattered up outside the gate, and the next thing I knew he had burst onto the front porch, breathing hard, and dragged me into his arms.

"Gale! What is it?"

He just stared at me for a moment. "I've gotta ask you something."

"Yes? Whatever is the matter?"

He lifted me off my feet and swung me twice around in a circle. Out in her front yard covering up her roses next door, old Mrs. Hinckley gasped and dropped her spectacles.

He set me on my feet, sucked in a big breath and blew it out. "How'd you like to sell this house?"

"Sell it? To whom?"

"To me."

"Gale, you have a cabin out at the ranch. What do you need with this house?"

"I don't need it, by myself. But *we* do."

I caught my breath. "Gale, stop. You make a hundred and thirty-five dollars a month, you told me so yourself. You can't afford to buy this house."

"Yes, I can. I sold one of my paintings. Did you know I paint pictures? Anyway, I sold one. For twelve thousand dollars!"

He stopped suddenly. "Unless you don't want to marry me. Do you? I mean, will you? Marry me?"

"But—"

"Sell your house to me, Lilah. That way I can support you."

"But you work for the Rocking K."

"Not anymore. My cabin's not big enough for the two of us. We need room for you to write. And for me to paint. I can sure as hell support a wife on twelve thousand dollars. And that's for just one painting! God, I can hardly believe it."

I stared at him. "Gale, you're bubbling like a little boy with a new toy."

"That painting was a portrait of you, Lilah. And I just finished a second one."

"I know."

His green eyes widened. "How could you know?"

"I cannot tell you."

"Alice," he murmured. "She shipped that painting to the gallery in Chicago and—"

"Gale."

"And she must have—"

"Gale?"

"Yeah? Lilah, let's get married right away. Today."

I circled my arms around his neck, stretched up on tiptoe and kissed him very, very thoroughly. Mrs. Hinckley dropped her spectacles a second time.

"Take me to bed, Gale."

"Huh? But what about getting married today?"

I kissed him again. "Today is Christmas Eve. We can get married tomorrow."

"Don't know if I can wait," he whispered near my ear.

Suddenly I felt as if I could fly, just spread my wings and soar up off the porch and over the town and look down on the snow-blanketed roofs and wish that everyone in the world could be as happy as I was. And all it took was one kiss from Gale McBurney and another whisper in my ear before we wound our arms around each other and stumbled upstairs to my bedroom, where we gave thanks for laughter and for love.

And for being with each other.

Epilogue

For weeks following the wedding of Lilah Cornwell and Gale McBurney, the entire county talked about the event.

Whitey Poletti, the barber, strolled around dressed in a spangly Venice boatman's costume, playing Italian love songs on his well-used accordion. The Ness twins, Edith and Noralee, somehow convinced sawmill owner Ike Bruhn to construct them each a pair of eight-foot stilts, and the girls cavorted about tossing paper flowers down on the assembled guests.

A heavily masked clown juggled Alice Kingman's best china dinner plates, at one point tossing six in the air at the same time, whereupon Alice had to sit down and fan herself. The guests all wondered who it was, and to this day, no one knows for sure.

Musicians who usually performed at barn dances, a fiddle, two guitars, a banjo and a washtub bass, played the "Wedding March," accompanied by a children's chorus of comb-and-tissue-paper kazoos.

And when Gale and Lilah stood hand in hand before Reverend Pollock and repeated their vows, there wasn't a dry eye in the room.

After the ceremony, waltzes and polkas reverberated through the church hall until long past midnight, when Gale lifted his bride into his arms, white lace gown and all, and strode out the door and down the snowy street to the house with the orange picket fence.

* * * * *